THE NEED TO BE FAMOUS

THE NEED
TO BE FAMOUS

Barbara Toner

*To Mark, Mindy,
Georgie, Nicholas
& Jayne Wales.

with much love
from Barbara X
21/4/88.*

Macdonald

A Macdonald Book

Copyright © Barbara Toner 1988

First published in Great Britain in 1988 by
Macdonald & Co (Publishers) Ltd
London & Sydney

Toner, Barbara
  The need to be famous.
  I. Title
  823′914[F]   PR6070.04/

  ISBN 0-356-15299-5

Printed and bound in Great Britain by
Richard Clay Ltd, Bungay, Suffolk

Macdonald & Co (Publishers) Ltd
Greater London House
Hampstead Road
London NW1 7QX
A Pergamon Press plc Company

Chapter One

The Brewsters were blessed. Where other families suffered from vile obesity, savage wrinkling or debilitating hair loss, their bodies were lean and desirable, their complexions were clear and kissable and their hair gleamed with attention and money. They flourished. They prospered. They glowed with good health, good looks and good luck. But they were blighted by a condition as hideous as it is invisible. They were crazed by the need to be famous.

They looked normal. They looked better than normal. But that's appearances for you; it takes circumstances to expose the truth and Neville, his wife Penny and Jeremy and his wife Fern all vied for circumstances in which they could expose themselves more to wilder and louder acclaim. They pursued the circumstances without rest which should have caused alarm but they called the circumstances opportunities and themselves hard-working and everyone believed them because of the appearances.

Neville was an actor with some impressive credits, a handsome face and impeccable diction but he might have been a taxi driver. Penny was the star of the oldest programme on television but there were many people who thought she was someone who had died. Jeremy, the dashing former teacher now journalist, broadcaster, columnist and singer, could have been any old man in a shirt advertisement. And his wife Fern, clever, witty and fascinating if short, was just like any mother with a teenage daughter burgeoning into a thing of beauty, though she was a poet. They all looked as sane as could be; sanity was part of their corporate image.

They didn't set out to fool anyone. People were simply prepared to be fooled because the Brewsters exuded that brand of good fortune which feels contagious but they fooled everyone, themselves into the bargain. They were blind to the natural consequences of their acting.

They acted so much they no longer knew what it was like not to. Any wonder they failed to see the danger in a consequence so inviting that it appealed to all of them simultaneously and irresistibly. Another family would never have seen opportunity in anything so shocking but another family was never as afflicted by so overpowering a need.

It began in all innocence, in a tunnel of ancient dust where Neville found himself smiling. 'What am I to do, then? What about my wife and child?' he demanded, with feeling. 'We need a roof over our heads.' He paused. 'You know what my wife is like.' He ran his fingers through his hair, grey with soot and a smattering of passing years, and he allowed a shaft of light to cut across his elegant profile, flattering his nose and chin.

It didn't cut much ice with Kenny Vertigo who scraped the end of his pickaxe wearily. 'Look,' he said, 'I'm doing this job as a favour. I don't know what your wife's like and I don't care what your wife's like. I've got enough trouble with my own wife. I should be over with Stan and Mick doing a Gothic conversion. I'm only here because I promised Toby. I'm doing my best.'

It didn't feel like the beginning of a circumstance or even the glimmer of an opportunity and if it had, there wasn't much Neville could have done about it. 'I know, I know,' he said. 'And I'm grateful to you and to Toby. All I'm saying, Kenny, is that I will have nowhere to live after Tuesday. I need this house.'

It could have happened to anybody. 'And all I'm saying,' said Kenny, 'is that I've got three other jobs to finish before I can bring more men over here and quite frankly Neville, it's a dump, isn't it? There's months' work here.' He drove his axe into the wall and pulled a large chunk of it away. 'Tell your wife. Months' work. At least.'

Neville sighed. He groped for words. He eyed Kenny's solid features with hate which he masked with genuine concern. 'Look,' he said. 'I can see your problem. Naturally. But you know television. You know the stress. You're the best builder in the business. My wife deserves the security of a roof over her head.'

Kenny sighed. 'Who is she?' Neville could see he didn't care who she was.

'Miss Penny,' he spat. Some of the wall had lodged in his throat.

'Never heard of her,' Kenny said.

'Miss Penny. *Kidding About*. You know, *Kid's Corner*.'

'Oh her,' said Kenny, 'I thought she was dead.' Neville threw back his head and laughed with great charm.

'She'd be thrilled,' he chortled. 'She's not even unconscious a lot of the time. Seriously. How about it? How about taking one or two men off the conversion and speeding this up a bit for her sake? You were a kid once. We'd both be very grateful.' Kenny laughed with less charm. He shook his head.

'I'd like to Neville,' he said. 'I really would. I liked your work in *The Iceman Cometh* but it can't be done. Sorry. You don't get a Gothic job every day of the week and, frankly, this one's important to me. I don't want it cocked up in my absence.'

'Fair enough,' said Neville graciously. 'I know you'll do what you can for us. Whose is it, anyway?'

'Marty Cork's,' sniffed Kenny proudly.

'Ah,' said Neville. 'Well, he's a good man. I don't blame you.'

It was sometimes assumed Penny Brewster was dead because she had been Miss Penny for nineteen years, even when her name had been Maureen Cartilage, and many children who had watched and loved her had coasted into middle age, not appreciating that she was where they had left her, tethered to her youth by a striped scarf. Miss Penny's scarves struck exactly the right note of carefree enthusiasm for *Kid's Corner*, or *Kidding About* as it came to be called, and as the years passed, they hid the tiny suggestion of crêpe on Miss Penny's neck.

She didn't wear them at home where she was able to act her age which was early to late thirties and where she could be herself. At home she was a beautiful, dedicated mother to Glen, the off-spring of her first marriage to a session musician and a loving wife to Neville who adored and cherished her for herself. The scarves were superfluous at home, when she had a home. Due to an unlucky miscalculation, she found herself suddenly without one. Circumstances do creep up on you, no matter how keenly you keep an eye out and she was a woman who prided herself on knowing an opportunity when she saw one.

'Damn,' she said, tremulously. 'What are we going to do?' She had deliciously pink lips that curved upwards in an expression of perpetual happiness and goodwill towards men, a happy combination with her large, well-shaped breasts, especially in a crisis which is where she now appeared to be.

'I'll fix it,' said Neville, kissing her lightly. 'Leave it to me.' He liked to think of her as his dear little nineteen-year-old, scarf or no scarf, home or no home. She burst into tears. 'Oh darling,' he said, 'please don't cry. I'll talk to Kenny again. You know what builders are like.' But Penny continued to cry, sweet little sobs into her hand. 'Penny,' he said. 'Come on, love. It's not the end of the world. I could put the Plimsolls off or if the worst comes to the worst, we can live among the rubble. Plenty of people do.'

'We can't put the Plimsolls off,' she said. 'She's had the baby and we've exchanged contracts.'

'I'm aware of that,' said Neville quietly. 'I am aware of that Penelope. But these things happen. We sold the house knowing we were taking a slight risk and we bought Mandarin Street knowing that it needed work. Didn't we?'

Penny nodded. They had. 'It's just that I didn't expect to find myself homeless and out of job at the same time.' She shuddered.

'We won't be homeless,' Neville said, taking her shoulders. 'We'll still own Mandarin Street. We just won't be able to sleep in it for a while. What do you mean, out of a job?' Penny began to cry again, silently, because she knew nothing sounded more unattractive than a woman her age lowing.

'I am, I am,' she said. 'He shouted at me in front of everyone. He said if I got the children to gallop one more time, he'd walk off the show. He said children hated galloping, he knew from experience, and even those morons who wanted to gallop didn't want to every time I forgot what was coming next. He was horrible. He's a pig. I hate him. I wish he was dead. I wish I was dead. He's only been in the business a week. I hate him. Honestly Neville, I can't go on. I can't take the abuse. I can't stand those snotty little brats with no sense of rhythm.'

'Shsh,' said Neville. 'You're tired. It's not a problem. Go and see Robin and he'll sort it out. You know he always does. Now there's a good little love. Wipe your eyes, blow your nose and sit down while I tell you what I think we can do about the house. Gin?' Neville smiled at his wife and ruffled his hair as he caught sight of it in the mirror above the fireplace. He was looking good for thirty-seven, even if he did say so himself and being sweet to Penny always made him feel strong. 'There's absolutely nothing to worry about,' he said, 'because I'm going to talk to Jeremy. I'm sure he'll take us for a day or two.'

Penny smiled up at him mistily. 'Do you think he will?' she asked breathlessly. 'Oh God, that would solve everything. But what about Fern? She loathes me. She resents me, you know she does.'

'You are lovely,' said Neville handing her a glass, 'and I love you and you must leave Fern to me.' Then they sat down together to watch a tape of the day's show and to assure each other that Penny's understanding of it was miles beyond the comprehension of any pipsqueak producer brought across from Current Affairs.

Neville wasn't at all sure that Jeremy would solve everything. He had only mentioned him as a diversion. Jeremy was really the last person who might help them, given Fern, but Jeremy had sprung into his mind as Penny wept and then out of his mouth to shut her up.

His attention hadn't had to stray far from his wife on one channel to his brother on another where the problems of survival and progression were the same. 'I'll ring him immediately,' he said, but he didn't which was just as well because he wouldn't have found him in and he would have had to make polite conversation with Fern who terrified him.

Jeremy was standing outside a former banqueting hall in a shabby seaside town staring into the sky, lost in composition. 'Here in this shabby seaside town,' he thought he might say, 'exactly twenty years ago today, this country saw the worst natural disaster in the history of modern engineering.' No ... 'This country ...' no. 'This once proud banqueting hall is the scene of the worst engineering disaster the country has seen.' He said it aloud to hear it.

'You've said scene twice,' said McEvoy, the sound engineer who was crouched at his feet.

Jeremy was darker and leaner than his brother and if people thought him more handsome, his diction was less impressive. This was only fair, he thought since he was the more intelligent and better versed in the ways of the world. 'I know, I know,' he snapped. 'Here, in this shabby seaside town, twenty years ago today, ninety-four people died when ... when what?' he said to McEvoy. 'Was it the roof or the chandelier?'

'God, they're everywhere,' said McEvoy, toppling as another camera crew shoved past looking for a superior perspective. The town was crawling with camera crews. There wasn't a mourning relative, a still-shocked survivor, a vicar, an architect, a former Lord Mayor or chandelier manufacturer left in the place uninterviewed. There wasn't a pebble on the beach unruffled by the relentless tread of a television reporter declaiming into the wind or an inch of the banquet-

10

ing hall, now Macdonalds, unfilmed, unlit or unadmired for still standing.

'Let's do it round the back,' said Jeremy. 'I'll stand in front of the back door that people tried to hammer down in their desperate efforts to escape. No one else is round the back. They're all doing the beach or the front entrance.'

'Four has done the top of the hill,' said McEvoy.

'Have they?' said Jeremy thoughtfully. 'Which hill?' He considered carefully. Did he want a hilltop? 'We don't want a hill.' He hurried around the back ahead of McEvoy and the cameraman. 'We'll do it here,' he said. 'This is fine.' He was oblivious to any circumstance involving his brother, let alone one which might concern his brother's wife and child. It would never have occurred to him that such a one could exist outside Christmas.

He mumbled to himself and studied the scrawled notes on his hands as McEvoy and the cameraman organized themselves. 'Right?' he asked, when they appeared to be ready. 'No, not right,' he cried. 'Hang on.' He puffed up his hair and slicked down his eyebrows, then he held up his sunglasses to examine his reflection. He pulled a stick of make-up from his inside pocket and wiped it across his forehead, nose and chin, a nose and chin as flattered by extra light as his brother's.

'Right,' he said again. He cleared his throat and arranged his face. He concentrated on blocking the Macdonalds' smell from his nostrils so that he could more effectively convey the scope of the tragedy.

'Chandelier disaster, back door, take one,' McEvoy muttered into his machine.

'Twenty years ago today,' Jeremy began, his eyes ablaze with sincerity and a hint of world weary sexuality, 'in this shabby seaside town overlooked by time, the outside world, and the main flight path to the Atlantic, on this very spot, commemorated now by Ronald Macdonald and celebrated over the years by countless Big Macs and Chicken Nuggets ... we're here. Piss off. We're here. You can see I'm here. I'm doing my report and we got here first. I don't give a shit if it is the back door through which the desperate tried

11

heartbreakingly to escape. I was bloody well here first, now piss off.' And the crew from Central did piss off because they could see he meant it and he wasn't a man to tangle with.

Some people said Jeremy Brewster was ruthless. He said he was professional and he didn't see anything wrong with ambition. Yet had he been merely ambitious, he would have been, at the age of thirty-five, a darn fine headmaster or maybe a darn fine don. But he had fled from teaching at the earliest opportunity, which he had created by abusing an old university friendship. He had nagged and nagged at old Bill Frisbee, whose brain had exploded at the age of thirty-three from too much striving, and finally old Bill had let him do the God spot on Channel 5 last thing at night. He had made it so inventive and himself so appealing that he was fairly soon offered a reporting job on *The News As We Speak*, an early evening round-up of the day's events.

Not that News was where he wanted to be. Access to the public is limited on News but he quickly became the best-looking, toughest and most incisive reporter on the team so he was given all the best stories and then, bewilderingly to many, he had offered to read the *News for the Deaf* on the side. The *News for the Deaf* made a large feature of his diction and paid pleasing attention to his face. He enjoyed *News for the Deaf* but he had his eye on Arts and Drama. He wanted to be a personality.

Not long after he had seen off the lot from Central, he lay on his bed in a hotel bedroom, sipping whisky and listening to Fern. 'Well I'm not going to get home tonight, am I?' he said. 'You'll have to collect her yourself. What's she doing going out in the middle of the week anyway? I thought you said she had to stay in ... did he? What did he want? Didn't he? When are they moving? Didn't he? Give Ruby my love then. Bye.'

Fern Brewster, who was an Honours graduate, didn't give Ruby her father's love. She forgot. She kicked the sofa in her large elegant drawing-room and straightened a picture. She didn't want to drive through the night to fetch her daughter from a birthday party. She had her career to think of as well.

She wandered into the kitchen and sat at the long pale kitchen table. Her career was a secret which confirmed her intellectual superiority over just about everyone. She didn't think that was boasting. It was a statement of fact. If she had been vain, she would have shown her verse around, but she didn't. She wrote for her own pleasure because she could and that was enough. At university, someone had remarked unkindly that being clever was important to Fern because she was ugly. But that wasn't true. She was short, yes, but she took her intelligence for granted.

She rose from the table and poured herself a glass of wine, then she took her special roller ball pen and her special lined paper, lit the small candle next to the silver cruet, turned off the light and began to write. She hardly hesitated. She would write an appreciation of the African in *vers libre* and she would call it *Black Rod*.

'*Black Rod knocked thrice,*' she began. The phone rang. 'Yes,' she said. Her mouth tightened. 'What's up?' she said. 'No disco?'

'Don't be silly,' said Jeremy impatiently. 'I've just been thinking. I'd better give old Nev a ring, hadn't I, if he's trying to ring me?'

'Why?' she asked.

'He is my brother,' said Jeremy. 'He is trying to ring me. I think I should call him back. Will you find me his number?'

'Where is it?' said Fern. 'Hurry up Jeremy. I'm busy.'

'In your book, isn't it? Why are you busy? I thought you could have a nice, lazy night with me and Ruby out of the way.'

'It isn't in my book. He is your brother. If you don't have him in your book ring Directory Enquiries.'

'I have,' said Jeremy. 'They hung up.'

'Then ring the office and get them to find it for you. I'm really too busy.' She spoke bluntly because she always did when she was working. Everyone took it for her generally off-hand manner which they put down to her cleverness. Well some people did. 'I can't think why you're bothering,' she said. 'He'll ring again if he wants something and there's no reason at all to think that he doesn't.'

13

'You are bloody rude,' Jeremy said. 'Just a minute. I have to go. Room Service is here. See you tomorrow.' Room Service brought him supper on a tray. It made him feel lonely. 'I've lost my brother's telephone number,' he told the waitress.

'Oh,' she said. 'I don't have a brother.'

Chapter
Two

Because Jeremy believed he had the advantage over Neville in years, hair, height, looks, charm, fat, the lot, he was generous. He didn't see much of his older brother but when he did he liked to think they were fond of each other. He would say to Fern 'He's a nice old thing, really.' And she would say, 'Who?'

He had been married to Fern for sixteen years and still she talked as if he had been raised in an orphanage. It was ridiculous. He was pleased to acknowledge her family with a monthly cheque to a nursing home.

'Neville,' he cried when he finally spoke to him a day later from the warmth and safety of his London newsroom. 'What news upon the Rialto?'

'Good news,' said Neville. His voice shimmered down the phone from his rib cage, every utterance an audition. 'Very good news. I've been offered *The Pyjama Game*, in Guildford. A six week run, then maybe Cheltenham and with any luck, the West End. Thank Christ. Otherwise it was *The Mousetrap* again. The bit of cheese this time.' He laughed loudly with boyish enthusiasm.

'Huh huh,' Jeremy sniggered, agreeably but with difficulty because he didn't know why Neville was laughing. 'That's good. Very good. Who's doing it?' He tossed aside a pang of envy. He might have been an actor himself if the pay hadn't been so ridiculous.

'Toby Gospel,' said Neville. 'He wouldn't have dreamt of offering it to anyone else he said. I know what everyone thinks about Toby but at least he delivers.'

'Who cares what everyone thinks?' said Jeremy. 'You can't afford to let what everyone thinks bother you. Did you see my disaster special?'

'Missed it,' sighed Neville. 'Sorry. How did it go?'

'Very well, but that's not the point. The point is everyone else did theirs from the top of a hill or the beach but I said 'Why should I do what everyone else is doing?' and I did mine round by the rubbish bins where the back door stuck, trapping hundreds and it was exactly right. Everyone said.'

'Brilliant,' said Neville. 'Brilliant. Everyone was rushing round to the top of the hill on the beach but you found the back door. Bloody brilliant. Wonderful mood. I bet it was a wonderful mood. The least obvious place. Brilliant.'

'Everyone else did the sea front or the top of the hill,' Jeremy explained again because he was rattled by Neville's ardour. There was something wrong with Neville. 'How's the lovely Penny?'

'Lovely,' said Neville. 'As ever. She's been driven mad by the new producer they've brought in who thinks he knows it all. And of course she's very upset about the house. Otherwise she's wonderful.'

'What about the house?' Jeremy asked idly. 'I thought you had moved.'

'Almost,' said Neville. 'We've been unlucky. There are some structural problems we didn't know about - no walls.' He laughed again. 'Anyway we can't live in it until they're fixed which is a bore, to tell the truth, because we've sold Bucket Road and we have to get out.'

'Where will you go?' Jeremy enquired, and in the brief pause thought he sensed a circumstance which was far from promising and was possibly appalling.

Neville said, 'We're working on it. Nowhere obvious springs to mind. It's only for a matter of days, of course, but a hotel is

16

out of the question. Penny couldn't stand a hotel.' Neville waited, hoping he wasn't going to have to spell it out. He sometimes told himself he was close to his brother but then, again, he sometimes knew that he wasn't.

Jeremy dived in. 'Who is he?' he asked. 'Who is Penny's new producer?' He knew he should offer to have them. He knew his house was big enough and that it would be the decent thing. But then, he asked himself, would it be fair? Would it be fair to Fern to inflict his family on her and in such numbers? Would it be fair to Penny who was a cretin. Even he couldn't tolerate a cretin for long and he would shout at Penny who would be miserable and would that be fair to Neville? He heard Neville clear his throat and he heard the question form in it. He thought 'He is my brother.'

'Why don't you come and stay with us for a while? I know Fern would love to have you,' he said. Afterwards he couldn't recall making such an obviously silly remark.

'Oh Jeremy,' Neville said. 'That really is incredibly nice of you. It would get us out of a hole and when I say hole, you ought to see it.' He chuckled. Jeremy flinched. 'We'd need to move in at the weekend if that's O.K. with you.'

'That's fine,' he said. 'I'll put Fern on red alert.' It wouldn't be difficult, he thought uncomfortably. She was easily alerted.

Fern didn't devote as many hours as she would have liked to her career. But that was part of its charm, grabbing at it whenever she could and dashing off something straight from the heart. She believed it benefited from being illicit and on the morning Jeremy invited his family to stay, she said so to Ralph Fantoni who was one of the very few people allowed into her confidence. She had to let someone in. Someone has to know you are writing secretly, even if no one is allowed to read it. Images must be projected, when they are images you have of yourself, if only on the narrowest ray to the smallest screen.

Ralph said, 'Like adultery. Like illicit lust.'

'Just like it,' she said and blushed. Ralph thought she was

gorgeous. He thought she had the most entrancing glint to her eyes, the most suggestive twitch to her lips, the most sensuous pitch to her voice and he longed to wind his fingers about the strands of hair that fell carelessly in tendrils from her comb down her long white neck. He didn't care that she was short. He wasn't very tall himself. 'More coffee?' she asked.

Ralph was in graphic design. He worked from home. His wife was in banking. She worked in a bank. They had two children, one of whom had gone to school with Ruby Brewster. Ralph had fallen in love with Fern on a school run, through car windows. 'Morning Ruby,' he used to cry lustily, but he'd only ever had eyes for her mother.

Fern knew he loved her. She said she loved him. But she said she didn't love him like that. Once she'd said she did love him like that but wouldn't do anything about it because it would destroy their friendship and she valued the friendship more than she valued a passing pleasure of the flesh. Perhaps she should have gone for the flesh but she didn't. He'd said, 'Why passing? Why passing, Fern? I will love you forever.' The knowledge that underneath she did love him that way sustained him, though he had moments of despair when he thought she was frigid. But then, he told himself, she really couldn't be.

Jeremy wasn't the sort of man who needed to stay married to a frigid wife. He could have had his pick of all the wives in the neighbourhood. He probably did. Ralph liked to torment himself with the thought that he did and once he'd tried to suggest to Fern that he did but she had put an end to that with a silence so icy that he told himself she was frigid from top to bottom. Everything froze sometimes with Fern. She was Hungarian, someone said, but whenever he asked her she would say 'I'm English, Ralph. What a daft question.' The Brewsters were the kind of family about whom rumours sprung up because people liked to talk about them. Fern being Hungarian was just a rumour.

'The trouble is,' she said, refilling his cup with the thick black sludge she drank all day, 'there's so much else to do. You don't know how lucky you are. You're left alone during

18

the day because everyone can see you are a graphic designer who needs time to work. No one leaves me alone because they think I've got all the time in the world.'

'I'll go then,' he said, and put his cup to his lips with a simper.

She dropped a kiss on his head. 'Not you,' she said. 'You keep me sane.' She knew how to keep a man at her feet, frigid or Hungarian.

'Fern,' he ventured. 'I have something to ask you.' She turned her small, shiny eyes upon him with a challenge that delighted him. 'I know you won't like me asking but I'm going to.' Her lips twitched invitingly.

'Well?' she said. She put her elbows on the kitchen table so he could see the tiniest suggestion of her breasts clenched, in anticipation, he told himself.

'You know I've mentioned my friend Bud Fenchurch.' She smiled. Of course she did. Bud Fenchurch was the one friend of his she was even remotely interested in. 'I've also mentioned you to him, obviously. As a matter of fact I've told him all about you. I know you're going to say I betrayed you but just hear me out.'

'Ralph,' she protested but weakly. He grabbed her wrist to shut her up and she allowed him to hold it and run his thumb along the inside of her arm. It was tantalizing.

'He wants to see your poems and I said I would get them to him, by force if necessary.' He watched her carefully. She watched him. She pulled her wrist away.

'You had no right to,' she said. 'You had absolutely no right to and now you're going to look very silly because I'm not going to let you have them. They're not for publication. I've told you. They are for me, for my own amusement. I thought you understood.'

'I do understand,' he said. 'I understand better than you think. For one thing, I know I wouldn't be a graphic designer if I could sell my abstracts. And I know you won't let anyone see your poems because you think they might be bad.' She laughed.

'You don't know much,' she said. 'My poems probably are bad. But they're my business. If you had any guts you would

19

paint abstracts and be done with it.' She was flushed. They had never had such a dangerous conversation. 'I don't need approval.'

'Oh yes you do,' he said. 'That's why you need me. You like me approving of you. You give me little snippets of your poems so I will approve of them and I do approve of them. You know I approve of you.' He placed his coffee firmly on the table and stood up. He took her wrist again and held it tightly. He stared down at her which wasn't far but a respectable distance for a man hoping to look forceful. She chewed her bottom lip. He pulled her to him pressing his free hand into the small of her back. Another tendril fell from the comb. He squeaked with desire. The phone rang. It was always ringing at the Brewsters'.

'Don't answer it,' he whispered.

'What?' she said. 'The phone's ringing.' She broke free and answered it. 'Did they?' she said. 'Did they? Did he? Well it was good. No, of course it was good. I told you last night it was good. Oh, did you? What did he want? The bloody cheek. You told him it was out of the question, of course. You what? Jeremy, you what? Well you'll have to get out of it because I don't want them here. What's that got to do with it? We put my mother in a nursing home. Look I don't want to discuss it now. I'm busy. Make an effort to get home for supper and we'll sort it out then. That Penny's a cretin. It's out of the question. Good bye.'

Ralph wasn't stupid. He could see the spell was broken. As she put the phone down he strode across to her, took her chin between his fingers and looked longingly at her lips, then away. He said, 'I will see you soon.' And he left her, feeling he had made some progress. He truly believed he did understand her. He thought he saw her need. He didn't guess she was mad, only that she was a tease and the person she teased most was herself.

Penny wasn't as cretinous as all that. Penny was a survivor which, in the parlance of children's television programmes, means someone who knows how to gallop without hesitation or someone who knows who to sleep with. Penny hadn't had many useful lovers but she had cleverly used her talent for extending sympathy, so that men who agreed behind her back that she was a pain in the arse, vied for her attention face to face when their wives left them or didn't leave them, when their babies stayed awake all night or when their bank managers took away their credit. She was wonderful at making them feel worthwhile despite everything.

This isn't to diminish her sex drive. It was as prodigious as anyone's is when they need to be famous. But, being happily and devotedly married to Neville, she simply diverted her excess from the bed to wherever she could use it most effectively: behind sets, in Wardrobe and Make-up and in executive offices where she nodded, crooned and made suggestive remarks to boost strategic morales with the utmost discretion.

The problem with her new producer was the same old one of ambition and boredom. Bright sparks or drunks were always being shunted across to *Kidding About* to mark time and the occasional one would see it as an opportunity for glory or salvation and suggest that a few changes be made round here. They exhausted her. She hated them. She knew changes weren't what was needed. More publicity was what was needed.

She said to Robin Powder, Head of Children and Sundries, 'I'm all for change as you know. But the right sort of change. I'd like to do more filmed inserts. I've told you that before, haven't I? But you know what I mean. Filmed inserts would be astonishing.' Robin Powder gazed out of his executive office which adjoined the boardroom and sniffed. It was the sniff of a man with a nose for evasion.

'Expensive though, dear,' he said. 'Costly. And budgets are the thing at that time of day, aren't they? You know that even better than me.' He studied her affectionately. He had slept with her; one of the few who had when she was between husbands. This had nothing to do with her long service to children's viewing because he wasn't that loyal, or even that powerful but he had always appreciated her grace in allowing the affair to begin and then to end without tears.

'I want to do more drama,' she said. 'Another play.' She

21

studied him too, with less affection but as long a memory. She enjoyed being taken into his confidence on matters of delicacy regarding programming, appointments, the state of his wife's hernia and his own digestion but she expected it to cut both ways. Well it was a friendship and what is friendship if it isn't something cutting both ways? She wanted him to cut the new producer down to size.

He said, 'When you say other. Do I remember which other?'

'Of course you do,' she smiled. '*Dick Whittington.* You remember me doing *Dick Whittington.* It wasn't that long ago.'

'Oh, the panto,' he said. 'Of course I remember. It was a disaster. Why on earth would you want to do another one?'

'I don't,' she said. 'I want to do a play, a proper play with a proper part. I know I can do it. And think how good it would be for the show. It would be wonderful publicity.' Robin sighed and smiled.

'What sort of play?' he said. 'Do you mean in the theatre, or what? You know my hands are tied with Arts and Drama here. You know how funny they are.'

'They're not that funny,' Penny said softly. 'Not really. Not once you get to know them. And I don't mind auditioning. You don't mind if I think about auditioning do you, if I hear of something?'

'Of course not,' he said drumming his fingers on his vast empty desk so she would leave. 'And don't worry about that other thing. I'll have a word with him. I'll tell him not to get carried away. I've always enjoyed your running-around bits myself.'

In many ways Penny was the opposite of cretinous. She was, more than any other Brewster, resourceful and one of the resources she conserved best was her courage. She was marvellous at appreciating what she could or could not stand. This drove her, shortly after her pleasant conversation with Robin Powder, to telephone her husband. 'I've been thinking,' she said before he could get a word in edgeways, 'I don't want to stay with Jeremy and Fern. I don't like her. It would be horrible.'

'Well that's brilliant,' said Neville, 'in view of what I have

22

just agreed with Jeremy. And it's a little late, considering what you said last night.' He spoke crossly because he had been looking forward to her gratitude and admiration. 'I've just this minute thanked him and said we will be moving in at the weekend.'

'I'm sorry, darling,' she said. 'Honestly I am. But I don't think I could face it. She's so nasty. She should be in hospital. It would be unbearable.'

'That's stupid,' he said, less than considerate now no one would acknowledge his triumph. 'No one likes Fern. She's awful but we can put up with it because it is free accommodation and if you want a whirlpool in the second bathroom we have to take whatever free accommodation we can get.'

Jeremy had nothing as persuasive to put to Fern, except the obligation of blood towards blood. 'Maureen isn't blood,' she said. 'Nor is that lumpy thing she calls her son. We will have Neville if you insist but I'm not prepared to have Maureen.'

'She hasn't been Maureen for years,' Jeremy protested.

'It makes no difference,' snapped Fern, taking out a comb and ramming it into her skull to prove to her head that she meant it. 'The thought of her hanging round the kitchen whinnying away while I try to get on with my life nauseates me and I won't have it.'

'I'm sorry you feel like that,' Jeremy said, 'because I have already invited them and I am not prepared to uninvite them. That is final. If it makes you feel any better you can invite your mother for the weekend when they have gone.' He knew it would not make her feel even a tiny bit better. 'You will hardly see them anyway because Neville has been offered *The Pyjama Game* in Guildford, the boy will be at school and Penny leaves for work at the crack of dawn and goes to bed the minute she gets home. If you're not prepared to put up with it you can go to a health farm until they leave.'

It was a lost argument, Fern knew, because Jeremy had right on his side and money. She wasn't all that desperately concerned about right and she told herself she could take or leave the money but she did care about appearances. By not consulting her Jeremy had deprived her of a choice. They had to come or she would look mean and mean was not something she cared to look, not to anyone, not even to cretinous Penny. Fuming, she took herself off to her room and wrote another two lines of *Black Rod*:

'*The members stiffened and rose as one.*
For it was their intention to enter the ancient chamber.'

It calmed her. She put her pen in her mouth and wondered if it was the African she was still writing about. She would have to wait and see she told herself.

Chapter
Three

Neither Ruby Brewster, nor Penny's son Glen who was also called Brewster for convenience, needed to be famous. It was very odd they should have that in common. Yet while not even appearances seemed to bother Ruby, both appearances and circumstances mattered to Glen, they mattered a lot, and everyone should have noticed but no one did. They were certainly very good-looking children. Glen wasn't at all lumpy.

Ruby was tall and slender with Persil-white skin, knowing blue eyes and black hair which fled from her skull in a tangled mass, terrified, possibly, of the contents of her head. She knew her own will and imposed it with a spirit which both pleased and worried her parents. They said on the one hand 'For God's sake, she's only fifteen,' and on the other 'Well she's fifteen, for God's sake.' They had brought her up to be aware of her own importance.

Unable to settle down to her work, Fern looked to her for support on the matter of the Neville Brewsters. 'You won't believe what your father has done. He's invited Neville and his family to come and live with us,' she said. Ruby was watching television in the small sitting-room off the large drawing-room. 'Did you hear what I said?'

'Neville who?' said Ruby.

'Your uncle,' said Fern. Your uncle, his wife and her sad child.'

'Has he?' asked Ruby. 'Why?' She didn't look at her mother. She toyed with the brown rice and salad on her lap and the cat beneath her feet and she smiled at the screen.

'I don't know,' said Fern. 'They've nowhere to live, he says. It's going to be a nightmare. That Maureen's voice will be bleating all over the house and God alone knows what the boy will be up to. He's at a school for the mentally disadvantaged.'

'Where will they sleep?' Ruby asked. 'I won't have to give up my room, will I?'

'I don't suppose so,' said Fern. 'There's the spare room for Neville and Maureen and the boy can have Jeremy's study; or the conservatory; or the garden shed. I hope he's not destructive.'

'The garden shed,' said Ruby decisively. 'It has a padlock.' Fern accepted this as allegiance of a sort but you could never tell with Ruby. She always spoke with conviction even when she couldn't possibly have had any.

Glen was as convinced. 'I'm not going,' he declared with his face fixed dreadfully against his mother. 'I don't want to talk about it. I want to watch this. I'll go and stay with Ants' Nest.'

Penny sometimes thought Glen was dreadfully difficult and she put it down to his having come from a broken home. He was not, however, at a school for the mentally disadvantaged. He was at a good Public School, on a sports scholarship it's true because of his astonishing physical advantages, but his brain certainly wasn't to be sneezed at.

'Darling,' she wheedled. 'Ants' Nest is a juvenile delinquent. His mother couldn't manage the two of you.' She smiled at him. She adored him, even if he could be tiresome. He was a marvellous figure of a youth: broad shouldered, slim waisted and long legged, and his face already promised to be heart-stoppingly craggy. His deep-set eyes glittered enticingly, with sexual innuendo although he was only sixteen. She considered it was a tragedy he had given up modelling and she prayed he would return to it.

'Well I'm not going to Jeremy's and that's final,' he said. He chuckled at the television which encouraged her.

'I don't want to go either,' she sighed. 'But we have to. Neville has arranged it and it wasn't easy for him. It's only for a few days. We'll manage.'

'If it wasn't easy for him, why did he bother?' Glen growled. 'We should go to a hotel or rent a place. Why aren't we renting a place?'

'Our money is tied up,' Penny said. 'You know that as well as I do.'

'We can use my money,' Glen said. He had made a packet from modelling. 'I'd rather spend all my money than go somewhere I'm not wanted.' He took a swig on his can of Coke.

'Don't be so silly,' Penny snapped. 'You will want your money for a sports car or a deposit on a penthouse. Coca Cola is very bad for your skin.' He groaned derisively. 'You wait and see ... You mightn't think so now but I know you will in a year or two. I know what men like and I know what you will like. You'll need your money.' She surveyed the lack of impact she was having and started again. 'Look,' she crooned, 'look, it's worth the sacrifice, believe me. I know sacrifices and this one is worth it.'

'But you don't mind going where we won't be wanted,' Glen said. He dragged his eyes finally from the screen to glare into hers which upset her. She hated bad feeling. She told anyone who cared to listen that she wasn't just his mother, she was Glen's friend. They had a special relationship, she had said to the reporter who had interviewed her when Royalty appeared on *Kidding About* to talk about sickness. They had come through a lot together.

'Of course we'll be wanted,' she lied. 'They wouldn't have asked us if they didn't want us. And even if they don't want us, so what! We can put up with that.'

'I can't,' said Glen. 'I'm going to Ants' Nest's. You mightn't have any pride but I have.'

27

'How dare you,' Penny cried because she was tired. 'After all we've been through together. How dare you speak to me like that. How dare you tell me I have no pride when I supported you for eight years, single-handed. Where do you think my pride was all those years? I couldn't afford pride all those years; that's where it was. Pride is a luxury in this world and the sooner you realize that the better. You are coming with us to Jeremy's and you will behave politely and as if you are wanted. That's what I have always done and it's what you are going to do.'

It was a missed opportunity which Penny, who had flounced to the bathroom to pluck her upper lip, dimly perceived. She knew she had been dishonest. In all the years she had spent raising him single-handed, she had never had to swallow her pride. She had walked away from her first marriage of her own accord; she had always enjoyed the admiration of countless men whose beds she could take or leave and, though she feared rejection, there had always been someone to shield her from it.

Still, she told herself with a snappy pluck in the small unsatisfactory bathroom in Bucket Road, she had dealt with him beautifully. It had been brave and dignified, insistent but not excessive. She wondered if it was a performance worth building on. She wondered if there was a character in there she could develop, of a brave, struggling mother, perhaps a prostitute but then again, perhaps not. She thought she saw an opportunity there, somewhere, but it was the wrong one.

Glen wondered what he had done in the womb to deserve her. He didn't think he would ever recover from having a mother who was called Miss Penny. Not only had he not inherited the family obsession, he despised it. He despised himself for having modelled sailor suits and for having grinned his way through baked bean and toothpaste commercials. He despised his mother for marrying a man with an ego that was like an enormous balloon, stretched to the point of popping, as huge and as frail as her own. He despised himself for saying his mother was someone who had died. He despised all Brewsters.

He telephoned his friend Ants' Nest but Ants' Nest's

mother said the boy had been taken away. 'I believe he is now in a home,' she informed him. 'Sad, isn't it?' she said. At least she sounded normal, he told himself. At least she wasn't called Miss Penny.

Ruby did not despise her parents. She thought she could see through them but she thought she could see through everyone. On the whole she was fond of them. Fern had never encouraged her to model because Fern thought modelling was asinine and Ruby was inclined to agree with her. Jeremy said Fern, being the mother, knew about matters of that sort. Glen didn't have a father to speak of so no one was anxious to interfere on the matter of his modelling. He would have appreciated having a father to chat to about this and that.

'Well,' said Jeremy, grinning broadly, 'your old man's going to be a star, after all.'

'Good, Daddy,' said Ruby. 'What in, *News for the Mentally Disadvantaged*?' She was now in her bedroom sprawled on the floor with her homework in front of her and the cat under an arm. Her father was sitting on the end of her bed.

'*Tempting Fate*,' he said with satisfaction. 'A totally new concept straight from America. No one over here has thought of anything like it. It's a quiz programme for the more or less literate. They want me to host it because they said I have credibility from News, compassion from *News for the Deaf* and wit from my newspaper column. I can't tell you how pleased I am. I'm really, really pleased.' She could tell. His eyes were bloodshot with pleasure and the smile on his face curled about his nose and cheeks, giving him the look of a garden gnome although he was better proportioned.

'I thought you said that game shows were only one up from doing *What's On In The Sewer*,' she said, studying him with interest. 'I thought you wanted to get into Arts and Drama.'

'I did,' he agreed. 'I do. But all in good time. This is special. It's a cross between *Mastermind* and that thing where they say, "Come on down". You won't get on our show with an IQ of less than 100.'

'That's Maureen's son out, then,' Ruby sighed. 'I've told

Mummy to put him in the shed. In case he's violent.' Jeremy stopped looking pleased with himself. He frowned.

'That's not funny,' he said. 'I don't know why you're both being so unkind. As far as I know there is nothing wrong with the boy. Well you know there isn't. You met him that time we all went to see *Puss In Boots* and went backstage to meet Puss. Toby Gospel directed it, you remember.'

'I remember going to see *Puss In Boots*,' Ruby admitted. 'But I don't remember him. What's his name, anyway? It's Dean, isn't it, or Lesley, or Kent.'

'It's Glen,' said Jeremy. 'And his mother is called Penny, even if her name is Maureen. So we must call her Penny and not make her feel uncomfortable. There is nothing to be gained from awkwardness or rudeness when we are offering hospitality. I have asked them to our house because they are without one and Neville is my brother. I hope you and your mother will be kind enough to help me honour my family obligation.' Ruby might have interrupted in the very slight pause here but her father gave her no chance. He was simply changing pitch.

'You are an only child Ruby, which, as I've said before, was not my choice. I would have liked you to have had a brother or sister because brothers and sisters are people you can turn to in an emergency when there is no one else. That is the power of blood. Glen isn't blood of course but I don't see why you shouldn't treat him as the brother you never had, love him if you can, at least until they get a new roof on their house.' He gazed at her with considerable emotion and Ruby gazed back. He had articulated beautifully and though she was used to his articulation and immune to it she was moved by the combination of his noble sentiment and his new career prospects.

'Of course we will,' she said. 'You know we will. Anyway I've said at school that I would like to work with mentally handicapped children. I'll treat him as a work experience project. Tell me about the show. When does it start?'

'Not for a few months yet,' said Jeremy. 'It's still at the top-secret stage so for God's sake don't tell anyone. They're talking to a couple of other people about it of course but it's

30

only a formality. *Tempting Fate* is what I've always wanted.'
He really was very, very pleased. His pleasure enabled him
to look at the imminent invasion of his house and his slightly
less than nuclear family with the peculiar belief that everything would be fine. Pleasure is a funny thing for colouring
circumstances.

Fern, being less pleasured, was less inclined to mistake the
feeling in her bones. What she feared most of all was the
open-endedness of the arrangement. What she dreaded was
that it would go on and on and there would be no escape. 'We
will never get rid of them,' she cried as they sipped a little
brandy before going to bed. 'Oh God!'

Jeremy would have liked her to have been more delighted
about *Tempting Fate* but he had long ago abandoned any
real hope of impressing her. Sometimes he guessed he did but
she never made it obvious because she hated anything
obvious. She liked everything to be understated except her
own irritation which she understated in a very obvious way.
'Where do you think they are going to sleep, for one thing?'
she carped in her low, husky voice which she imagined might
have been like Sylvia Plath's, had Sylvia Plath not been
American and almost certainly high-pitched.

'That's easy,' said Jeremy, buoyant with guilt because her
mother was in a nursing home and not in the conservatory or
the garden shed. 'Neville and Penny in the spare bedroom
and Glen in my study.'

'You hate people in your study,' protested Fern triumphantly. 'You've always said no one could use your study and
now you are allowing a boy with some sort of brain damage to
live in it. I am amazed. But I am grateful to get the importance of your study into perspective when I have always
wanted a study but have had to make do with the kitchen
table.' Jeremy laughed pleasantly.

'Oh Stubble,' he said, for this was his affectionate name for
her, 'you never miss a trick, do you? What do you need a
study for? You can write your diary in bed, the shopping list
on the kitchen table and letters of complaint wherever you
feel angriest. You don't need a study. I do.' Fern looked at
him from beneath her long dark lashes with her chin held

high in a gesture of contempt which he couldn't be expected to understand because he didn't know about the poetry.

'And what do you need one for, apart from the bills?' She couldn't be blamed for feeling bitter. Jeremy patronized her because he was successful and he thought she had no need to be.

'That's unfair,' he said. 'You know I do a lot of work from home. You know I need a private place to work. But I'm prepared to give it up because my brother has asked for help. Now let's be sensible about it. I will empty my desk of important files and lock them in the safe and then he will be perfectly comfortable.'

'I am glad,' said Fern. 'His comfort is the most important thing.'

'You look especially plain when you are sulky,' Jeremy said. 'Now I'm going to bed. If I get bags under my eyes no one is going to want to watch *News for the Deaf.* Cheer up! You're very shortly going to find yourself married to a star.' Fern took a turn about the house before going to bed herself and wondered if Ralph Fantoni loved her enough to run away with her. She asked herself what she had to lose when she appeared to be in possession of so very little. Only the blessed can be so easily ungrateful.

Penny, on the other hand, was untroubled by thoughts as down-hearted and her own position, all things considered, was not so much better than Fern's. She was sound asleep when the telephone rang in Bucket Road well after eleven. Neville leapt out of bed and dashed down the hall to answer it before it could disturb her. 'It'll be for me,' croaked Glen, who also appeared in the hall. 'I am expecting a call.'

But it was Kenny Vertigo, returning an earlier one of Neville's. 'Sorry it's so late,' he said. 'I went straight from the conversion to the National and I tried to get you at the interval but I ran into a friend who's just had a play accepted by the Lyric and he wanted to talk about it and you know how things are with writers. Now what can I do for you?'

'Well it's nothing too urgent, you know,' crooned Neville.

'Just an update, really. We were wondering where you stood with our little job.'

'Up to my arse in muck, if you'll forgive the expression,' Kenny said. He had been drinking, Neville gathered. 'As I think I told your wife, it's going to be months and there's nothing I can do about it. If you want to give the job to someone else then it's perfectly O.K. by me. I mean it really is, Neville. And I hear you're doing *The Pyjama Game* with Toby.'

'Right,' said Neville, pleased. 'Absolutely correct. Who told you, just as a matter of interest?' Even an inkling that there had been a conversation about them to which they had not been party fed the Brewsters' need. Neville and Kenny talked shop for a few more minutes and gossiped about Tony Gospel and what everyone said about him and then Neville hung up feeling warm and at peace with himself, unconcerned by the failure of their house to become more habitable. He had no intention of swapping builders. An actor in his position couldn't afford to, as he and Kenny well knew.

'Who was it?' asked Penny, rolling over as he climbed back into bed.

'Sorry darling,' said Neville. 'I tried to get to it before it woke you. It was Kenny, about the house. He'd heard from Toby about me getting *Pyjama Game* and Toby said he wouldn't have thought of anyone else. That was kind of him, wasn't it? He needn't have said it but he did. The one thing you can't fault Toby for is his frankness.'

'No,' Penny agreed. 'Did I tell you what I said to Robin? I told him I wanted to do another play. I was thinking of asking Toby. I thought I'd ask Toby about *Private Lives* or something. What do you think?' Neville was spared from telling her by the phone which he scurried to answer again. But Glen picked it up and turned his back as he spotted Neville who hovered anxiously by the stairs in case it was someone else who had heard about *The Pyjama Game.*

'Yeah,' he heard Glen say, 'Yeah, yeah, just for a few weeks. Your mother told you, did she? Yeah. Well what about your place? I can't get a court order, can I? Not quickly. I can pay, though. What about if I pay? Oh. No. No. Right. Oh, right. See you.'

'Who was that?' he asked.

'Ants' Nest,' said Glen and he sloped off to bed before anything else could be demanded of him.

'It was only Ants' Nest,' said Neville to Penny. 'God I'm tired. What's he ringing for at this hour? If you ask me he should be in a home.'

Chapter
Four

Madness can be in the blood. Paddy and Boyd Brewster had been a mind-reading act, a fine act too, but they had petered out for want of an audience, so they had turned to faith-healing from which they had made their modest fortune. Faith-healing never invaded their sons' blood. Their sons' blood inherited the gift of memory and lusted after the glory of earlier times. Maybe it inherited the madness but there was no knowing. Paddy and Boyd had died before they could be held responsible for the sins of their sons. They had gone within hours of each other, shortly after Jeremy's first God spot. 'I would like to speak of death,' he had said, never guessing what they might make of it. He had meant nothing by speaking of death. His only intention had been to make an impact.

They hadn't been deaf though he had told Nancy Dipswitch in Publicity that they were. 'It might make a diary item for someone,' he had suggested winningly, prior to taking on the news for the hard of hearing. It wouldn't have mattered if they had been because hearing wasn't essential for mind-reading or faith-healing. It was the eyes that mattered; eyes, memory and touch.

'This was Dad's, wasn't it?' said Neville, tenderly stroking the mask of tragedy he'd removed from the wall of Jeremy's study to which the brothers had retreated not long after several trunks had been deposited in the spare room. 'I've got comedy, somewhere.'

'Have you?' Jeremy asked in surprise. 'I wondered what had become of it. I looked everywhere for it. I thought I'd taken the pair of them.'

'No,' said Neville quickly. 'No.'

'No,' said Jeremy. He laughed. 'Funny isn't it, sleeping under the same roof again? We haven't done that for over twenty years. Penny O.K. now?'

'She's lying down,' Neville said. 'She was a bit overwrought, I think. She gets tired easily.'

'Well she's got a lot on, hasn't she, with five shows a week. It must be a strain. Do you think Glen will be comfortable in the shed?'

'He'll be fine,' said Neville. 'He's a tough lad.'

'We got Mrs Burt to give it a good clean-out. I told her to look for the comedy mask as a matter of fact, while she was about it. But she didn't find it because you had it. Fancy that. I'd love to have the pair of them.' He sighed and smiled at his brother but Neville only smiled back.

'So would I,' he said. Paddy used to say that Jeremy looked like the tough one, but it was Neville. Neville never gave an inch. And Boyd used to say that Jeremy was more driven. He used to say drive was what counted. Then Paddy would say but Neville is gifted and Boyd would say Jeremy is cleverer and sometimes they would end up hitting each other.

It was funny how rarely they saw eye to eye about their sons. Maybe this was mad when they were a mind-reading act. Maybe this was the root of it but maybe not. Lots of parents have favourites whom they back like horses and lots of children in the same family clamour for the same light to shine on them.

Penny was lying down because she was overwrought about her son being assigned to the shed. She was flat out on the wide, hard bed in the guest room thoroughly depleted by the turn of events which she might have anticipated, did anticipate, but couldn't persuade Neville to believe would come to pass.

Fern hadn't come to the door to greet them. Jeremy had. 'Come in,' he had said. 'Come in. How lovely. Come in.' Glen had lingered at the gate. He hadn't spoken for three days. 'Cheer up,' Neville had said in the car as they had edged across London, laden with luggage and foreboding. 'It's only for a week or two and at least you'll be comfortable. At least you'll have your own room.' But then Jeremy had said, 'Right! Now, Glen, isn't it? Fern thought you'd probably prefer the privacy of your own small apartment in the garden.'

'It's the shed,' Penny had hissed. Even she hadn't imagined a shed. Neville had ignored her.

'Great,' he had cried. 'Just the thing. The very thing for a boy, isn't it, Glen? It's the very thing.' But Glen had gone pink. He had stared at her; his irises had spurted venom at her. He had said politely, 'Right. Fine. Thanks.' Then he had taken his bag across the threshold and closed the door in their faces.

Fern had appeared eventually, in dismal but gracious brown, smiling distantly. 'Coffee, anyone?' she had said. 'Where is Glen? I thought he was coming too. We had the garden shed cleared out specially.' It had been too much for Penny. She had had to lie down, in the spare room which Fern had shown her to, murmuring, 'I've put some fresh flowers by your bed. Oh dear, they won't make you sick, will they?'

Penny remembered now that she feared and hated Fern because Fern never gave her a chance. She never allowed her a second in which she could charm or flatter or sympathize. Fern confronted the world with banter, wit and a slightly amused expression and Penny could never be sure she wasn't the butt of the joke. 'Help,' she said quietly, on the bed. 'Help.' It made her feel better. 'Help, help, help.' Help usually came when she asked for it.

She wondered what Glen was doing. He hadn't given her a chance either, slamming the door on her before she could explain it wasn't her fault that his Aunty Fern was a cow. She could hear voices in the garden and decided it would be wise to reappear, wan but determined.

'Ah,' said Neville when she did, 'darling! You're looking better already. Doesn't she, Fern? Better already.' He kissed her. 'You remember Ruby, don't you? She's grown a lot but she's as gorgeous as ever, isn't she?' Penny beamed, used to Neville's flattery but uncertain as to how it would be received by his family.

'Oh Neville,' she said. 'I haven't grown that much, just a little on the behind. Where is Glen? A lie down would do him good as well. He's been worn out all week. I suppose you get worn out too, do you, Ruby?' Ruby laughed politely. 'Glen?' Penny called, banging on the garden shed. 'Glen, come out and say hello to Ruby. She's awfully pretty. You'll love her.' She winked at Ruby and Ruby winked back. 'Come out, darling.' But nothing moved inside the shed and the door remained locked and the Brewsters outside the shed would have stood there looking at each other and the shed for ages had Fern not suggested they go in for lunch.

'Guess what, Fern,' Jeremy said. 'Guess where I found the other mask? Neville's had it all the time. Bloody comedy was with Neville all the time.'

Neville was the one who had always wanted to be in showbusiness. He was the one entitled to both the masks. His mother would have been the first to say so. Paddy was the one who had said, 'Look, if he doesn't want to be a chemist it's no use making him. Let him go into acting. He's a natural, you can see it.'

Jeremy had done what his father had said he should do. His father had said nothing could beat a good education, talent was two a penny. Jeremy had gone to university because he was the brainy one. He wasn't the theatrical one. Neville was the theatrical one. Neville should have had both masks. But he didn't say so as they strolled happily across the lawn. He laughed deeply. He said 'How lovely the garden is. How lovely everything is. How kind of you to put us up. We really do appreciate it, you know. Isn't it lovely, darling?'

'Lovely,' Penny agreed. 'Lovely. I expect Glen just wants to have a rest.'

Ruby didn't follow them into lunch. She hung about by the garden shed. She sang to herself loudly and she eyed the window which now had curtains drawn where only last week it had been blocked by the debris of sixteen years of married life. She was longing to see Penny's sad son, longing to take him in hand and perhaps reclaim part of his brain, providing of course he didn't dribble. She was sure she could handle anything mentally disturbing. She was less confident about anything physical.

Glen, sitting on the tiny collapsable bed piled with sheets and blankets, unmade-up, unwelcoming, too small and plain insulting, listened to her singing and thought about burning the shed down. It would be easy. He could set fire to the pile of magazines in the corner and sprinkle the lot with kerosene from the container on the shelf. He could scramble to safety out the window or die tragically in the fire. It would make no odds, he told himself.

'Glen,' Ruby called. 'Glen, are you coming to lunch?' He ignored her. He intended to ignore everyone. He would buy his own food and eat it in his own time and he would stay away from everyone since that was what was expected of him. He put his head in his hands. How could his mother have done it? How could she? It would have been better if she had died in childbirth. Then he could have loved her memory. Then she would never have married a Brewster. Then she wouldn't have abandoned him from choice.

Ruby tapped on the door. 'Do you want me to get you some salad? I could bring it out to you. I could bring us both some and we could have a picnic?' She sounded repellent. She had a ridiculously patronizing voice and she was only thirteen or something. Who on earth did the Brewsters think they were? 'You must be hungry. I bet you're starving. I'm starving and I haven't had to move today. I didn't get up until twelve. Glen?'

He went to the window and pulled back the curtain a tiny bit. He saw her, stretched out on the grass doing exercises, waving her long, slim, pale legs in the air so he could see her underwear over which she was wearing a long white top and a loose pink skirt. It was pretty obvious to him, as he watched her, that she wasn't thirteen. She was fit, too. Suddenly she stopped exercising and looked across at him. 'O.K.' he called. 'I won't be a minute. Hang on.' He did his hair in the mirror over the bed and washed at the tiny basin. 'I was asleep,' he said as he walked towards her. 'You must be Ruby. Where's everyone else?'

'Having lunch,' she said. She smiled at him in disbelief. 'You're not at all how I remembered you. You're much bigger.' She laughed.

'So are you,' he said. 'Much.' He couldn't think of anything else.

'I hope you don't mind the shed,' she said. 'It was my idea. I thought you'd be more comfortable, having some privacy. You're much better off out of the house because we're awful close up. You wait and see. You'll be grateful.' She spoke lightly but with spirit. Glen shrugged.

'The shed's fine,' he said. 'I like sheds, as a matter of fact.' He smiled at her. As he walked with her through the conservatory, he decided to be polite to Ruby for his mother's sake. She wasn't dead, when it came down to it, and she was only doing her best. 'I'm only staying for a couple of nights anyway, then I'm off to a friend's place,' he said. 'We're going to Jerusalem for a while in a week or two.'

'An Israeli exchange,' said Ruby.

'Sort of,' Glen agreed.

'Oh,' Ruby remarked. 'Lucky.' For a mentally unhealthy boy, she thought, he was awfully independent.

The Brewsters senior might have thought their grandchildren lacked imagination. Jeremy and Neville had spent their childhoods writing plays and acting them, concocting special effects, building sets and writing tickets which they charged for. They might have thought Glen and Ruby didn't know how to amuse themselves and that what did amuse them was odd. They might have been able to teach them a thing or two but Paddy and Boyd were dead. There was no getting away from it. A great many of their relics were in the garden shed. In any case, what good had come of it? What good does come of relying too heavily on the imagination? It only encourages unrealistic expectations.

40

Jeremy and Fern's was a very big house, with a very large garden and the garden backed onto a park. The rooms were very big because Fern had knocked down lots of walls to achieve three bedrooms, three bathrooms, a study, a drawing-room, a small sitting-room, a dining-room, a kitchen and a conservatory, where once there had been space for a Victorian family of twelve and its staff. The whole was a miracle of cleverly placed RSJs. To emphasize the new dimensions, she had employed pastels, mirrors, *objets*, lamps, subtle fabrics and mahogany recovered from generations of paint. The very best of everything had been used, painstakingly searched for and found in places no ordinary poet would have bothered to look. It was a tribute to early prosperity and the expectation of more to come. In an understated way it suggested high hopes. Had it not been for the tiniest hints of showbusiness on the study walls it might have been the home of a high-flying don with a private income.

'Light is all important, isn't it?' Fern said to Penny as she showed her around in the late afternoon and sun poured in from the west. 'Light and space.' She was talking to herself more than Penny. She didn't honestly expect Penny to appreciate it.

But Penny murmured reverentially. 'It has been your life's work, hasn't it?'

'What?' said Fern.

'The house. You have turned it into a work of art.'

'Good God,' Fern cried. 'What a disgusting thought. Of course I haven't.' She glared at Penny and Penny thought about bursting into tears. 'Honestly! I've much more to do with my life than spend it on a house. That's just too depressing for words. That's almost the most depressing thing I've heard all day.'

'Sorry,' said Penny. 'Sorry.' She would tell Neville to tell Jeremy that he was married to a snake. 'I just thought, you know, that since you don't work you've had the time to make it beautiful. Women with careers just don't get the time. I didn't mean to offend you. I've just never had the time myself, you know, with my career and everything. I would love to have a house like this. But I've never had the time.

41

Bucket Road is pretty, of course, and fashionable. But it's not beautiful. I was only saying that this is beautiful.' She put her hand to her throat and when she found there was no scarf there, she twiddled the bit of loose skin under her chin.

'Thank you,' said Fern. 'I am flattered.' Penny knew she wasn't. She should have told the truth. She should have said how like a morgue it was and how little luxury there was, despite its size and the size of Jeremy's income, despite the taste Fern was supposed to have and all the time she had on her hands, despite all the stuff that had been bequeathed to them by Jeremy's parents.

Bits of furniture worth thousands of pounds, looking as if they might have been picked up from junk shops, were left carelessly in halls and bedrooms where she, for one, would have taken them for bits of junk. There were paintings on the walls which gave no suggestion of importance or style or money. They were just faint blobs of colour which meant nothing to anyone. 'Oh, I love this,' she cried in front of a large pale canvas which was much like all the others. Two thin splats of red and yellow ran from top to bottom in parallel wavering lines. 'This is wonderful,' she said. 'What's it called?'

'Blood and Pus,' said Jeremy coming out from his study. 'It's by a friend of Fern's called Ralph Fantoni. You'll meet him. He's always hanging about the place, waiting to grope anything female that gives him a second glance.' He laughed and Penny laughed too.

'Shut up, Jeremy,' said Fern. 'It's called *Study 3*, as a matter of fact, Penny. Jeremy is being unkind because he has no talent to speak of himself.'

'But luckily,' he said, 'I have legs which are longer than my arms, unlike Ralph Fantoni.' Jeremy was no fool. He understood Fern's watchfulness and Ralph's ever presence. At least he thought he did. And he thought he met it with just the right touch of ridicule.

Penny giggled again, relieved to be with someone who wasn't frightened of Fern and who knew how to put her in her place. 'You are silly, Jeremy,' she simpered. 'You've got loads going for you. Talent, looks, legs, everything, hasn't he,

42

Fern? You have to admit.' She slid her arm around his waist and squeezed it and immediately felt comfortable again. Jeremy grinned at her.

'You aren't so bad yourself,' he said. 'Is she Fern?'

'I'll go and see to the supper,' Fern said and she hurried back to the kitchen where she intended to resent the assumption that she would happily do it all on her own.

'Fern,' Neville yelped. 'You startled me. I was just slicing up a few potatoes. I thought I would do some dauphinois. What do you think? I've stuck the garlic in the lamb but I can't find the rosemary. Where do you keep the rosemary?'

'In the garden,' she said. 'But the lamb's for tomorrow, Neville. It's lasagne tonight because we're all tired. We always have a roast for Sunday lunch.'

'Oh dear,' said Neville. 'Typical. Sorry, Fern. Sorry, dear.' He stood helplessly at the sink, wearing one of Fern's aprons. 'We don't go in for Sunday lunch ourselves. We don't usually get up till well after two. But never mind. I adore lasagne.' He grinned at Fern and waited for approval because Penny would have said something encouraging at a point as difficult as this. But Fern merely put the lamb back into the fridge.

'Actually Fern,' Neville said, 'I think Penny might just like an egg or something because she can't take pasta. It bloats her. She swells up poor little thing and I have to jump on her stomach to get her back into shape again.'

Who knows what another family would have made of it? It is rare for two marriages to fit comfortably under one roof, sharing the same food and drawing-room, wandering through the same conservatory, keen to get their hands on the same mask of comedy and trying to please each other into the bargain. It offends all sense of territory and hospitality to have a strange brother-in-law hovering anxiously by the double drainer, determined not to be a nuisance or an encumbrance, anxious not to disturb the usual running of the household even though the introduction of his family has doubled its size. And it's hard to avoid bitterness when a boy is banished to the garden shed yet made to feel as if he's been offered an empire. But it is all made so much more difficult when there is mania as well. Mania isn't easy at the best of times.

43

As they settled down for their first night under the same roof in twenty years Jeremy and Neville said to their wives, 'I know, I know. But we have to put up with it, don't we?' And when this wasn't readily seen to be the case they said crossly, 'Look we don't have a choice. I don't have a choice and you don't have a choice so let's just leave it at that.' They both felt badly served by wives they considered should have known better. They both told themselves that things couldn't get any worse so they would have to improve.

And matters might have improved, even among the Brewsters, had certain fundamental mistakes not already been made which set a series of unfortunate balls rolling. Penny, only too aware that she had landed herself in a hostile environment just to secure a spa bath, drew on her infallible instinct for survival and astonishingly wooed the wrong ally. She chose to charm Jeremy because he was by far the more easily charmed but she chose wrong.

Neville, seeing that Fern needed to be charmed, chose out of the blue to remind her of the days when he had been the brother she favoured and declared with passion over the lasagne, apropos of his wife's tendency to bloat, 'I can honestly say Fern that you've kept your figure better than any girlfriend I ever had, present company excepted. It's as trim as I remember it and God alone knows, I remember it.' Fern didn't find this charming. Nor did Penny and nor, as a matter of fact, did Jeremy. Glen did, but that was small comfort. Glen hooted for far longer than was necessary or even comprehensible and Ruby took Glen's hilarity for the first clear sign of his handicap.

'At your school,' she said chattily, 'is psychiatric counselling part of the curriculum?'

'Ruby!' her mother had cried. 'What an offensive question.'

And Penny had said, determined to win another friend, 'I'm sure she didn't intend it to be. Do you have therapy, Ruby?' And what with one thing and another, the tension rose and might have gone through the roof, taking the wretched circumstance with it had not Neville stilled everyone's tongue by saying, 'Look, we're all very tired. But Glen,

Penny and I want you, Jeremy, Fern and Ruby, to know how grateful we are for the spare room and the shed and to thank you for making us as comfortable as you have. We intend to treat your house as ours because that is the best way to return the compliment and I would like us all to raise our glasses. To us.'

'To us,' everyone agreed.

'And with our champagne,' Fern said later, in bed. 'He toasted us with champagne we paid for.'

Chapter
Five

Bad blood or no bad blood, there is a life beyond the family and opportunities must be seized since they never arise. If Miss Penny had taught Merilee Bawdle anything, she had taught her that and in gratitude Merilee had waged a campaign on Miss Penny's behalf every year because she believed Miss Penny deserved a Fertile Fruit Television Award.

She could never credit Miss Penny's failure to carry off a single trophy in fifteen years of being nominated. Nor could Miss Penny who wondered whether it had anything to do with her audience. When she considered who else staggered home under the weight of the children's banana each year she could only assume that her appeal was to a mass market incapable of putting pen to paper. She made this assumption with good reason.

Kidding About's greatest appeal was to children under the age of three who were placed in front of it by mothers desperate for a cigarette and a few minutes on the phone. Merilee had been just such a mother when she had first written to a Miss Penny so young and joyful that she'd had no need of a scarf and could gallop higher and harder than any toddler on the set.

'*Dear Miss Penny,*' Merilee had written, '*I've never sent anyone a fan letter before but I simply had to let you know how much my little boy Buck loves your show. He sits in front of it good as gold and doesn't move an inch or make a single sound the whole time you're on. He loves the galloping bits. I wonder if you could send him a photo with your name on it. We could stick it on the end of his cot and maybe he would be quiet all night as well as all day. Ha ha.*'

Buck was now older than Glen and could put pen to paper really quite well but Merilee continued to write because she had never forgotten how kind Penny had been when she had sought advice about her divorce. '*Dear Miss Penny,*' she had pleaded, '*You were so good about the worm treatment, I haven't hesitated to ask you what I should do next. I want to leave my husband who is asleep on the divan. We have nothing in common any more.*'

Penny, by now experienced in divorce herself, had replied, '*It is my belief that if there is a way out and you can take it for the best, then you should. Thank you for the lovely photo of little Buck. He reminds me so much of my Glen.*'

Merilee, freed from the ghastly strictures of marriage to a somnivolent, had come into her own, completing her schooling then taking teacher training which thrust her into a position of unimagined power and influence. She was now the headmistress of a small but well-connected school in Sunderland where she remained Miss Penny's greatest fan.

'*Dear Miss Penny,*' she wrote at the very hour her heroine was lying in some distress on the spare bed in her brother-in-law's house begging the thin air for help, '*You will be pleased to know that so far 459 people in the Sunderland area have agreed to vote you Children's Personality of The Year in the Fertile Fruit Television Awards. This is 304 more than last year when you were nominated for The Most Popular Female which I feel now may not have been appropriate. I'm sure that when the Sunderland region votes are added to the nationwide figures we will have enough for you to win. Here's hoping. You deserve it. All my best wishes, Merilee.*'

Her letter was an opportunity to be wrung if at all possible. 'The thing is Robin,' Penny said, wriggling forward to reach

47

halfway across the large empty desk, 'I've been nominated for the fifteenth year and I do think we could do something about it, just to give it a little push. It would be marvellous if I could win something, just once, don't you think?' She didn't mention the letter. She wasn't sure if it was legal but she took advantage of the hope it offered. Robin stared out of his window down onto the car-park with a lack of interest he hoped she would put down to ethics.

'I know you're doing them again this year,' Penny burbled, 'and I don't want to embarrass you in any way but I do think it's important, for morale you know. Not for me, so much as for the show, the whole team. They've worked so hard over the years. I was thinking of those filmed inserts. They would clinch it, I'm positive. We could get some really good publicity with film stories. And we have the time. They're still voting, aren't they? We want to get the older voter, viewer, who might write in. I've talked to Dave about it and he said he thought it would be marvellous to do some film and a bit less galloping. He's all for it. He did come from Current Affairs, let's face it, so he knows what he is talking about.'

'You've sorted out your differences then,' Robin said drily.

'You know I can get on with anyone,' Penny declared without a trace of embarrassment. 'If I put my mind to it. I respect his judgement. He knows a lot about documentaries.'

Robin sighed. 'What about the play? How is the play doing?'

'What play?' Penny asked. 'No one's offered me a play. I'm not doing a play. I'd love to, of course. But I'm not.'

'Oh,' said Robin. 'I thought you might have lined one up. I daresay you've been too busy, what with your move and what have you. How is the new house?'

'We're not in the new house,' she said. 'It's a shambles. Kenny Vertigo is doing Marty Cork's Gothic conversion so we have to wait until that's finished before he can start on ours. We're staying with Jeremy.'

'Jeremy with the wife,' Robin said in awe. 'Well that must be nice for you.' He tugged at his fingers until they clicked. 'I heard someone say Jeremy was moving over to L.E., to do a new game show. Is he? It'll be a disaster if he does, of course.

Journalists can't do Light Entertainment any more than stars can do documentaries.'

'He's a star already though, isn't he?' Penny said. 'Now come on Robin, let me do some film, please. Please. I could go to factories and things to see how butter is made. Or maybe I could go into the playground to ask children what they think of the Queen or somebody. You must see the potential.'

Robin sighed again, louder. 'Listen my dear, it's the Powder law of staying on top. Stick to what you know. That way you'll avoid catastrophes. Believe me. You are a star. Stay one. Stick to the galloping. And you can tell Jeremy I said so.' So Penny went back to her dressing-room, sad beyond belief that Jeremy would never be a star, delighted that Robin still thought she was one, but dissatisfied, definitely less content than she had hoped to be. She was under par anyway, what with the tension at home. She was doing her best to stay on top of it, but frankly, how high and how long would she would have to stay?

'*Dear Merilee,*' she wrote at the little desk she called her office because the *Kidding About* offices did not include space for her, '*How lovely. How truly lovely and loyal. Will you thank every one of those 459 people and tell them that all I am doing is my best and that I am working hard to improve it. I hope to be putting little news stories into the programme soon so I can get out of the studio and among the people. I think the viewers would love it, don't you? And keep your eye out for a little bit of serious theatre that I'm shortly to be involved in. It's early days yet but something to look forward to. Perhaps you could bring Class Mauve down on a coach. I'm sure it would be a marvellous experience for them. Which reminds me, could you thank them for the gorgeous bottle-top snowman. We will try to show it sometime next week. And could you mention to Samantha's mother that while we don't do tap dancing on the show we do like to do musical movement and, provided Samantha is no taller than the average four-year-old, being eight is not necessarily a handicap. She might like to write to the producer whose name is Dave Caster, as in sugar, though I'm afraid sweet is not the right word for him. Must dash, the cameras are about to roll. Much love to you and yours, Miss Penny.*'

Then she rang Toby Gospel. She was sure Neville wouldn't mind. Why would he? Toby had come to their wedding and it wasn't as if they were competing for the same parts. She would never do anything to hurt Neville, just as he would never do anything to hurt her. They respected each other far too much.

Neville, even when he was behind the wheel of Madge McGuire's taxi, liked to think of their marriage as a partnership to which they contributed equally. Penny's income was of course far more predictable than his and much larger, if it came to that, but this was really only a matter of luck, a matter of the right break at the right time in front of the right person. Not many people would dispute that he was the more talented.

Of course he always denied it when Penny said so because he knew it upset her to think she had abandoned a promising stage career for children's television and that had she not, she might have achieved fame in plays the calibre of those he was offered. But he knew, and he thought she knew in her heart of hearts, that the theatre promised her very little and that her acting ability was already extended by the three minute story she told at the end of every *Kidding About.*

Only the other day she had been tormented by *The Three Billy Goats Gruff.* 'What is the troll thinking about?' she had cried in a frenzy of alternatives. 'I mean, maybe he didn't want to hurt anyone. Maybe it was all territorial and he only wanted to stop the bridge from falling in. It was the roof over his head, wasn't it? We wouldn't want anyone running over our roof, if we had a roof. And it was very fair of him not to eat the smaller goats, wasn't it? I mean he might have been a good guy underneath, just misunderstood.' She had the same trouble with Rumpelstiltskin. Neville had laughed and tried to advise her. 'You are sweet,' he had said. 'Just read it. That's all you have to do. Follow the autocue and you can't go wrong.'

He didn't have any trouble with motivation himself. He just acted. He took his script, learnt it, learnt the songs if there were any, learnt the movements and did them. He could even do an American accent if it was called for. He didn't need to worry about motivation. If there was one thing he was confident about it was his natural ability.

What did worry him was why it wasn't more widely recognized. He had his allies, of course, like Toby Gospel and Madge McGuire but he couldn't honestly say he had hit the big time. Not the very, very big time where his name was household and his foibles legend. No one told Neville Brewster stories yet, or at least none that he was proud of.

In Madge's taxi, to which he had retreated when Fern had made it plain that she expected him to retreat, he pulled at his nose and wished his part in *The Pyjama Game* was slightly bigger. He'd have loved the Rock Hudson role, but then again, maybe not. He revved the motor and started to whistle. It was only a matter of time, he told himself, only a matter of luck, only a matter of getting into the public eye. He pulled away wondering about the public's eye and where it was to be found and it came to him, so quickly and painlessly that he laughed out loud. It was obvious. He could read the *Kidding About* stories. It would save Penny the agony and it would be a regular exposure for him: every day, for three minutes. He would get her to ask Robin. Or possibly he would get Madge to ask Robin. It could be fantastic. He might become a cult figure. So pleased was he by the inspiration that he decided to drive straight over to ask Madge what she thought. He wanted to tell her about Jeremy having that mask of tragedy anyway. He told her practically everything. That's what agents are for.

'Toby?' said Penny. 'Thanks for calling back, darling. What? No, no, Neville's fine.' She smiled at herself in the mirror and pulled her little black scarf with the red spots further to the side. 'I wasn't ... no, actually there were a couple of things. I wondered if you had any power over Kenny Vertigo. Yes darling, I know and we're awfully grateful but we're stuck at Jeremy's and the dreaded Fern's ... no she hasn't ... and I don't think I'm going to be able to take it much longer.'

She leaned towards the mirror to examine her teeth. She had very nice teeth though they were inclined to yellow which was worrying. She avoided yellow scarves for that very reason. 'At the weekend,' she said. 'What? I know but Gothic conversions can't take forever ... Will you? Thank you. You are wonderful. And the other thing was this ... you wouldn't know of the teeniest, tiniest, squidgiest thing going that I could do ... no, theatre ... in anything ... God no, nothing like that, I've got a contract until the end of the year, my darling. I just wouldn't mind a bit of something else.' She found a tiny blemish on her chin and scraped at it with a carefully manicured nail.

'Now that's very crude,' she giggled. 'Stop it at once. Of course I can sing. You've heard me. I do twelve variations on "The Wheels of the Bus" and I can do a three-part harmony, on my own, of "Five Little Ducks". Will you have a think? Will you? You are lovely! How are the children? Oh! How horrible! Never mind, I'll hear from you, then. Bye bye darling.'

She didn't laugh out loud, as Neville had done but she did allow herself a small contented smile because she felt that she was in command of her own destiny which is a privilege not always accorded to stars. She had not only taught Merilee the importance of seizing opportunities, she understood the need to create them. She had that over Fern, at least.

Fern's poor reputation in Neville's and Penny's circle wasn't altogether fair. Her unwarranted rudeness was famous only because she had been overheard to remark at their wedding that she'd never seen such a vulgar display of mediocrity in the whole of her life. No one liked her after that. No friend of Penny's and Neville's had a kind word to say about her. Had she known she would have said she couldn't have given a toss but she would have been lying, because underneath Fern was as sensitive as the next writer. She was stung by criticism. She was stung by the repulsive way Penny had patronized her.

'You would have been sick,' she told Ralph Fantoni. "I am a career woman," she said. "You are not." The woman has a brain the size of a germ. I should have slapped her.' She was sitting in the garden on an ancient but valuable swing, with a small tapestry on her lap into which she inserted a needle and thread every so often, almost without noticing where and to what effect. She was feeling very beautiful, injured, but strong.

Ralph stood behind her, leaning casually against one of the cast-iron supports, giving the swing a nudge every now and again so that a tiny breeze rippled about Fern's creamy white neck, blowing the loose tendril of burnished hair hither and thither. 'You've only got yourself to blame, my little love,' he said. 'If you came clean and admitted you were the world's greatest unread poet you wouldn't be in the pickle you are today.'

He pulled the swing to a stop and moved to stand against her then he massaged the back of her neck with hard, probing fingers until small blotches of pink began to appear and she said, 'You have healing hands. You have an artist's touch.'

And he gasped, 'Then let me touch you a little more, a little longer and a little lower.'

And she whispered, 'Oh stop it. You know the state of play' and stood up quickly to get more coffee.

'What is the state of play then?' he said. 'Are you going to let me show Fenchurch the poems or not? Do you want to let Miss Penny get the better of you or not? Come on, Fern. You're grown up now. You can take rejection on the chin. Or can you? Maybe you can't. Maybe that's where Miss Penny has the edge over you.'

'There's no comparison and you know there isn't,' she called, having moved across to the elegant white wrought-iron table by the gloriously weeping willow. 'She isn't exposing herself in the same way. When she's rejected, it's not her soul that is scorned. It's only her galloping.'

'The woman has no soul,' Ralph murmured. 'And you have no heart.' He had crossed to the table to place himself perilously close to her, all but on top of her and Fern, gripped by their intimacy and his profound understanding of her, suddenly put down the coffee pot, laden with the sludge of uncertain but expensive origin and put her arms around his neck with a small, breathless cry.

It had nothing to do with Penny's outrageous flirtation with Jeremy. It had nothing to do with Neville reminding her of the charms of her youth. It had nothing to do with either of those things which she could not bring herself to mention to Ralph. She simply felt compelled. She stood on tiptoe, though it was only just necessary, and she placed her mouth, fractionally and bewitchingly open, onto his and she allowed it to linger there, full of promise for nine seconds.

'You can have three poems,' she whispered huskily and so low that Glen in the shed who had timed the kiss could hardly hear her although his window was wide open.

'Which ones?' Ralph gasped. 'Which?' His lips were in her hair, lost, Glen feared as he peered over the sill, for she had masses of it. Fern pulled away though she continued to gaze at him and Ralph put his fingers to his mouth, as if to hold the kiss in place but actually, Glen saw, to remove several long strands which he had bitten from the copper tendril.

'Which do you think?' Fern asked. 'Which ones might he like? He might loathe them all. Oh God, I'm not sure. He could loathe them all.'

'That's enough. You must show them,' said Ralph. 'And you will. We'll let him see *The African* because that's your newest, *The Organ Grinder* because that's your longest and *Ophelia* because it's my favourite.'

He looked across towards the garden shed and for one horrifying minute Glen believed he had been spotted. But Ralph's eyes were half closed and he began to recite moodily,

'*Ophelia smiled and said, for a runt,*
He made a good job of watering her garden.'

'How could he not love it?' he asked. 'It's brilliant.' Then he followed Fern who had collected their cups and the coffee pot onto a delicate ceramic tray and was heading across the garden to the conservatory. 'I read Jeremy's column this morning,' was the last thing Glen heard him say. 'He doesn't really believe all that crap he writes, does he?'

The true answer to that question was maybe. Jeremy was never sure because he could argue any case so cogently and so powerfully that on the one hand he believed what he wrote and on the other he could quite see why he mightn't. He wrote what he thought would go down best on the day, whatever would provoke the most correspondence because

54

provocation was the whole point. Each Tuesday he sat down and wrote for the Thursday a pithy five-hundred words which he hoped captured the mood of the nation as he saw it from behind the television news.

He had been doing it for years, ever since his success on the God spot had convinced a short-lived editor that he could and should do it. Incoming editors, too nervous of their positions to act decisively, let him stay, pleased when the letters came in, nervous when they didn't, but persuaded that his face on the box justified their publishing his unspeakable waffle. Every year they hoped he would be named the Fertile Fruits Television Reporter of the Year because then there would be no question of their great good sense in having him.

Fern only sometimes read the column because she knew he was capable of thinking anything that suited him and it only amused her occasionally to see what it was. When Ralph had left and Glen had sloped off unseen to school with a forged note from his stepfather and in the sure knowledge that he had £603 in his football boot, she sat down with the newspaper at the kitchen table.

'*One has to ask oneself in this day and age,*' Jeremy had written, '*what God intended for Woman. We know for a fact that he didn't intend her to eat from the fruit in the Garden of Eden. But did he honestly intend for her to eat from the fruit intended for Man? I believe he did.*' He was striking out in defence of a worker sacked from a pizza parlour. '*No woman is less feminine for boldly trudging where most men fear to trudge. There's a place for a woman's touch, in even the roughest of houses and I am speaking now of the infamous Peesa Pizza. It wasn't easy for little Juanita Hobbs. Like all mothers who help earn the family crust she made sacrifices and her courage surely entitles her to a job, whatever the job, wherever the job. Women should have jobs. I go further. A woman with a job is as good as any man. God, I am sure would see a woman with a job as a complete woman. Eve might well have been a market gardener.*' It was, as Ralph had said, crap.

Fern wasn't in the habit of telephoning him at work and she didn't telephone him now. She took her special roller ballpen and her special lined paper and she composed her letter of revenge. '*Dear Sir,*' she wrote, '*How curious of your columnist Jeremy Brewster to find a woman with a job a complete woman. What does he think a woman without a job is, half a woman? I wish he would explain as I am unemployed and choose to be so. Does he find me lacking? Yours sincerely, Fern Brewster (Mrs).*'

She addressed the envelope and she posted it with some pleasure. If there was one thing she loathed it was to be unfavourably compared and Jeremy, she told herself, was comparing her to the dullard Penny. If there was something she loathed more it was to be accused of falling short. She intended to show Jeremy and to show Penny and to show Neville that she had more to offer the world than a fine house and she didn't intend doing it in a crude scene across the dinner table either.

She would give her poems to Ralph for his friend Fenchurch and she would show them where real talent could get you when it was teamed with taste and brains. As she strolled back from the post box she thought she might rag-roll the garden shed into the bargain so that when Glen had moved out it could be her private retreat. This was not so much creating an opportunity as indulging an old habit. The house was her forte, like it or not.

Chapter
Six

Perhaps Paddy's and Boyd's contribution was negligible. Maybe all they provided was a humdrum existence for their sons. Like Juanita Hobbs, formerly of *Peesa Pizza*, the young Brewsters may have been mesmerized by the tiny specks of limelight they remembered from their parents' past and so the course of their lives was fixed.

Miss Hobbs, overwhelmed by the adulation she received from her friends and family now she was a public figure, telephoned Jeremy to say how grateful she was and how everyone had seen it in the paper and said how good it was, though it was a shame they hadn't used a photograph because she was thinking now she might be a model. No, she hadn't got her job back but even so, she wanted to thank him for being so nice. Jeremy said, 'Not at all.' He found it as gratifying as could be, defending a young life which otherwise might have been lost.

'It's what it's all about,' he said to Julian Fortescue when they met for lunch and Julian laughed and said it wasn't half as gratifying as his *Tempting Fate* contract would be. Julian said, 'We're delighted to have you on board, Jeremy, we really are. We're all convinced this one's a winner. You know that, don't you? The pilot's just a formality.' Jeremy asked him to dinner at once. He rang Fern and he said, 'One more for dinner, Stubble. And tell Neville and Penny to be there. I'm sure they'd love to meet Julian ... No, he's not that one. I don't think he has a wife. I forgot to ask and he didn't mention it.'

After five days under the one roof the Brewsters believed they knew where they stood. Crude scenes had been avoided because they avoided scenes of any sort. Neville avoided Fern, Fern took care that Jeremy avoided Penny and Neville made sure that Fern and Penny were never in any room at the same time. He took care that Penny left early in the morning, came home at supper time, refused Fern's cooking and took a sandwich to the spare room where she watched the spare television though she complained to him bitterly that she was lost without a spare video. Since he was not yet required for rehearsals, he forced himself to spend a lot of time in the ruins of Mandarin Street or in Madge McGuire's taxi and so horrible was this that it didn't occur to him that Glen might have been festering in the shed. It didn't really occur to anyone. They were all too grateful that crude scenes were being avoided though all of them indulged in crude thoughts. They pursued their various interests, forgot completely about Glen and they grumbled. If anything felt remotely uncomfortable, nothing felt at all ominous. He was only a boy.

On the fifth night, shortly before the dinner to which everyone had agreed to come to meet Julian whoever he was, Fern spoke up in the privacy of their bedroom. 'What's wrong with his jaws?' she asked angrily as she pulled black tights up her short but well defined legs. 'No one normal makes that much noise when he eats. Wasn't he ever X-rayed as a child?'

'I know,' said Jeremy agreeably. 'It's shocking. I think he was born with too much saliva.' He was lying on their great white bed, dripping with lace and cushions and bathed in carefully constructed shadows, at peace, satisfied, unaware of his wife's letter in the post, untroubled by his brother's saliva, pleased that he had done his duty by his brother and the girl from Peesa Pizza and delighted with the impact he imagined

58

Julian might have on his family. Julian was living proof of his success.

'He hangs around the kitchen all day,' Fern said. 'Always snuffling for food. What happened? Wasn't he breast fed long enough?' Jeremy laughed.

'You are mean,' he said. 'Poor old Neville. He can't help being greedy. But Penny hardly eats a thing. We can't complain.'

'Huh!' Fern scoffed. 'She takes chocolate to her room. She only pretends not to eat. She pretends to be a bird but she is a pig.' She examined her face carefully in the vast gilt-framed mirror that lined a wall of their *en suite*. 'That's why she has such rotten skin,' she added.

'The boy seems nice enough,' Jeremy said, unwilling to defend Penny's skin when he knew it was a sensitive area.

'Considering his problems.' Fern admitted. 'He's completely neglected. Have you noticed? Any wonder he has problems! But at least he can look after himself. She makes him do all his own meals.'

'I bet he appreciates you cooking for him while he's here,' Jeremy said, squirming comfortably, enjoying the sensation of goodness and kindness.

'I don't' said Fern. 'I've hardly even seen him. I told you. He looks after himself.' She smiled affably because she was as happy as he was. She didn't harangue him about his column or complain about his cloying attitude to Penny. Revenge was at hand and knowing it was she could pretend she didn't know there was a column or an attitude. She revelled in her secrets.

'Really?' said Jeremy, less comfortably. 'Ruby was right, then. She said he would prefer the shed. Ruby's always right.' Then he rose from the bed. 'Haven't you finished in there, yet?' he said. And he stood before the mirror assessing himself in the way men and women do when their bodies are commodities or if they aren't, really deserve to be.

Penny, three doors along, on the opposite side of the richly carpeted hall, frowned into the mirror of her *en suite* with a similarly critical eye though hers was a much smaller mirror and less flattering, she thought. 'I would hate that,' she

59

shrieked. 'I would hate it and you are not to do it. We're not a double act.' She rubbed *crème pour le cou* into her throat. She rubbed so hard that new wrinkles appeared and she coated them with *crème* as she spotted them so that within minutes her whole neck was a mass of white slime. She wanted to scream.

'I know we're not,' said Neville who was staring out the window. 'I know we're not and I never said we were. For God's sake Penny, I'm not trying to take over anything. All I'm saying is that we can help each other. You hate reading the story. I could do with the exposure. It would take some of the strain off you. That's all I'm saying.' In the half light that glowed from the delicate flower lamps which sprouted from the wall above the bed, he could be taken for an astonishingly good looking man though the fact was unnoticed by his wife who was about to pass through the mirror so absorbed was she in the folds of her flesh.

When the *crème* had all finally disappeared she tossed her shiny peach dressing-gown back from her shoulders and draped it about her breasts exposing as much of her cleavage as she could without revealing anything as unseemly as a nipple. She put her head to one side to study the effect. 'Do you know,' she said, 'I think I should wear my dresses lower cut,' she said. 'What do you think?'

'Very nice,' he said without looking at her. He wanted to punch the pillow so overwhelmed was he by frustration and dismay. He was close to shouting at her when he never shouted at her. He had so few really good ideas.

'You're not even looking at me,' Penny complained. 'You have to look at me to get the effect.'

'I am looking at you,' he said. 'Very nice. I don't understand you, Penny. I don't understand why you're over-reacting. All I'm suggesting is that I sit on a stool, read the story, then straight back to you. You don't even have to name me. I could just be the person who does it. I could be Uncle Neville. You'd only have to say, "Now it's time for the story. Ready, Uncle Neville?" And I would say, "Ready Miss Penny and may I say how pretty you are looking today." Then ...' He flicked his fingers and pointed to an imaginary stool with an imaginary Uncle Neville sitting on it ... 'into the story.'

'No,' he added, examining her breasts very briefly. 'I don't much like it. I think the scarf is better.'

'I don't mean for the show,' said Penny. 'For off duty or for other work. I don't just do *Kidding About*, you know, Neville. I am an actress, or have you forgotten? I rang Toby today and asked him to keep an eye out for something, as a matter of fact.'

'Did you?' he said. 'Did you really? What sort of something? And did you mention it to Madge as a matter of fact?' He knew she hadn't. 'What do you suppose Madge would have to say about that?' He wished she had phoned Madge and he wished she had heard Madge say, 'Now listen Penny, love, you're doing well where you are so let's not tempt Fate.'

'Darling,' sighed Penny. 'In ten years Madge has got me one pantomime. I don't think I need to consult her about anything.'

'What did Toby say, anyway?' asked Neville. 'Did he mention me?' He threw himself into the tiny antique chair by the door with fury clinging to the lining of his throat unwilling to be dislodged because fury was alien to his role in the marriage. 'Was he friendly?'

'Very,' said Penny. 'He said he'd find something for me since I had the best bosom in the business. And I don't think he mentioned you. Where are you going? Please don't hurry down to dinner. I can't stand the pressure. Fern does everything crossly and glares at me whenever I offer to help.'

'Free accommodation isn't perfect,' he said. 'I will see you down there.' And he left her to her cleavage which she admired again since the mirror was completely free.

Glen and Ruby had not been asked to dinner but Jeremy had said Ruby should come and have a small glass of wine and meet Julian before buzzing back to her room to do her homework. She was often called in to impress his friends and contacts and she invariably did with her exceptionally fine eyes and with the startling freshness of her expression which was untramelled by disappointment or failure.

'I've asked Glen to come over too,' she announced to her parents as they sat with their pre-drink drinks in the conservatory enjoying the evening sun, the smell of honeysuckle, the absence of Neville and Penny and the certainty that, despite the current imposition, they were blessed.

'Oh darling,' cried Fern. 'Why? What a mad thing to do.'

'It wasn't,' said Ruby. 'There's nothing wrong with him. I've studied him very carefully. He's not at all disadvantaged you know. He has a wonderful body.'

'Honestly,' laughed Jeremy.

'When?' said Fern. 'He's never here. When have you studied him? He stays in the shed.'

'Lots of times,' Ruby shrugged. 'It would have been awfully rude not to. He is our guest, isn't he? I think he should eat with us more often.'

'I can't think of a single good reason why,' Fern said.

'Here he is now,' said Jeremy.

'With Julian,' said Fern. 'What on earth is he doing coming round the back? You'd think he'd knock at the front door, wouldn't you?' They all stood, smiled, walked out onto the lawn and called 'Hello' so their voices echoed and hovered hospitably in the still evening air.

'Hello,' cried Neville bounding through the conservatory door before Fern could offer Julian her second cheek. 'Glorious night, isn't it, absolutely glorious.' And everyone agreed that it was and that drinks should be taken in the garden where Fern had carelessly arranged half a dozen chairs about the wrought iron table and where she sincerely hoped to herself Penny would be unable to find them. She took the roses Julian offered and casually placed them with perfect aim among the white daisies in the small vase waiting on the table.

'They're divine,' she said. 'Thank you. I'd adore champagne, Jeremy. Be a love, Glen,' she said, 'And give Jeremy a hand. He's not awfully good with the ice bucket. No, you stay, Ruby and keep us elderly people company. It's lovely to see you again, Julian. I don't think I've seen you since last year's perfectly disgusting awards.'

Fern knew how to be gracious even if she wasn't reputed to be and didn't care to be to her husband's relations. She welcomed Julian so effusively that he began to wonder if Jeremy had been divorced and this was a new wife whose hand touched his arm far more often than was usual for manners. He laughed cautiously and enquired after Ruby's progess at school.

Ruby said, 'Very slow, thank you. But it must be endured.' She didn't smile. She studied him seriously. He looked like a creep, she decided. 'Glen is the clever one in the family,' she said. She spoke with a drawl which delighted Julian as it had delighted many guests before him.

'I am the clever one in family,' roared Neville playfully. 'I've been trying to remember where we met before, Julian. You weren't by any chance with the Burlington Rep were you, twelve, fifteen years ago?'

'God no,' said Julian. 'My background's in Sales.' He was a slim, balding man with a fat moustache which failed to flatter his prominent teeth but he carried himself with assurance and spoke with all the confidence of a man who could rise above anything, if pushed.

'Sales,' cried Fern. 'How fascinating. And how clever of you to have made it from Sales to Light Entertainment. That can't have been easy.' She had him by his elbow which he kept a close eye on. He wondered what she was getting at, blinking like that and touching him.

'It wasn't,' he admitted, dimpling at her, harmlessly he hoped. 'But I am ambitious in my own weedy way. I made sure I got where I wanted to be.'

'And are you where you want to be?' asked Fern, peering at him in the twilight and challenging him throatily so that he really was very puzzled and obliged to seek help from Neville with a toss of his head.

'She wants to catch me out,' he said. 'And here is the man with the drinks.' He leapt to his feet. 'Well done Jeremy, well done.' Jeremy laughed because he felt he had done well. He made a small speech announcing the pilot of *Tempting Fate* and his delight in working with Julian of whom everyone spoke so highly and his genuine thrill at branching out from News to Light Entertainment. Then Julian proposed a toast to Jeremy, to the show and to fame and fortune and they all lifted their glasses just as Penny teetered through the conservatory crying 'Oh you naughty people. You've started without me', causing Ruby to catch Glen's eye which narrowed dangerously.

'Penny, my love,' cried Jeremy. 'You look exquisite.'

'As always,' Neville said. 'We are drinking to Jeremy's game show, darling. Come and join us. Julian this is my wife Miss Penny. Penny, this is Julian Fortescue, Jeremy's executive producer.' Penny bent across the table to shake Julian's hand and her breasts heaved awesomely.

'How lovely to meet you,' she sighed. 'And how sensible you are to snap up Jeremy before anyone else.'

'Careful,' shrieked Fern. 'The table. For a minute I thought it was going to go over. Take Glen's chair, Penny. It's a little bit stronger than the others and Glen you don't mind sitting on the grass, do you? Tell me, Julian, is *Tempting Fate* the pinnacle of your career or not? I'm not prying. I'm just fascinated by pinnacles.'

'Your wife has the most worrying line in small talk,' Julian said loudly and Jeremy replied, 'Be grateful. You only need worry when she starts to talk big', a remark which appealed so hugely to Penny's sense of humour that she almost fell from her chair, despite its sturdiness.

'I used to work with your lot,' Julian said to Penny. 'In Sales. Before I moved to Production. What's Talcum up to, still doing the awards, I bet?' Penny squealed with glee.

'He's still doing the awards,' she agreed. 'You don't call him Talcum,' she cried. 'You are wicked.'

Julian laughed and dimpled. It was safest to dimple at random. 'Doesn't everyone?' he asked.

'Penny hasn't been there very long,' said Fern. 'She doesn't know what everyone does yet.'

'Do you know Kenny Vertigo?' Neville enquired. 'Everyone does.'

'No,' said Julian. 'Tell me, Mrs Brewster, are you at the pinnacle of your career?'

'I am an actress. I've a long way to go,' sighed Penny as Fern said, 'I have no career but funnily enough, I have decided it's time to look for a pinnacle.' She raised her voice towards the end of her sentence in order to drown Penny's breathless modesty and her declaration rang quite clearly about the garden, demanding recognition though it was faintly embarrassing.

'Terrific,' said Julian.

'We all need to aim for something,' said Neville. 'But only the very top in my case,' he laughed. 'What are you aiming for, brother?'

Jeremy sipped his champagne as he considered his reply. 'I've often asked myself,' he said. 'And I suppose it is recognition. I want to be recognized as good at my job, whatever it happens to be, whether it's in News, as a columnist, as a personality or even as a singer. I simply want to be recognized as a professional. And if I'm truly honest,' he paused to laugh charmingly at himself, 'by as many people as possible.'

'A singer!' shrieked Fern but everyone pretended she hadn't because it was Jeremy's night and he was the one they were celebrating, after all.

'I'll drink to that,' said Julian and as they did the children bade them all goodnight and crept away from the floodlit terrace, across the lawn to the shed, though Fern cried to Ruby that it was rather late and she should go to her own room.

'Nice kids,' said Julian. 'They look like each other too, don't they?' He wasn't listening when Neville tried to point out there was no reason why they should. And he didn't listen to a single thing Neville said all night, though Neville's diction was at its most impressive. He had no need to when Neville hadn't been nominated for a Fertile Fruit and seemed unlikely ever to be.

'I'm up for one myself, I gather,' he said between the first and second courses which Fern produced miraculously with a minimum of fuss and fanfare although they were of a quality rarely found outside Provence.

'I've been nominated fourteen times,' said Penny. 'Oh Fern, no sauce and no vegetables for me, thank you. I'll just have a tiny spoonful of the meaty stuff and a little bit of bread and butter.' Then she embarked on a long, directionless account of the time her greatest fan, Merilee Bawdle, once a single parent now a respected Sunderland headmistress, came all the way down to London, bringing with her a party of twenty pensioners and five members of the P.T.A., to see her in *Dick Whittington* in which she played the cat, for which she received several very good notices, by the way, only to find she had a sore throat that day and the whole Sunderland party had been reduced to tears at finding an understudy had taken her place.

'I know Penny. You've told me before,' said Neville whose eyes were the only ones she could catch by the time she drew her tale to her close.

Julian's attention had been taken by Jeremy who wanted to tell him about the story for which he was being nominated this year. 'There was some luck, of course,' he was saying. 'There we are stuck by the side of the road while our driver tries to repair the spare tyre which is even flatter than the flat, when along comes this police car and who should be in the back but the widow, on her way back from identifying the body.

'Naturally, while the police driver is helping our chap, I say to the widow, "I know it's a time of grief. I know what you are going through but I truly believe that you would be doing the world a favour if you gave me an interview now, on the spot, by the side of this lonely road. The only way future tragedies can be avoided is by the public witnessing your suffering." It was bloody moving actually.'

'Must have been. Must have been wonderful in it's way,' Julian agreed. 'And it's exactly that touch we're looking for in *Fate*. The human touch. What you have that the others don't have is the capacity to be witty without being flippant, the ability to be intelligent without sounding like a smart arse and the humility to be compassionate without being sickly.'

'I know,' said Jeremy.

'Jeremy,' said Fern, 'I can hear the drains. Listen! I don't think I can live with that slurping. You'll have to get Mr Burt ...' She stopped mid-sentence and listened a little longer, her eyes glued to Neville's jaws which were working hard on the slightest of strawberry soufflés. 'Oh!' she said. 'It's all right It's not the drains.'

Julian was not without compassion himself. 'Working?' he

said to Neville whom he saw suddenly it would be kinder to acknowledge. But Neville's mouth was full and all he could do was nod.

'Almost in rehearsal,' Penny explained for him. 'He's doing *The Pyjama Game* with Tony Gospel. I'm hoping for something in it myself, as a matter of fact. I know it's time I extended myself. It's ages since I've done anything other than *Kidding* and one gets lazy when something comes to one so easily. If you hear of anything,' she said, smiling at him with astonishing good will given the brevity of their acquaintance, 'you know where you can reach me.'

'Oh my God,' cried Julian. 'Marty Cork. I've completely forgotten to return his call. 'Listen,' he said, 'It's been lovely but I really must get home. If I don't listen to my telephone messages before midnight I will be in deep trouble.' And he left, abandoning Fern, Penny and Neville to an empty feeling in the pits of their stomachs of having been cheated out of something they had worked for. Fern wasn't sure why she should feel so wretched. She despised showbusiness. She didn't know what had got into her. Ralph definitely hadn't but she felt as if he should have.

Jeremy on the other hand felt fulfilled. 'Wasn't he fun? He's a very decent bloke and I'm jolly lucky to be working with him,' he said. Then, full of good cheer, he went out to the garden to bring in the empty glasses and on his way back thought he glimpsed his daughter, sneaking in through the kitchen door, pausing only to wave back to the garden shed where a tall muscular figure, naked from the waist up, waved back.'A very nice bloke,' he said to himself again. 'I'm lucky.'

Chapter
Seven

Ruby's concern for Glen's mental handicap had not lasted long despite her earnest wish to do something constructive about it. Within a very few minutes of meeting him she'd realized that he had overcome it, whatever it was or had been and that whatever it was or might have been was easily compensated for by his physical perfection. On the same hand, Glen had discovered that as Brewsters went, Ruby was an exception. She was big-headed, he admitted, but her big-headedness was less vanity than the simple acceptance of her own natural ability and she certainly seemed to have bags of that. She was beautifully endowed, he thought.

In short, Glen and Ruby had formed an immediate attachment for each other in the garden shed. Ruby's passion, evident but undirected for so long had found a target, and Glen, desperate though he had been to join Ants' Nest in the home for delinquents, told himself he could hang on for a couple more days. He could leave whenever he liked he assured himself and, had it not been for Ruby, he would have liked. The longer he stayed in the garden shed, the more disgusted he became with the adult behaviour in the house and garden. He hated Fern most of all. He hated Fern as much as he resented Neville.

He blamed Fern for the garden shed. Fern was sneaky. He despised Fern for whatever she was doing with Ralph. She was like his mother only sneaky and sordid. Those poems. Those poems! They were revolting. How could a mother write poems like that? He'd have liked her better if she was called Miss Fern.

Even Ruby was embarrassed by her mother's rudeness and contempt. And when Glen had pointed it out to her over drinks with Julian Fortescue, she believed she too could detect the horrible spectre of their parents' egos colliding noisily and stupidly about the place without a single thought for anything other than their own importance or anyone other than themselves. 'They are obsessed', Glen told her. 'They are mad. You wait and see.' He wanted her to wait until the awards. He had had fifteen years' experience of the madness at award time.

If Ruby thought this was slightly hysterical, she didn't say so. All she remembered about the awards was a flurry of expectation followed by a week of excuses and the colder than usual atmosphere in which her father accused her mother of upsetting his career. They were nothing very out of the ordinary. She found Glen's view of the world persuasive because she was pleased to be persuaded by him but she had reservations. She had never seen her parents in the light he threw on them.

'My father wants me to treat you like the brother I never had,' she said in his defence the night Julian Fortescue came to dinner. They were leaning on the window ledge gazing back at the conservatory as he took a breather from weight-training. His back glistened with exertion and his muscles glowed with fine tuning. He turned to face her.

'Does he?' he asked. 'And how do you want me to treat you?' Her stomach turned over under his gaze and she put her hand to it.

'No supper,' she laughed. She had been eating erratically since he'd moved in, avoiding family meals to have supper with him only to find he had his on the way home from school. Sometimes she took food across and shared it with him but mostly she was hungry.

'How do you?' he insisted. He could feel her firm upper arm against his and his heart throbbed.

'I never much wanted a brother,' she murmured. They smiled out at the garden but it was a nerve-wracking business, taunting each other in this way, both believing themselves to be in love with a step cousin with whom any liaison could only lead to trouble. They had been taunting and thrilling each other from the very first day, if Fern had only known it.

'They probably can't help themselves,' Ruby sighed.

'They are crazy,' Glen repeated. 'I'm going into banking. I want to be a grey, faceless man in a bank.' He put his arm about her shoulders and felt her tremble under it. He wanted to protect her. He wanted to spare her from her mother's liaison with Ralph Fantoni and her mother's smutty poetry. He wouldn't abandon her, he told himself, no matter how bad things became. When he said goodnight to her he kissed her chastely on the top of her head then he lay on his narrow, fragile bed and flicked through the copies of *Men Only* he'd bought from Bucket Road. They made him homesick.

'Do you think Glen is all right in the shed?' Penny said to Neville just before she went to sleep.

'He didn't address a single remark to me all night,' Neville replied. 'What a prick. What do you make of him not knowing Kenny Vertgo? Penny?' But Penny was asleep. She had worked very hard all day.

Naturally Fern's letter wasn't published. After it had been passed all around Features and most of News and everyone had had a good laugh, it was passed on to the editor who telephoned Jeremy. 'Roy here,' he said. 'We've had an interesting response to yesterday's column. I've got one especially interesting letter in front of me from a Mrs Fern Brewster.'

'Very funny,' said Jeremy. He was sitting on his desk, sipping coffee, designing a wardrobe for himself and his new persona.

'I mean it,' said Roy. 'Do you want to hear it?' He read it. 'Good, isn't it?' he said.

'It's a joke,' Jeremy laughed. 'I'll get her for this. Sometimes she doesn't know when to stop.'

'I was wondering,' Roy said, 'if we could have a bit of fun with it. I was wondering if your wife mightn't like to do a reply for us. Mrs Brewster Replies. It might be a bit of fun.'

'Come off it,' Jeremy said, chuckling again in case his voice betrayed his alarm. 'She's a simple woman, my wife. I don't think she'd want to take it any further. It's her idea of a joke. She wouldn't want anyone to take her seriously.'

'Are you sure?' sad Roy. 'With the awards coming up I thought it might be a useful bit of publicity.'

'Hardly useful,' said Jeremy firmly. 'But thanks anyway. Have you seen Tuesday's yet ... on The Family? It's very strong, I think, and a nasty letter from the wife wouldn't do it any favours.' He laughed again. 'She really is the limit. Let me know what you think of Tuesday's, O.K.?' It was a narrow squeak Jeremy was quick to perceive. But it was a squeak. He rang Fern at once to confront her with her folly and as he waited for her to answer, his mind wandered back to his new persona and after a bit his anger faded and he replaced the receiver and telephoned Julian Fortescue instead.

'Far be it from me to sound pushy,' he said after the usual pleasantries. 'But if you want a vocal on the *Tempting Fate* theme I'd like to have a shot at it. My singing teacher reckons I'm up to it.'

He should have taken a good hard look at Fern's letter and asked himself why. He might have checked Fern in her stride before her foot had even a chance to leave the ground in search of her pinnacle. But he didn't and when he finally suspected that she was about to take off, it was too late. This is how circumstances are. Jeremy, spotting an opportunity just as his wife saw an opening in her future, devoted himself to it rather than her and decided as the day wore on and he still hadn't spoken to her that the letter could be put down to a bit of silliness which he imagined she had concocted with Ruby who was a great one for cheeky japes.

When he saw her at last, late on the night after Julian Fortescue had come to dinner, he had long forgotten any reference she might have made to a pinnacle, and all he said was, 'Roy thought your letter about my column was very funny but I didn't. I found it embarrassing. I know it was only a joke,' he cried before she could tell him it was no such thing, 'but jokes like that can backfire and I shouldn't have to remind you that that column is important to me. It's a very good shop-window.'

Perhaps anything he said would have been futile. Fern was a strong-willed woman and though she may have suppressed her ambition, or genuinely not had any ambition, for sixteen years, perhaps there was nothing anyone could have done to stop her once she glimpsed her chance.

While Jeremy was sleeping, she crept out of bed and down to the kitchen where she pushed aside a large rubber plant and removed a secret panel from the wall beneath the gas meter. From the tiny safe, she took her velvet-covered folder and from the folder she took a sheath of beautifully inscribed paper which she placed in a large envelope and then she took the envelope back to bed with her to sleep on the knowledge that Fenchurch would see all her poems, every one. She could have fetched them next morning when everyone had left the house but Fern was as tempted by dramatic gestures as much as Penny, Neville and Jeremy.

'There's someone creeping about the house,' Penny whispered to Neville. 'I can hear someone in the hall.' She couldn't sleep so Neville couldn't sleep and for some time they had lain with their eyes firmly shut discussing the wisdom of waking Jeremy up to ask for a Mogadon. 'Jeremy must be getting himself a Mogadon,' Penny said. 'I really need one. Go and ask him for one. Please Neville.'

'You don't need one,' Neville whispered back. 'You have given them up so you mustn't start again. This is the first night you haven't been able to sleep for months.'

'But I do need one,' said Penny. 'You know I do when it gets to be two o'clock. I can't sleep and I know I won't go to sleep now. I will look awful in the morning and Dave will shout at me and we'll do the galloping all wrong and I won't be able to read the story and I will get my contract torn up and we won't be able to pay for Mandarin Street and we'll have to stay here for ever and ever.' She began to moan pitifully. 'Please, Neville get up and ask him. I can hear him, getting himself one.'

'He doesn't take sleeping pills,' Neville said. 'There's no one there. Now just relax and think of nice things. Think of counting money. Think of an audience and count all the faces.'

'There is someone there. Listen.' They listened. But they

72

could hear nothing because Fern was down in the kitchen and well out of earshot.

'Close your eyes,' yawned Neville 'and think of an audience. Go on Pen. It's very late and I need to sleep as well.' Penny began to count aloud, determined that Neville shouldn't go to sleep before her.

'One, two, three,' she murmured. 'Oh God,' she cried. 'They're all getting up and walking out. Please Neville, go and see Jeremy. They're bound to have something.'

So Neville, because he loved his wife and didn't wish humiliation on her whatever the hour, crawled from his bed just in time to see Fern disappear along the hall and into her bedroom carrying a large manilla envelope. He might have called out to her but he could tell from the way she was tip-toeing and clutching her package to her bosom that she didn't want to be seen, that whatever she was doing in the middle of the night when everyone else was asleep, she was doing because it was in the middle of the night and everyone else was asleep.

He waited for her to close her bedroom door then he crept along to the third bathroom, at the very end of the hall by the second flight of stairs and, as quietly as he could, he sifted through the contents of the cupboards either side of the dainty handbasin. 'What on earth are you doing?' Ruby asked, switching on the light. She stood in the doorway with her tennis racquet raised, quite willing and able to administer a hefty smash to the back of his skull.

'Damn,' hissed Neville. 'Sorry, sweetheart. I'm looking for something to help Penny get to sleep. She's in a bad way, I'm afraid.'

'What sort of something,' Ruby said. 'There's nothing in here. Hardly anyone uses this bathroom. You'll only find soap, toothpaste, some *Rive Gauche*, maybe a bottle of *Au Sauvage* and a spare razor. Mummy doesn't believe in drugs.'

'Of course not. Nor do I,' said Neville, pulling himself to his feet. 'Nor does Penny most of the time.' He smiled at her awkwardly. He had scarcely spoken to her in six days.

'You could try hot milk,' Ruby said. 'Would you like me to get you hot milk? Or have you tried that already? Was that you in the kitchen a minute ago.'

'No, I haven't tried milk. Penny is allergic to milk, as a matter of fact. I don't think there's anyone in the kitchen.' He spoke from a wild desire to please Fern by keeping her secret though he knew she would be furious that he shared it.

'I definitely heard someone,' Ruby said. 'I'd better go down and make sure everything's O.K.'

'I'll go,' said Neville. 'You go back to bed.'

'Do you want this?' She offered him the tennis racquet.

'It's O.K.' he said, grinning bravely at her. 'I can look after myself.' He headed confidently down the stairs and when he got to the kitchen had a quick rummage through the herbs in case there was Mogadon next to the marjoram before calling for Ruby's sake. 'Anyone there?'

No one replied because no one was there but as he turned to go back up the stairs he tripped over the panel Fern had failed to replace over the gap beneath the gas meter and he brought down the vast rubber plant Fern had used to conceal it. He cracked his head on the large white pot causing Ruby who had been waiting with the tennis racquet at the top of the stairs to come running down crying, 'The police have been called. Stay where you are. The police are on their way.'

It was an accident of course and not a circumstance that left much to choice, so no one could have been blamed but it affected matters as surely as Jeremy's reluctance to pay serious attention to Fern's letter. The appearance of a secret panel created only the mildest stir. It was assumed Neville had dislodged in when he fell. The furthest-reaching effects were caused by Neville's concussion which confined him to the house. 'A week would be wise,' said the doctor who was called while Penny snored quietly to herself in the spare bed, finally bored to sleep by the length of time it took Neville to come back with anything useful.

'He can't possibly expect me to look after him,' Fern said to Jeremy over breakfast an hour after Penny's taxi had collected her to take her to the studio next day. 'Oh God, think of all the meals he's going to be here for. I don't know if I'm strong enough.'

'It's not very serious, but quite spectacular.' Neville told Madge McGuire, and she insisted on tipping off the diaries, two of which ran items, less about his head accident than about him staying with his brother, Jeremy, whom, they noted, seemed to be on the brink of a new career in Light Entertainment when his strength had always been probing but sensitive news coverage. It beat the diarists why a man of his talent would want to make the change.

'Jeremy's going to need an agent,' Madge said to Neville when she had finished reading the pieces to him. 'Now he's headed for the brighter lights.'

'He doesn't want one,' Neville said shortly. He retreated to the garden, anxious and upset.

'Hullo Neville,' said Ralph Fantoni. He strolled across the lawn and threw himself to the grass alongside the cane banana chair on which Neville was outstretched with Jeremy's panama hat tipped forward to shield his eyes from the sun. 'I gather we have something in common.' He had wandered into the garden to occupy himself while Fern talked on the phone to Bud Fenchurch.

'What's that?' asked Neville. He had said nothing to anyone about the frequency of Ralph's visits to Fern which he had been unable to avoid noticing as he convalesced. Fern had said briefly that Ralph was her best friend which she indicated by her tone was enough to account for his generous access to the house, the grounds and most parts of her anatomy.

Ralph smiled. 'Someone, I mean,' he said, nodding his head towards the house.

'Sorry?' said Neville. 'Oh Fern. Yes, she said you were close.'

'Did she?' Ralph asked eagerly. 'Did she, indeed? Now what did she mean by that, I wonder?'

'What?' said Neville. He didn't like Ralph. He didn't like Ralph's familiarity. He didn't know Ralph from a bar of soap and he didn't want to, however friendly he was with Fern. He took liberties, Neville thought and he gathered he was taking liberties with Fern but if that was the case, he didn't want to know, anymore than he wanted to know what had been in her package the night the pot fell on him. He loathed secrets. They were especially dangerous when they belonged to someone like Fern.

'What else did she say?' Ralph smirked. He was lying flat

on the grass now as if the grass was his, as if he owned the earth.

'When?' asked Neville. He wondered what Fern saw in him. She had been so particular once.

'When she told you we were close?'

Neville considered. 'I don't know,' he said eventually. 'I think she asked me if I wanted a sandwich. Yes,' he said after further reflection. 'She asked me if I wanted a sandwich and if I did she said she would take it up to my room so I could eat it there.'

Ralph gave a small yelp of amusement. 'Did she? She is a fine woman. I'm going to ask her to make me a sandwich.' He stood up. 'I don't suppose you would like a sandwich.' He grinned suggestively. Neville wanted him to go away. He wondered if Jeremy knew what was going on.

'I don't want a sandwich, thank you,' he said and he watched Ralph walk slowly back to the house, every so often stopping to examine the turf as if he had planted it himself.

Fern was no longer on the phone. She was sitting at the long pine table in the kitchen staring into space. 'What's up?' Ralph said. 'You should be over the moon.'

'I feel terrible,' Fern said. 'And I feel wonderful at the same time. I don't know what I feel.' She gazed up at him, her dark eyes brilliant with uncertainty. 'Are you sure he means it. Are you sure he will publish them'?

'Of course I'm sure,' said Ralph. 'You heard him. He wouldn't say it if he didn't mean it.' Then he pulled her to her feet and tried to kiss her but she turned her head away because she could see Neville in the garden and she didn't know what Neville could see through Jeremy's panama hat. 'I want to take you to bed,' Ralph whispered, pressing himself to her.

'I know,' she said.

'Let me,' he urged her.

'One day,' she said. Then she called, 'Oh Neville, I was just about to send Ralph to ask you. Do you want a sandwich?'

'He doesn't want a sandwich,' murmured Ralph spitefully. 'I don't think he would know what to do with one even if you gave him one on a plate.'

Chapter
Eight

Penny should have seen what was going on in the garden shed but what mother sees more than she can stand to see. She wasn't deliberately neglectful. She never had been as she had explained to Glen so often in the past. For years they had seen each other only at chance meetings. Their schedules were different. School hours were not her working hours even if they were close. The difference, now she was under Fern's and Jeremy's roof, was that he wasn't precisely, so they ran into each other less. In the normal course of events, when they were in their own home, they ran into each other more. That was all. If they had run into each other more she might have seen how unhappy he was. But if they had run into each other more he wouldn't have been in the garden shed so he would not have been unhappy. It wasn't her fault if he was unhappy. It was Fern's.

'Well,' she said, perching herself with difficulty on a small ladder draped with his clothes, 'this is cosy.'

'It isn't,' he muttered. 'There's nowhere for me to hang anything, there's nowhere for me to do my homework, I don't have enough room for my weights or enough space to train properly, the bed's too small and there's nowhere for me to eat.'

'Darling,' Penny giggled. 'You're only supposed to sleep here. You should come over to the house for everything else. No one expects you to spend all your time in here.'

'They don't want me over there,' he said. 'It's obvious, isn't it? They put me out here because they don't want me over there.' He had his back to her which she found offensive but it was difficult to complain when she couldn't help observing the shed was poky and horrible by the standards of a normal bedroom.

'Look,' she said, 'if you'd rather be over in the house, I'm sure they wouldn't mind.' She wasn't at all sure, as he was well aware. 'But it's not so bad, is it? At least you have some privacy here. I don't know where they could put you over in the house.'

'I could sleep with Ruby,' he said.

'Glen!' she squealed. 'That's a terrible thing to say. Don't even say it as a joke. Ruby is only a little girl and you are still a boy, though I know you are a big boy. You must never say that again and I mean it. Fern would have you arrested.'

'I was joking,' he said. 'And Fern can't talk. She's the last person who could talk.'

'What do you mean by that?' she said, tired suddenly, depleted by the barrage of anger that poured from her son. She joined him by the window and was instantly distracted.

'Look, there's Jeremy,' she cried. 'I'll see you later, darling. I want to talk to him about something very important.' She kissed him before she left and told him to come to her room to visit her whenever he liked, then away she dashed into the cool night air calling, 'Jeremy, Jeremy, could you wait a minute? I want to ask you something.' She had been making free use of the house and grounds since Neville had concussed himself, unrestrained by his caution and readiness to bring her food in bed.

Jeremy, who had seen very little of her given the number of days she had spent in his house, smiled warmly when he saw her. He had begun to believe he really was quite fond of her and though intelligence was not her strong suit, he told himself, she was very fetching and very sweet. He put his arm about her as they walked together towards the house. He

78

could quite see why Neville had married her though he most definitely hadn't at the time.

'Had a good day?' she asked, gazing at him with a radiance Fern never displayed.

'Very good,' he said. 'Five separate people congratulated me on my Family column. Did you see it?'

'It was wonderful,' Penny said. 'I read it three times and I showed it to Dave Caster who said it was excellent. He said he didn't know why you wanted to go into Light Entertainment when you could do so well in Arts and Drama.'

'Did he? Did he?' asked Jeremy. 'Who's Dave Caster again?'

'My producer. I used to think he was horrible but he seems to know an awful lot about documentaries. He's been brought over from News which is very flattering to me, don't you think? He says you're under-achieving.'

'Why don't you have him over for a drink at the weekend?' Jeremy said as they arrived arm in arm in the kitchen. 'That would be nice, wouldn't it, Fern, for Penny to have her producer over for a drink.'

'Why?' asked Fern. She was sitting at the table, peeling and chopping vegetables and Neville was watching her with a bandage on his head, keeping his end up with sensible remarks about seasonal fruits.

Penny tutted. 'Oh Fern,' she said. 'You are funny, "Why?" For a start he admires Jeremy hugely. And B, it would be a big help for me to see him away from work because I really want him to think about a new look *Kidding About* with filmed inserts which would use his talents as well as stretch me a bit. I'm so bored with the show at the moment. I want to drop lots of it. I want to get rid of the galloping and the story. I want it to grow. Do you know what I mean, Jeremy?' She didn't so much as blink in Neville's direction.

'When did you decide all that?' he asked, wondering if he had missed a large chunk of his wife's career in the ten minutes he had been unconscious. Perhaps he had amnesia and no one could bring themselves to tell him.

'You know I've been wanting to for ages,' said Penny. 'I've talked to Talcum and he doesn't seem to have any objections,

79

not serious ones, anyway. He's not happy about the expense but I'm sure we can work around that, don't you think Jeremy, with a bit of common sense? I look at it this way, Fern. It's my show and if I don't keep it interesting no one else will. Do you see what I mean?'

Jeremy said he definitely did and Fern said to Neville, 'I think kiwi fruit is desperately overrated, but if you like it, I will order a crate.' Then she turned to Jeremy and said, 'You can have who you like on Saturday but don't forget it's the second in the month and we will have Mummy.'

Later, in Jeremy's study, Neville said, 'I wonder if I could ask Madge McGuire for a drink as well? I know she wants to talk to you and frankly Jeremy, I really need to sit down somewhere with Madge and talk about where I'm going. I don't know anymore, Jeremy. Maybe I should be looking for a new agent. I've been with Madge so long I think she's forgotten that I'm serious. I mean, *The Pyjama Game* at my age! I should be doing *Macbeth*.'

'Oh I don't know, Neville,' Jeremy said. 'You have a fine, light touch. There's nothing wrong in sticking to what you're good at. What's she want to talk to me about?'

'I don't know,' said Neville vaguely. 'This and that. But where's it getting me? That's what I want to know. I'm thirty-seven. I should have done Broadway by now. I should have my own television series. I should be winning awards like you and Penny. I don't know where I've gone wrong. How many people have heard of the fine, light actor, Neville Brewster?'

'You have your following,' said Jeremy uneasily. He wasn't comfortable with anyone else's career. He was really only comfortable with his own which he understood for all its intricate subtleties. Taking aim and firing was how he saw his career. 'It's just a matter of breaks,' he said. 'You know that. You've been in the business long enough. It's different for me. I can make my own breaks. I can go looking for opportunities and I can create them if I want to. You have to wait until you're offered something. That's the way it is. But if you stick to what you know and keep on doing it as well as you can, then you can't fail, can you?'

'You bastard,' said Neville suddenly. 'You utter bastard.

You don't stick. You dodge and weave like a bloody rattle-snake to get where you want to be and you know it works. I don't want to stick. I want to move on. I've got the talent and I want it recognized.' He put his head in his hands and wished a little blood would colour his bandage though he knew it wouldn't because his wound was almost healed.

Jeremy sighed. 'You're tired,' he said. 'Want a drink?'

'I'm not tired,' Neville snarled. 'I am sick, I've had enough. Life is unfair. Look at me, look at you. I don't even have a house and you live in a palace.'

'I'm going to have a drink,' Jeremy said. He didn't want a heart to heart. He knew what was eating Neville because it had been eating him all their lives. He had never come to terms with the arrival of a younger brother. 'Look,' he said, calmly, because he was utterly confident of his superior position, 'you're too nice a person, that's all. I told you the other day. You care too much about what people think. I don't care.'

'Don't give me that,' said Neville. 'Of course you care. What's your life all about? Applause applause, the same as mine. You just look for it in a different place.'

'Hang on, Nev,' said Jeremy. 'I do what I'm good at. I like to do my best. Being good at what I do is important to me, being the best at it. That's where the satisfaction is.'

'Then why aren't you a teacher?' Neville snapped. 'You were a great teacher, everyone said. The audiences were too small, that's why.' It was ungrateful to say the least.

'Come on,' said Jeremy pleasantly. 'Let's go and join the women. They're probably wondering what on earth we are up to.'

'I'll ask Madge for Saturday then.' said Neville sulkily.

'Fine,' said Jeremy. 'We'll make it a party.' He couldn't have been more gracious.

Neville naturally regretted his outburst within minutes. You cannot enjoy jealousy without remorse and the come-uppance is more immediate than food poisoning. During dinner which they all ate together now that he was on hand to watch its preparation, he left his place and walked around the table to where Jeremy was savouring a morsel of steamed

81

chicken. 'I am sorry,' he said, resting his hand on his shoulder. 'I am sorry. I behaved like a beast.'

'That's all right,' said Jeremy. 'Don't give it another thought.' But he did, of course. Everyone did. No one believed for a minute it would stay under the carpet where Jeremy appeared to have swept it.

'You should have slung him out on the spot,' Fern said as she wiped make-up from her face before getting into bed. 'It's the most appalling cheek. How dare he when he is taking advantage of our hospitality to save on rent, not to mention food and fuel. Why didn't you order him out?'

'I wanted to. But I couldn't,' murmured Jeremy, pleased to have his patience so duly noted. 'He was wearing a bandage and he looked so pathetic. He has always known how to look pathetic.'

Penny, lying on the floor beside the spare dressing table to relax her back, said, 'Oh Neville, how awful! You must have a brain disorder.' She lifted her head and studied him with genuine concern. 'Does it ache a lot?'

'Quite a lot,' Neville said. 'I don't know what came over me. One minute I was sitting there thinking I should offer him the mask of comedy, the next I was in the grip of this irrational rage. It's a terrible thing to admit, Penny, but for a minute I wanted to kill him.' He gazed about the spare room, apparently unseeing, desperate for an explanation to appear from the shadows. 'I felt such a failure.'

'You are not a failure,' Penny said, climbing on to the bed beside him. 'You are my husband. Look how well you are doing. You've got *The Pyjama Game* coming up. Lots of actors would give their right arms for the part.'

'It's all right. It's quite all right,' said Neville. 'I don't need bolstering. I know exactly where I stand and I know that at my age I should be standing a lot further up the ladder. But that's the trouble, there is no ladder. You can't climb. One month you seem to have made it. The next month, crash, there is nothing. There's nothing to build on. Let's face it, you could lose *Kidding About* tomorrow and where would you be? Hoping for something else, the same as me.' He stroked her hair vacantly until she sat up.

'You are right,' she said. 'But I have realized something. Survival isn't the thing. Change is what it's all about and you must take risks. Look at Jeremy. He goes after things all the time. I'm not going to spend my life galloping in circles. I want much more than that and I'm going to see I get it.'

'Exactly,' said Neville. 'And I bet you will.' He smiled at her fondly. 'But you won't do anything rash, will you.'

'No,' she promised. 'And you must stop insulting Jeremy. You will apologize won't you, or Fern will make him throw us out.'

Fern tried but Jeremy wouldn't, not ever. He was a man of honour and there were the appearances to consider. Had he had even the smallest inclination to do so, it would have vanished completely when Kenny Vertigo arrived shortly before everyone was expected for drinks on Saturday to fill in the panel which was no longer required as a hiding place. 'You'll soon be over at Neville's I gather,' Jeremy said.

'Sorry Jeremy,' Kenny grinned. 'I'm still at Marty Cork's and to be frank he's mucking us about. Gothic is one thing but now he wants a folly in the garden. I don't have a good folly man, when it comes down to it, Jeremy, and I was at my wits' end until I remembered that bloke from the R.S.C. I can't see myself getting to your brother's place before the month's end and it's a shame isn't it, because I can see he's not a well man.'

'Oh, he's all right,' Jeremy said. 'He's raring to go as a matter of fact. You know he's doing *The Pyjama Game.*'

'I don't think so,' said Kenny, slapping plaster across the wall. 'I would say that was very much in doubt myself.'

'Why?' asked Jeremy. 'It's only a small wound. He fell over a pot plant.'

'That may be so,' said Kenny. 'That may be all too true Jeremy, but Toby Gospel is having a spot of bother. I daresay your brother will be hearing from him in due course if not before. I remember your brother in *The Iceman Cometh.* It was a fine piece of work. I remember saying so at the time.'

Although he was pressed, Kenny wouldn't stay for a drink.

He said, 'Lovely to see you again Madge, it really is believe me. Your roof holding up all right? Great, great. Any time.' And he said to Neville, 'I won't rush into your job. I can see you are comfortably set up here.' Then he winked broadly and disappeared because he didn't want to be around when Madge broke the news of Toby Gospel's spot of bother.

'I blame myself,' Madge said. 'I should have seen it coming. Toby is not to be trusted any more though I hate to say so. You don't like to say that about anyone who's done so well in the past. But you mustn't worry. There's a lot coming up that will interest you ... ah Jeremy, I was just saying to Neville how thrilled I am that you are moving to Light Entertainment. It's a very shrewd move. Congratulations.'

Madge McGuire was sixty-two with curling hennaed hair and a liking for clothes just an inch too young for her. She could afford them. What she hadn't made from her agency, she had accrued from her fleet of taxis and she had done extremely well from her agency by clutching to her, at a tender age, three extremely successful players who found themselves tied to her umbilically and quite unable to move because they feared an actor's life without the security of the taxis to fall back on. Neville wasn't one of them though she cared about Neville in a similarly possessive way. 'Do you have someone looking after you?' she said to Jeremy.

Jeremy took a seat beside her. 'Isn't the weather awful?' he said.

'But this conservatory is lovely,' she replied. Neville said nothing. He wanted Jeremy to go away.

'You don't handle people like me,' Jeremy said, knowing she would be the last person he would go to even if she did.

'I don't,' she agreed. 'But I can certainly advise you. I've been in the business for a very long time and I know a good bet when I see one, don't I, Neville?' She smiled at Neville and he wondered who she meant.

'Jeremy,' called Fern, 'Excuse me Madge, will you? Could you come and meet Mrs Plantaganet. Mummy has promised her she can go on *Tempting Fate*.'

'God!' said Jeremy. 'I said it was a mistake letting your mother bring a friend.' But he went anyway because what

84

with one thing and another, he was in no position to argue.

'Look at them,' said Ralph Fantoni a little later when he finally trapped Fern between the fridge and the hobs. 'Look at them fawn.' He was above fawning himself. He placed himself among those who might one day be fawned over so would not stoop. He contented himself with glory by association.

Mrs Plantaganet was fawning over Neville whom she remembered in *The Iceman Cometh* before her hip went. Dave Caster was fawning over Jeremy and his own wife, Rebecca Fantoni, was fawning over Miss Penny. 'You taught all our children to gallop,' she was enthusing. 'Honestly. You were marvellous. Well you still are, I'm sure. Do you still gallop?'

Penny said, 'Do you know Dave Caster? Come and meet him. He's my producer.' Then she said, forgetting she had Rebecca in tow, 'Now Dave, you must ask Jeremy. Ask him what he thinks about me doing filmed inserts. Go on. Ask him if he thinks they would be a good idea.' She was wearing an astonishingly chilly dress given the weather.

Dave smiled at her and then at Jeremy who also smiled though he was breathless with admiration at her gall. 'What do you think?' Dave asked.

'I think she would be marvellous. I think it can't do any harm and provided she wears dresses like the one she's got on, the ratings will soar.' Jeremy kissed her loudly on the neck. It made them all laugh, hysterically.

'That settles it, then,' Dave said. 'Now I must be off. I've left the wife in the car with the children. But we'll have lunch, Jeremy, all right? I'll be in touch. And Miss Penny, you can consider it done.' As he weaved his way across the room Penny wrapped her arms about her brother-in-law and said, 'Thank you, thank you, thank you. I don't know how to thank you.'

'Look at your mother and my father,' Ruby said from the conservatory.

'No thanks,' said Glen. 'I would much rather look at you.' And Fern, hearing the exchange from the clinch she was in behind the boiler, sensed danger which gave an edge to the kiss she exchanged with Ralph Fantoni which quite took his breath away.

Chapter
Nine

The multiple blows Neville sustained to his head and ego might have felled a lesser man or a saner man, but Neville was neither less nor sane. He was driven, spurred by the success which seemed to be his brother's for the taking and his wife's when she put her foot down. The need swells and pulsates with envy. Two days after hearing that *The Pyjama Game* was to be shelved, he woke in acute agitation and ripped the bandage from his skull.

'Look,' he said to himself in the mirror, 'a dear little scar.' He didn't shave. He washed his hair, ruffled his bristles, put on a smart white shirt with a stiff upturned collar and a pair of pale jeans which hugged what remained of his figure, and he climbed into his taxi determined to find Kenny Vertigo. 'I will not be beaten,' he said to himself. 'I have talent. Penny, bless her, has limited talent, so she can read her own sodding stories or she can shove the stories anywhere that suits Dave Caster. I will not be beaten.' He put his severe attitude towards his little wife down to his head wound and told himself it was not before time.

He caught Kenny at the gate to Marty Cork's. 'Just passing,' he said. 'I was returning Madge's taxi, as a matter of fact and I thought, "Good Lord, there's Marty's place. I wonder how Kenny is getting on."'

'Hullo, Neville,' said Kenny. 'What do you think? Are you a Gothic man?'

Neville laughed. 'You've done a great job. Is the chief about?'

'Playing golf in Marbella,' said Kenny. 'But Suzie's indoors with the designer. Why don't you wander up?'

'I don't think I'll bother,' said Neville who didn't know Suzie or even Marty, though he had met them of course. Marty had been the host of *Who Can We Talk To Now*, a mid-week, mid-evening chat show whose appeal to the public was only moderate but had once been immense. He had made a comfortable transition from star to institution, by sensibly investing in property and, when he needed the publicity, in films. 'I gather he's got an interest in *Ravish*,' Neville mused, adding, 'That's a very fine flying buttress.'

'The Corks like it,' Kenny agreed, admiring his new addition to the large, late Victorian shell. 'Everyone's got an interest in *Ravish*. They raised the money the day after they thought of the title.'

'Casting now, are they?'

'I believe so,' said Kenny. 'Are you interested? I'll have a word if you like. I was only saying to Marty the other day how much I liked you in *The Iceman Cometh*.'

'Thanks,' said Neville, casually. 'I wouldn't mind. I've been looking for a film for a while, something a bit meaty.'

'It would be nice for you, wouldn't it,' said Kenny, 'what with the new house and Toby Gospel going the way he has? Again. Poor old Toby. He's asked me to do his conservatory but I'll be honest with you, Neville, I can't see that happening, either.'

'I'd be pleased if you would,' said Neville. 'I don't think it would do me any harm at all. I thought Toby already had a conservatory, didn't he?' Kenny shook his head and Neville smiled sorrowfully. 'He always was a bit of a big-noter. Poor old Toby.' They stood in silence for a minute before Neville said, 'Would you mind not mentioning anything to Madge? Things are a bit iffy there at the moment, if you follow.'

'I follow,' said Kenny then his eyes hardened and his jaw dropped as he studied the progress of a wheelbarrow across the jagged landscape of Marty Cork's brutally transformed Japanese garden. 'Get that sodding thing off there. Can't you see the red lines? You moron! You'll have to excuse me,' he said to Neville. 'I'll be in touch.' And he pranced as nimbly as any boy in the corps across the darkened sod to apply corrective measures.

Neville could create an opportunity from passing circumstance better than almost anyone. His mother had been right. And having created the opportunity he knew, almost better than anybody, how to follow it through. He didn't bother to inform Madge that he was returning the taxi and would never be taking it out again. He had no intention of reporting to her ever again.

Painful though it was he had decided to take charge of his own affairs from now on, to wean himself of Madge and her taxis. Madge had been his professional ruin. He could see it now. It was her fault that his career had rumbled to a noisy standstill in a room full of people in his brother's house. She didn't have a thought in her head as to where he should go next. She probably hadn't for years.

He thought about her phone calls: 'Neville my love, Billy's off to Spain to do a commercial and I was relying on him. You wouldn't do the ten-till-six shift, would you? Then pop by the office and let's have a little chat about some television.' And he would drive the taxi for a few hours because he wanted the money and to kill time and he would go and chat with her and television would come up but not usually in relation to him. He could name only one job that she could take credit for getting him in the last ten years. 'I've been a fool,' he told himself. He should have left her years ago. Now he would. He would fade her out as Penny had faded her out. It was a turning point. It was a crisis. The bump on his head had worked wonders.

He took the bus home, well able to cope with Fern, and Ralph Fantoni if necessary. He had as much right as Ralph to his brother's kitchen table. A tiny woman passing him in the street called 'Hello, haven't seen you for ages,' mistaking him for someone she thought she knew which he took for an omen. He felt fantastic. His prospects, he believed, were wonderful. He imagined the brilliance he could bring to a meaty role in *Ravish* and on the bus he planned the speech he might make at the BAFTA awards. It wouldn't be long. It would be short and poignant. 'Thank you mother,' he thought he might say. He liked the sound of that. But then again, he thought as he strolled from the bus stop home, perhaps something drily amusing would be better.

Ralph Fantoni was nowhere in sight as it turned out and Fern was alone at the kitchen table, smiling to herself. 'Neville,' she called. 'I'm just sitting here thinking about what to have for supper. Come and help me. I thought we would all eat together, *en famille*. I thought we would make the children attend. It's time we all sat down together, don't you think?'

This also filled Neville with pleasure, even if it was tempered by suspicion. Being party to Fern's secret life gave him good grounds for wondering about her motives for anything. But she appeared to have none as she smiled up from the recipe book, short of a good meal for everyone and there was nothing he liked better than making himself useful about the kitchen.

'We really had a very nice afternoon,' he reported to Penny later as she rested before going down to face the food they had lavished so much time and creative energy on. 'She can be very pleasant company when it suits her.'

'Can she?' said Penny. 'You ought to know. You had her before anyone else and she's still not much to look at.'

'That was years ago,' laughed Neville, surprised at the snipe and at how masculine it made him feel. 'She makes very good jokes and she knows when to be quiet. We just chopped away not even speaking for large parts of the afternoon. I enjoyed myself. Besides,' he added, 'she has something, Fern has. There's something Lauren Bacallish about her. No not Lauren Bacall. I'll think of who it is in a minute.'

'Humphrey Bogart,' Penny said. 'She's secretive, if you ask

me. I wouldn't be surprised if she was a kleptomaniac.'

Neville laughed again. He was happy. 'Anyway,' he said. 'She wants the children to eat with us. She wants Glen to come to supper.'

'Big deal,' said Penny. 'Why?' But Neville didn't know. Fern hadn't told him, or if she had he couldn't remember.

She hadn't. She had scarcely spoken to him at all because she was only vaguely aware he was there. Her mind was consumed with the meeting she'd had that morning with Bud Fenchurch. 'I have to tell you I haven't read poems as fine as these since I first discovered Pope,' he had said. 'They are witty, clever, satirical, polished, entertaining and best of all they are very, very commercial. I'm thrilled to bits with them. You,' he had added, after a ten second appraisal that had chilled her, 'are a very exciting woman.'

What was it, she had been asking herself as Neville had burbled on about his search for a suitable vehicle. What was it that men like Ralph and Bud saw in her? Surely she wasn't as desirable as all that. She had to suppress a giggle of satisfaction. Being desirable was never anything she had set out to be. She may once have been very attractive but she was a born academic. Everyone said so.

'And you'll buy your own taxi,' she said to Neville in order to be polite.

'Good heavens no,' he had said. 'I'm talking about a film. Professional vehicle, you know. Oh Lord. I don't suppose I was making myself clear. The old grey matter isn't working as well as it should be what with the concussion and everything.' Then he had lost her again as she returned to Bud Fenchurch.

Perhaps it was talent that made her sexually exciting. She controlled a grin with her teeth. Perhaps both Ralph and Bud were drawn to her in the way that women were drawn to politicians, though drawn to her talent and not her politics. It was possible. But was it probable? Was Ralph making fun of her? Had Ralph told Bud that she was good for a kiss in a corner? She flushed. She bit her lip harder and frowned. Maybe it was all a joke and both Ralph and Bud thought her poems were laughable but that it was fun to string her along because she was sexually available. 'Ouch,' she had said, peeling off a tiny bit of finger. She didn't hear Neville enquire after it. No, she told herself. There were plenty of sexually available women for them to toy with. They wouldn't do that to her. She was cleverer than both of them put together. If that was their game they must know she would see through it. Still, she would make herself less sexually inviting. She would freeze any overtures or compliments that were not directly related to her work and she would insist on a contract that was legally binding.

That resolve notwithstanding, Fern took special care over her hair and make-up for the supper she and Neville had prepared for the whole family because, despite herself, she was suddenly exquisitely aware of herself, physically, and she was aware as well of a new status, a new standing in the family which she would shortly reveal to them all. 'Oh,' said Penny, eyeing Fern's loose hair and darkened eyes, 'how unusual.'

'You look wonderful Fern,' Neville said, 'doesn't she, Jeremy? You look like a million dollars.'

'You look very nice, Mummy,' said Ruby. Ruby was grateful to her for having agreed to a meal *en famille*. Ruby had told her mother she was being beastly to Glen who showed not a single sign of a brain disorder and actually went to a very good school which required its pupils to be positively brilliant and because Fern had relented Ruby was grateful though Glen seemed not to be.

He laughed when Penny enquired of Fern sweetly, 'Have you found a new night cream?'

'No,' murmured Fern. 'Something much, much better. I've done you an egg Penny because I know you won't want what we are having.' This was unfortunate because Penny was starving and though an egg might have done very well had she chosen not to eat of her own accord, it seemed very meagre when thrust upon her. And Penny became unusually tense when she was hungry.

Jeremy said, 'So,' as he tucked into the mussels. 'How was everyone's day? I had some quite good news myself. I may be doing the vocals on the *Tempting Fate* theme music. Well when I say may be, it looks certain.'

'How fantastic,' said Penny. 'That really is wonderful

news, isn't it Glen?' She was determined to bring him into the conversation, whatever turn it took, to prove to him that she loved him.' I think singing is marvellous. My own singing teacher says I have a natural gift and I think Glen has inherited it. Do you remember having to sing that fish fingers solo. Music is so uplifting. I love to sing.'

'Penny does a very good "Row Row Row Your Boat",' Neville agreed, allowing himself a discreet slurp of mussel juice.

'That must be very uplifting,' Fern said, not wincing at the slurp because she felt well-disposed towards the whole world, including her brother-in-law. 'Do you do rowing actions, Penny, or what?' Penny glared at her and then at Neville. She didn't know what they meant.

'Julian's going to try to fix us a reasonable table for the awards, for once,' said Jeremy. 'I think he's going to ask Marty and Suzie Cork. 'You'll be with Robin's wife and Dave Caster, I suppose, won't you Penny, or is Dave up for an award himself? Did he do that documentary on walls? I think he did. No, he didn't. It was that oaf from Central. Do you remember he interviewed Kenny ... Kenny is amazing, isn't he?'

'I saw Kenny, today,' said Neville carelessly. 'At Marty's.'

'Oh yes?' said Jeremy.

'What were you doing there?' asked Penny.

'Is he starting work on your house?' enquired Fern. They all turned to him expectantly and their faces froze and their stomachs heaved as he tried to manoeuvre a mussel dangling from his lips back into his mouth with his tongue.

'Why were you at Marty's?' said Penny. 'You don't know him, do you?'

'Of course I know him,' said Neville. 'We met at Toby's, when Toby was doing *Puss in Boots*.'

'That was when I met you,' Ruby said to Glen. 'Before you grew muscles.' They smiled at each other and Fern's lips twitched uneasily. She wanted to tell Glen to go back to his shed but held herself in check.

'He's got money in *Ravish*, you know,' said Jeremy. 'How's the egg Penny?'

'Everyone's got money in *Ravish*,' Neville said. 'As a matter of fact I may be involved in it myself.'

'What?' said Penny who had finished her supper but had to sit through two more courses until everyone else finished theirs. She bitterly regretted having spent so much time on her own make-up. She might just as well have stayed in her room. 'How's the egg?' Jeremy repeated.

'Just right,' she smiled at him. 'What do you mean involved?' she demanded of Neville.

'It's early days,' said Neville. 'And I'm not going to go on about it. But they're casting at the moment and I'm in with a chance.'

'Oh well done,' said Jeremy. 'Well done. I think that calls for champagne. Let's break open some champagne. Fern? Bring a bottle up from the downstairs' fridge. It's not everyday we get two things to celebrate.'

Neville raised his hand. 'No.' he said. 'No, it's not settled. There's no point in celebrating yet. It's just a chance.'

'Okay,' said Jeremy. 'I take your point. It may turn out to be another *Pyjama Game*. We'll leave the film out of it. But get the champagne anyway Fern. We can drink to Penny's and my success in the awards. It may bring us luck.' And Fern went downstairs to get the champagne because she felt superior to them. She thought they were ridiculous. She thought their success, if there was going to be any success, was piddling compared to her own. She could turn out to be the best poet of her generation.

Penny shouldn't have drunk so much champagne on an egg. It immediately dissolved the single inhibition she had about showing herself up in public. 'Glen,' she said, 'Sing your fish fingers song. Go on, you haven't done it for ages and you know how I love it. It makes me cry. You'll love it, Fern, even if you do have a hard heart. Go on darling.' She began to warble herself. 'Some fings are fabulous, some fings are scrumshooless.' She really was quite musical.

'Shut up, Mother,' said Glen. 'You're being silly.'

'Im not,' giggled Penny. 'I'm just proud of you. You are handsome and gorgeous, isn't he Ruby? I think Ruby finds you almost as gorgeous as I do and who can blame her?' Her eyes focused unsteadily but triumphantly on Fern who realized immediately that the padlock would have to be used on the shed, whatever Ruby said about the boy. She distinctly remembered him having to have counselling as a child. She couldn't believe he had been cured. No one could be cured of a mother like Maureen Cartilage.

'Shut up, Mother,' said Glen again, causing Penny to stop giggling and put her hand to her mouth.

'Don't speak to your mother like that, Glen,' said Neville.

'Come on everyone, have another drink,' said Jeremy who might well have been ruthless in the fray but did not like the fray to intrude on meal times.

'You shouldn't speak to me like that, Glen,' said Penny. 'It was harmless fun. I don't know why you are so rude to me. You don't hear Ruby speaking to her mother like that.'

'I do sometimes,' said Ruby, anxious to be loyal when the shed might have been avoided completely had she not been so insistent.

'You don't Ruby,' Fern said. 'You have been brought up to know better.'

'Oh come on,' said Jeremy. 'This is supposed to be a celebration. I'll sing the *Tempting Fate* theme for you.' He rose and began to chant, 'Fate fate fate fate fate,' which seemed to be the first line.

'Shut up, Daddy,' said Ruby.

'That is quite enough Ruby,' snapped Fern. 'There is no need for copycat behaviour. I thought you had a mind of your own.'

'I do,' said Ruby. 'There is no need to be insulting.'

'To your room, I think.' said Fern. 'Jeremy you have given everyone far too much to drink.' She herself felt astonishingly sober.

'To your room, Glen,' cried Penny. 'I'll show everyone who is well brought up. When I say to your room, you will go to your room.'

'Room!' said Glen. 'Which room? Do you mean the shed? Do you want me to go back to the shed where you think I belong? Well don't worry because I will. I'm sorry I came. Thank you for the dinner Fern, it was delicious. Goodnight everyone.' And with the dignity and grace of a young Douglas Fairbanks — junior — he strode from the room. He didn't believe Ruby was responsible for the shed. He never had and he never would, even if she had been right about her family.

'Come back, darling,' said Penny. 'I didn't mean it. Come back. I probably was being silly.'

But Jeremy said, 'Leave him. He needs to cool down. Let's get on with our singalong. I remember "Some Fings are Fabulous",' And he stood again, keen to perform. 'Why don't you move to the piano, Miss Penny, to accompany me?'

'Oh honestly,' said Fern, glaring at Jeremy. 'You are pathetic. I don't know who led you to believe you were multi-talented but whoever it was made a serious mistake. You are going to make a complete fool of yourself before very long and don't expect me to hang around and say I didn't see it coming.'

'Fern!' cried Penny. 'How can you talk to your husband like that when he has provided this wonderful home for you. Millions of women, millons of my mothers from John O'Groats to Lands End would give their right arms for a house like this. He has, single-handed, supported this whole family for at least twenty years and what do you give him in return? I think you are ungrateful, even if it isn't my place to say so.'

'It isn't, Penny,' said Neville wearily. 'I think you should apologize. I'm sorry Fern. It was all that drink on an empty stomach.'

'It's quite all right,' said Fern frostily. 'She will soon have to eat her words. And there have been so many of them I don't believe she will ever be hungry again.' And with that, she left the room pausing only for a second at the door to cast a look of fury at her husband. It was a fine exit, as impressive as any Penny could have mustered in a properly sober moment.

'Excuse me,' said Ruby. 'I'll just make sure Glen's alright in the shed.'

Chapter
Ten

Penny didn't have the courage to apologize to Fern in person so she apologized to Jeremy whom she telephoned from work. 'Oh Jeremy,' she sighed. 'What can I say? I've been to see Sister and she took one look at me and said, 'Miss Penny, what have you been doing to yourself?' She said she's never seen me looking so fatigued. She said I must be very stressed and really, Jeremy, I think I must be. It's not any one thing, but a lot of little things: the awards, the house, the documentary, Neville, the seventy people from Sunderland who have written to say they are coming to London especially to see me and so on. I know you'll understand because we're in the same business, but I wasn't sure Fern would because she isn't though she is a wonderful cook. Could you make it alright with Fern for me? You know how fond of her I am. I truly didn't mean to hurt her feelings. I really don't know what came over me.'

An honest person might have said 'Champagne' but Jeremy wasn't very honest because he had never really needed to be. He said she wasn't to worry, that stress sometimes got to him too, though not very often and although it didn't get to Fern who was spared any of the professional tribulations that caused it, he was sure she would understand. Then he telephoned Fern who said, 'What stress? She is spoilt, idle, rude and stupid. She also has the sensitivity of a mallet. I want her out. I want them all out. I have too much on my plate. I cannot tolerate her and the boy is a sex maniac. You only have to look at him.'

Jeremy sighed noisily. 'That's an absurd thing to say,' he said. He also had quite a lot on his plate, Juanita Hobbs, for one thing, who was sitting in the corridor with a bunch of flowers waiting to thank him in person. 'He's a very decent boy. He's in the first eleven, the first fifteen and he is champion athlete. And dare I say, Fern, we wouldn't have this trouble if you'd let him sleep in the study in the first place.'

'Rubbish,' said Fern. 'There wouldn't be this trouble if you'd told Neville to stay in a hotel. You allowed them to move in and take over when you must have seen the havoc they would wreak. Look at them: a failed actor riddled with jealousy, a moron riddled with ambition and a sex maniac riddled with lust. You've seen the way he looks at Ruby. It's disgusting. I mean, how could you? Honestly, Jeremy, how could you?'

'I'm sorry, Fern,' Jeremy said. 'I have a news conference. I have to go. I will talk to you later.' And he put down the phone and paused only to flick a comb through his hair before going out to the corridor to greet Juanita as if she was an old friend. She really was very photogenic, he told himself as he bent to kiss her on the cheek.

Fern sat by the phone fuming and when it rang again snapped into it, 'What?' which surprised Bud Fenchurch who had anticipated a much warmer greeting from the woman he had decided he could easily make into a star. 'Oh dear,' laughed Fern, forgetting at once that she had intended to be distant. 'Sorry, I thought you were my husband.'

'That's alright, then,' said Bud smoothly. 'Husbands can take that sort of treatment but men who are wildly in love with you cannot.'

'My husband is wildly in love with me,' said Fern. 'He's wild about something, anyway.' She allowed herself a small, low laugh which she knew was entirely captivating to men prepared to be captivated. 'What can I do for you?'

'What can we do for each other?' Bud said. 'That is the point. You'll be interested to hear that I put your poems in front of a couple of people who are as excited as I am by them and we all agree that if we get this right we could all do very well out of them.'

'I don't believe you.' Fern said.

'I can understand that,' said Bud. 'Poems aren't usually anything much to get worked up about but believe me when I tell you yours are. What I would like to do is show you about the place a bit so that your face and name become familiar and I'd like to give people a very small taste of the sort of stuff they can expect from you, just a tease, something to whet their appetites. Then we can lead into a major push when we publish the first book. But what we must do now, immediately, is get together to talk about it. What about dinner, tonight?'

'I can't,' said Fern and remembering the strategy she had planned for protecting her dignity added, 'I won't. I don't want to be rushed into anything. I told Ralph and I'm telling you. I'm not sure it's fame and fortune I want.'

'Of course it isn't,' Bud agreed. 'But I'm sure you would like recognition. We all want to be recognized, even poets, and it's harder for poets than almost anyone else apart from glass engravers to be even vaguely noticed. You don't want to be vaguely noticed do you?'

'I'm not sure,' said Fern and she wasn't until she saw Neville striding across the grass and she remembered her fury at him, his stepson, his wife and his brother that she thought how blissful it would be to be able to spit in Jeremy's face, professionally speaking, and to win coveted awards while he was still being merely nominated. 'I certainly think we should talk about it,' she said to Bud. 'I could come to your office tomorrow, if you like.' So it was agreed and by the time Neville had come through the conservatory and into the kitchen where she had been redesigning the garden shed, both Fern and Bud were congratulating themselves on a move cleverly made.

'It's not that I don't love Jeremy,' Fern explained to herself. 'I just want to show him.'

'There's no doubt about Kenny Vertigo,' Neville said waving a script at her. 'He's as good as his word.' And he didn't even stop for a cracker topped with cottage cheese and chives but headed straight for his room where Fern soon heard him pacing to and fro, laughing and reading and preparing himself.

It was just as well for him and for Penny that she was diverted by the accolades being heaped upon her. They could thank Bud Fenchurch for the fact that she was only redesigning the shed and not plotting a serious accident. The scent of glory in the offing sweetened her. Even so, a small hard knot of fury sat low in her heart and as she returned to doodling on the large white sheet with her special roller pencil, imagining herself on television, the dinner table conversation of the previous night intruded again and again, and again she thought of sharper and crueller replies she should and could have made to Penny had Penny not swooned over her coffee. Fern would never forgive her. How dare she comment on her marriage to Jeremy. How dare she presume to know what went on inside it.

What did Penny know about grown-up, happy marriages, Fern demanded of herself and she threw down the pencil and headed across to the garden shed with the key. She was only playing at it with Neville. She and Jeremy understood each other. They even liked each other. They were content with what the other had to offer. Theirs was a mature arrangement between adults who accepted the shortfalls for the sake of the long run. They had been married sixteen years for God's sake. How dare anyone, least of all a screaming hysteric like Penny, assume that because they didn't sound as if they were content, they were not content.

She tentatively unlocked the shed door, aware that she was invading someone else's privacy. As she pulled it shut behind her and turned to examine the walls and their potential for stippling, the knot in her heart snapped, releasing a terrible flood of outrage and hate which turned it hard and fast against the Neville Brewsters and their sex-maniac son. If she

99

had been unreasonable about Penny, in the garden shed she found ample justification for her loathing.

Strewn across the frail camp bed, the floor and the shelves laden with half-used tins of paint and ancient mind-reading props were Glen's well-thumbed copies of *Men Only* and soiled garments reeking of teenage sweat. 'Oh my God,' she gasped. She had never even started a poem that encompassed anything so sordid. She tiptoed across the room, as if frightened of being contaminated and she picked up a magazine devoted entirely to the wonders of an enormous chest called Mandy. It revolted her. The tiny, seedy room bore out her worst fears, fulfilled the very grimmest pictures she had been able to conjure when she'd contemplated the bent of a youth so plainly over-sexed that it scarcely mattered whether he was mentally disadvantaged or not. She had only to compare it to Ruby's sweetly frilled and daintily polished suite with its well ordered compact-disc system, its elegant shelving for books and magazines and the absence of any obvious sexuality in the clothes draped across antique chairs. Glen was out of control. The room reeked of no control. The boy was a pyschopath.

If you are to be a poet of any note, you need this sort of imagination. If Fern's had run away with her it was only because of her extreme agitation that Penny had insulted her and Bud had flattered her beyond her wildest expectations. 'I must protect Ruby,' she muttered and she stormed back to the house fortified by Bud, Ralph, and even *The African* but scarcely mindful of them at all. She ran up the stairs and crashed into the spare room where she was greeted by Neville with a dramatic flourish.

'Woman of my dreams,' he cried. He had grown up with an unfortunate tendency to react inappropriately. It had driven his father wild.

'I don't mind you being in my house, Neville,' she yelled. 'You are blood and you are relatively clean and quiet. I can't pretend I like your wife but I'm prepared to put up with her dimwittedness and her insults for Jeremy's sake.' This was new but she didn't stop to admit it. 'What I will not tolerate,' she raged, 'what I cannot, Neville, cannot, tolerate is the filth in the garden shed. I know you are not related to him but you have introduced into our household something I am simply not able to stomach.' She paused and put her head in her hands.

'His football boots,' Neville sighed. 'I knew it. I said to Penny, "For God's sake remind Glen to put his football boots outside the shed every evening. They will stink the place out." I'm sorry Fern. He must have forgotten.'

'It isn't the boots. Don't be ridiculous. I can stand boots. You'll have to come and see for yourself.' And Neville who had been feeling better and tougher, with his feet more firmly on the ground than they'd been in years, had a horrible sensation that the rug was about to be pulled from underneath him. He followed Fern in silence to the shed. She kicked the door open and waited outside for him to go and see the depravity for himself. 'Go on,' she said. 'Go on.'

He saw only the usual condition of a room inhabited by Glen, though with the bizarre addition of the paint tins, the props and a wide range of gardening implements. He prowled around it carefully, looking for clues, wondering what on earth he could say to Fern who was clearly beside herself about something other than dinner the night before.

He had been avoiding her all day because he knew Penny's behaviour had been unforgivable and that Fern was even less forgiving than most people. He'd thought she was only waiting to catch him before telling him, as she had told him many years before, 'Well it's not working out is it. I think it's time to call it a day. You'll have to go.' He had been dreading it. Penny had clutched him during the night and sobbed onto his chest begging him. 'Please, please, Neville,' she had begged. 'Make it alright for me. I didn't mean to cause trouble. I was just hungry and she is such a cow.'

'We'd better pack our bags,' he had said. 'You don't want to stay, do you?'

'I hate it,' she had admitted in the tiny jerking gasps which were her speciality in times of trouble. 'But where will we go? How will it look if we move into a hotel now? Everyone knows we are here. Robin and Dave, the papers. What will they think? We have to stay. I really, really want a jacuzzi.' And she had begun to cry again, heartbreakingly, and he hadn't been able to stand it because he truly loved her even if she wasn't all that talented, perhaps because she wasn't all that talented, but earnt well.

'I'll do my best,' he had said eventually. 'But you'll have to apologize' and when that had brought on hysterics he had agreed that she could say she was sorry to Jeremy and hope that was good enough. But none of that seemed to matter now. Whatever it was that mattered, and mattered more than anything he could have imagined, was here in the shed. He must be blind, he told himself in bewilderment. He could see nothing. He picked up the *Men Only* on the bed and admired Mandy's enormous chest and he wondered vaguely if this might be it.

'See what I mean?' cried Fern from the doorway. 'You can see exactly what I mean. What if Ruby came across that smut? She spends hours over here with him just to keep him company. What is he up to? That's what I want to know. Frankly, Neville, he isn't fit company for Ruby and I won't have it. I don't want him anywhere near her. I'm sorry. You'll have to sort something out with Penny. But I can't have Ruby exposed to him.'

And because she could think of nothing else she wanted to say she headed back to the house, remembering only halfway across the lawn why she had come to the shed in the first place. Without a trace of regret she turned back and to Neville's even more acute bewilderment, began to measure the walls and rub her hands across their surface in a most disturbing way. She did that for several minutes without speaking then she left him again, sitting on the small camp bed without a single thought of anything positive to do. He put the copies of *Men Only* into a neat pile for a start. Then he decided to call on Jeremy at work. There was no one else really who could sort it all out.

Jeremy was almost never unfaithful to Fern and never ever in a way that he thought might threaten his marriage. He liked his marriage. He liked the things Fern had done to make it

102

comfortable. He didn't even mind Ralph Fantoni all that much because he thought if his wife was going to form an attachment to another man it might as well be with an undiscovered abstract painter whose works might one day be valuable. He took Juanita Hobbs to lunch because she was suitably unthreatening and she was very grateful and very, very pretty. He told her she had been wasted in a pizza parlour anyway.

'Why don't you come back to my office for a drink?' he said as they sipped the remains of their second bottle of wine.

'We're already having a drink,' Juanita giggled.

'A cosier drink,' Jeremy said. He smiled easily across the top of his glass and knew he looked fascinating. 'You wait here,' he said, 'while I make a quick phone call.' The newsroom wasn't exactly his own personal office and certainly no place for a cosy drink with a former dough-roller or whatever it was Juanita had been. He rang Julian Fortescue and asked if he could use his office for an hour in the afternoon. Compared to the newsroom, the *Tempting Fate* offices were The Ritz. 'I've got to write a column and really I just need a bit of peace and quiet for a few minutes,' he lied.

Julian, familiar with such lies, said, 'I need my office but you can always use the *Whoops Bang Wallop* office. There's no one there this week. Call by and I'll give you the key.'

It took Neville ages to find him. In News someone said they had seen him go to lunch but not come back and someone else said he was over in Light Entertainment with Julian Fortescue. Neville found Light Entertainment but not Julian Fortescue who had left for the day but Sally, Julian's secretary, was struck by a sudden thought and said if he wouldn't mind hanging on a minute she thought she knew where he was and she did, in *Whoops Bang Wallop* with his hand halfway up Juanita's long lean thigh. 'Oh,' he said with some surprise when she found him there because he believed he had locked himself in. 'This is Miss Hobbs who may be one of the hostesses.'

'Your brother is here,' said Sally, unmoved.

'Thank you,' said Jeremy and he waited for her to leave before telling Juanita that she had better go but he would be

103

in touch because, bore though it was, his brother being here probably meant trouble. And Juanita said she quite understood and that if he didn't phone her she could always phone him because she knew where he was, didn't she, and really she was dead keen to get some modelling work. 'Did you mean that about me being a hostess?' she asked.

'I'm afraid not,' Jeremy said. 'It's out of my hands.' Juanita took the fact bravely in her stride and left without another word, passing Neville in the corridor as she strode and throwing him a smile of resignation.

'Sorry to disturb you,' Neville said taking Jeremy by the elbow. 'Is there somewhere we can talk?'

They went back to the *Whoops Bang Wallop* office where they both sat on bean-bags and Neville explained the awful difficulty he was in, describing, to Jeremy's astonishment, Fern's weird communion with the walls. 'Oh God!' said Jeremy. 'What's wrong with the woman? We had her mother up and that Mrs Plantaganet. I even promised Mrs Plantaganet tickets for the first show.'

'I can take her point,' Neville said. 'I mean Glen is a good-looking boy and even I could see they liked the idea of each other. But we can't throw him out on his ear, can we? And I don't think Penny can take much more stress.'

'I like the boy,' Jeremy said. 'Of course we can't throw him out. Good Lord — *Men Only*. We used to have all those copies of *Nature* in the loft, didn't we? I don't know what's got into Fern. Leave it with me. I'll have a word with her. She may need to see a doctor.' So Neville thanked him and took himself off to Mandarin Street to kill time until Jeremy had the word and Jeremy went back to News, exhausted at the prospect of anoher awkward phone call.

Fortunately for him, he was spared it. Glen was less fortunate. He collided with Fern as she was leaving the shed for the fifth time that day, this time with tiny bits of material which she had been holding up to the light with a view to choosing blinds. 'Sorry,' said Glen who trod on her foot as she pushed past him. 'I didn't expect to find anyone in here.'

'Obviously,' said Fern. 'But since you have and it's me we might has well go back in because there's something I want to say to you.' And before he could sweep anything private under the bed, she presented him with her view of his suspect past, his sordid present and his lack of a future anywhere near Ruby and then she left him, aghast, afraid and alone. He didn't know what she was talking about, only that she appeared to hate him and that she certainly wanted him out of her house or, to be precise, the shed attached to her house. Where was his mother, he yelled silently to himself. Where was anyone who might take his side?

It was desperately unfair. Anyone could see it was desperately unfair. But Fern was blinkered by her overwhelming sense of territory which applied not only to her house but to her daughter. And she had no room in her heart for a boy who quite plainly had the wherewithal to charm her daughter while his mother was upstairs claiming the spare room.

Poor Glen. There wasn't much he could do, short of packing his bag. But he had no bag other than the one that was filled with school books and running shoes. So he unloaded it, stuffed it full of clothes and a couple of copies of *Men Only*, removed the money from his football boot and he left. He didn't even bother to leave a note. Apart from Ruby there was no one he wanted to communicate with and to communicate with Ruby he told himself would risk trouble for her. However he wouldn't abandon her. She would know where to find him. He could never abandon Ruby to a woman as treacherous as her mother, whatever her mother thought.

Chapter
Eleven

He wasn't missed for three days except by Ruby who said to her mother within hours of his leaving, 'I don't know where Glen is. He's not in his shed.'

'No,' said Fern. 'He's training. He mentioned he would be out training for a few days.' It was only a small lie. It could even have been the truth as far as Fern was concerned but if it wasn't the truth, it didn't matter. She was grateful the boy was keeping clear of Ruby as she had told him to. If it crossed her mind that he had run away, she didn't bother to admit it.

'That's funny,' Ruby said. 'He didn't say anything to me.' So Fern tightened the corners of her mouth and widened her gaze to suggest to her daughter that boys like Glen weren't to be trusted about anything.

'He probably has a girlfriend,' she said. 'He's the type.' It was easy for everyone except Ruby not to notice his absence. They were all very busy simulating their own, steering clear of each other to avoid the recriminations they imagined were coming as a result of the wretched meal *en famille* and they hadn't really noticed his presence. No one, except Fern, knew there would be no recriminations because she had decided the buck ended with Glen and had slung it at him. Both Penny and Neville assumed Jeremy had talked to Fern as he'd said he would and Jeremy told himself if he kept his head down and said nothing, Fern's mood would pass and, when it seemed to, he congratulated himself on his discretion.

At the same time, everyone except Ruby was thoroughly preoccupied with their careers which had simultaneously taken the most extraordinary leaps in the direction of the light they all craved. Glen couldn't have planned it worse. When he asked himself where his mother was on that hideous afternoon in the shed, he might have been gratified to learn that she, at least, was on top of the world. Robin Powder had been persuaded by Dave Caster, who could be extremely persuasive when he wanted to be, to allow Penny to have a shot at some filmed inserts.

Talcum had resisted of course because it was his job to resist. 'I'm against it. The whole point of *Kidding About* is that it's studio based. It's supposed to feel like home. Leaving home might make all those little viewers feel very insecure.' And Dave had said 'Crap, Robin. I want her off my back. I will help you out with the awards but only if you get her off my back.' He wasn't called Castor Oil for nothing.

The first assignment, arranged with great speed before anyone had time to change their mind about the wisdom of it, was an incisive look at How We Get Curtains, and a breezy but informative visit had been arranged to Window Dressing, a small family-firm owned by Angelica-in-Make-Up's mother. As Glen, several miles away, was shovelling notes from his boot to his bag, Penny was being briefed, though she was so excited she could scarcely pay attention.

'This is important, Penny,' Dave was saying. 'What you have to bear in mind is that we have three minutes to explain to our very young viewers how curtains are made so we don't need any long-winded interviews or complicated explanations. We'll let the pictures tell the story and you'll be there to turn the pages. Follow?'

Penny assured him she did. 'I'm not a complete idiot, you know,' she said to him. She hadn't opted for anything in the way of cleavage but an especially long and youthful scarf over a cowboy-check shirt, some snug jeans and a pair of coordinating calf high boots. 'What I'm trying to get across,' she said to Angelica, 'is joyful enthusiasm, you know, intelligent interest.'

Angelica said, 'If you could give a special mention to the Roman blinds ... they're sticking a bit at the moment. Mum thinks everyone's going back to pencil pleats.'

Curiously, it turned out not to be as easy as Penny had imagined and after several hours at Window Dressing she found herself very close to tears. 'All I'm saying,' Dave said to her between increasingly deep breaths, 'is that you can afford to be a bit more natural. You don't have to sound like the *Encyclopedia of Interlining.* And smile a bit more, okay? When you ask Brenda if it's hard to sew in a straight line, sound as if you really are interested.'

She tried it again. 'Now Brenda,' she said, 'I can see you are making curtains for some lucky sitting-room and you have to sew all the way up one side and all the way down the other. How high will these curtains be?' She grinned at Brenda who stared back at her, unable to comprehend the question, apparently.

'You say high, Penny. In what sense high?' Penny's eyes rolled sideways in her head in an attempt to catch Dave's.

'Keep going,' said Dave.

'How long will the seams be, Brenda?' Penny asked. 'And by seams, I mean the join between the bits of curtain.'

'I know what seams are,' Brenda said, looking in wonderment at Dave and at Angelica who had come to the shop to oversee Penny's make-up and keep an eye on her mother.

'I know you know,' said Penny. 'But we are talking to very, very young children who won't know.'

'Their mothers will though. And it's their mothers who will buy the curtains.'

'We're not here to sell them,' Penny said. 'We're trying to show the children how the bits of material that hang in front of their windows are made. . . .'

'Stop,' yelled Dave. 'Stop all this. We are wasting time. Now Brenda all you have to do is sew along the seams for a while. I'll tell you when to start and stop. Penny you come and stand near me. You don't have to say a word. We can say it all afterwards.'

'We'll do the interviews at the end, you mean,' Penny said with relief. 'Fine.'

'No I don't mean that, I mean there won't be any interviews. We don't need them. I'll just get some very nice film and you can explain it later. We'll dub it.'

'Oh,' said Penny. 'Dub, fine. We won't bother with the script then. Will you still show me measuring up a window and choosing material? Do you want me to do the bit where I say to Brenda what sort of curtains I want and ask her how long it will take and how much it will cost?'

'I don't know,' said Dave. 'I don't know. I want you to shut up for a while and let me get on with it.' And get on with it he did, leaving Penny slightly high and dry and wondering how much of her could be salvaged. She could see she was going to have to be firm about it. She was sure she could contribute a lot to the dubbing. She would do her best with the dubbing. Then it would definitely be a step in the right direction, she was almost certain. Before the day was out she had persuaded Dave to do a few takes of her leaping between steps in the procedure crying, 'Fantastic, Brenda' and 'Isn't this cotton absolutely amazing?' 'For enthusiasm and continuity,' she said to Dave. 'To turn the pages.'

'I'm so tired,' she said to Neville in the spare room a few hours later. 'I am utterly, utterly exhausted.' And she collapsed so realistically that Neville hadn't liked to mention that Fern believed Glen was a pornographic influence on her daughter and wanted her to do something about it. And no one said anything at all to her about him being missed so it wasn't her fault she didn't know.

'I am too,' Neville said. 'I've been working on this bloody script all day. I'm going to test for it tomorrow.'

Only Ruby wondered where Glen was that night because she crept across to the shed when the rest of the house was sleeping and found it locked and the window closed which it never was when he was inside it. She thought if he wasn't back the next night she would ask Penny about it. She didn't believe her mother. It was a lie about the training and the girlfriend. Ruby knew. She guessed Fern was up to something. She wondered if she might not be a kleptomaniac. She was the right age, give or take twenty years.

'What's in that carrier bag under the table?' she enquired with caution as she bade her mother goodnight. She had been studying the menopause in biology.

'Nothing,' Fern said. 'Nothing to do with you anyway. See you in the morning.' And she retrieved the large bundle and hurried back upstairs with it before Ruby could insist on examining the contents. It was her poetry in motion bag, the beginnings, middles and endings of thousands of poems which she was saving in the hope that one day they would all join together to produce a masterpiece. They were none of Ruby's business and if they looked like the loot of a kleptomaniac it wasn't her fault.

Bud Fenchurch was also struck by the air of mystery which Fern brought into the room with her the next day and he wondered if it could be communicated by radio. 'Down to business immediately,' he said, having detected from the previous day's phone call that grovelling and flirting might not be appropriate. 'We've arranged for you to do Friday's *Listen I'm Talking!* The only small problem is that they record at eight in the morning to go out at nine. How are you first thing in the morning?'

He gazed at her lips appreciatively. They weren't remotely menopausal. He imagined how tousled that long rich hair must be after a night's sleep and how tempting it would be to grab it in massive bundles and press her back into the pillow with the force of his lips on hers. Just why Fern inspired these frantic fantasies is anyone's guess. Penny didn't and she was infinitely prettier.

'What will they want me to do?' she enquired looking at him suspiciously.

'What do you think?' Bud said with a smile. 'Talk. Sam will introduce you as poetry's most exciting discovery of the year and express astonishment that your work is only just about to be published when Herbert Harrison has called you 'The inspired ginger in a generation of uninspired icing sugar.'

110

'I've never met Herbert Harrison,' Fern said.

'He's one of our authors,' Bud assured her. 'It's perfectly alright. I read him a line or two from *The African*. He doesn't mind saying whatever we want him to say.'

Fern flushed. 'Did he like *The African*?'

Bud's hesitation was fractional. 'Oh Lord yes. Loved it, I believe.' Fern contained the smirk she felt tugging her lips and took a deep breath to control the surge of adrenalin that lifted her spirits higher than they had been in years. She felt confident. She felt desired. She was a success. She half closed her eyes to study Bud as he spoke. He was much taller than Ralph and far more relaxed. His eyes were a heart-wrenching blue. 'Also,' he was saying, 'Arabella has fixed an interview with the *Sun*. I know *The Times* might seem more appropriate but having thought about it, your work does have a certain *Sun*-like ring to it and I understand *The Times* might be interested at a later date. Arabella will persevere.

'I won't be able to come with you to *Listen I'm Talking!* but Arabella will and she tells me someone from the programme will be in touch to confirm everything and to ask you one or two questions just to see which areas they ought to cover. In the meantime I will take the rest of these ...' He took from her a large folder into which she had placed a few of the joined up beginnings, middles and endings ... 'and we will get moving. That alright by you?'

'I think so,' said Fern. 'It's all happening so quickly.'

'Well it has to, doesn't it,' Bud laughed, 'if you're to be an overnight success.' And Fern laughed too. She laughed like mad.

Neville had always wanted instant stardom. From a very young boy he had imagined that he would be catapulted to fame on the strength of a single dynamic performance which would have the critics raving at the power of his raw, but undeniable talent. As the years passed, however, and some of his performances were admired by people close to him, and some were not, and occasional appearances were reviewed but only briefly, he had been forced to admit that when fame finally came, he would have served a long, hard apprentice-ship. It was an enduring disappointment. To have had to struggle to succeed is not nearly as satisfying as having your merit recognized instantly. To be professional and forty isn't the same as being brilliant and twenty. It counts for less. And you don't photograph as well.

'Working?' they said to him at Splendid Productions while he was waiting to read.

He shook his head, 'Recovering from an accident,' he said pointing to the scar. 'Forced me out of *The Pyjama Game* before Toby was forced to force everyone out of it.' Everyone laughed. They liked the sound of his voice and they admired the scar. It gave him a sort of battered look. They were looking for a battered look. Neville looked as if he had taken a small beating from life but had come up smiling, with his face, figure and voice, all of which were impressive, more or less intact. He had a vulnerable quality but an inner strength. You could see it. They liked him. They said so.

'Loved you in *The Iceman*,' they said. 'You're with Madge, aren't you?'

'Was,' he corrected them. 'She's wonderful, bless her,' he said. 'But my brother and I now work through the family lawyer. It makes us all so much richer, especially the lawyer.' They laughed again. He could tell it was going well. They all read Jeremy's column. They thought he was brilliant.

Of course he had spoken in haste. They didn't have a family lawyer. But he was sure one could be found if neces-sary and he was sure he had heard Jeremy say that his lawyer did all his contracts and that he wouldn't touch an agent with a barge pole. It was the sort of thing Jeremy would say if he hadn't already. It was a detail anyway. Jeremy would agree, if it came to anything, that it was only a detail.

Jeremy was standing at King's Cross station and declaring with fervour, 'Every year thousands of teenage children teem through these gates, some without luggage, some without money, some only with their dreams. All of them arrive with hope. They come from Liverpool, Glasgow, Birmingham, Nottingham ... you name it, they come from it, eager, excited, foolish, and as I stand here. ...'

'Just a minute, Jeremy,' McEvoy said. 'We've got a problem. Excuse me,' he said to a large boy with a portable stereo pressed to his head. 'Could you move away please. You're giving us a headache.'

'What?' said the boy.

'We'd like you to move,' said Jeremy. 'We're doing a news report here and you are in the way.' He smiled because he was recognizable.

'Well I don't want to move,' said the boy. 'I want to stand here. I've got the same right as you to stand here. I am listening to something and I want to stand here.'

'Jesus,' said McEvoy.

'No, it's alright. It's okay,' Jeremy said, aware that compassion for the boy was welling in his chest and that his intuition suggested to him that here was just such a lad as he had been about to describe. 'You're from Liverpool, aren't you?' he said.

'So what!' said the boy.

'Nothing,' said Jeremy. 'So nothing. I'm just interested. We're doing a news report on kids who come to London from up north. I was just interested. Have you been in London long?' He tried to suggest with a vague gesture behind his back that the camera should start to roll and the tape run and he could see out the corner of his eye that McEvoy had understood. A small spurt of excitement sharpened his glance and his tongue.

'What's it to you?' said the boy.

'What's it to your parents?' Jeremy asked gently. 'Do your parents know you're in London?'

'I don't have to talk to you,' the boy said and catching sight of the camera focused on him and McEvoy's mike, he cried. 'What are they up to?' He advanced on McEvoy. 'What do you think you're doing?'

Jeremy moved towards him and took him by his arm. 'He's not up to anything. I told you. We're doing a report on kids who come to London from the north. Would you mind if we interviewed you? You could see yourself on television tonight. You wouldn't mind being on television would you? It would be a laugh, wouldn't it?'

'Are you mad or something?' the boy thundered as a small

crowd slowed to stroll past the scene and peer at it without actually stopping to stare. 'What do you think I am? I don't want to be on television. What sort of a loon do you think I am?' He rushed at the camera and flung Jeremy from his arm causing Jeremy to be hurled backwards into the crowd and to land flat on his back in the middle of it. As commuters edged around him, confusing him for a drunk although he had a television crew with him, he looked skyward and through the haze of raincoats, unpolished shoes and grey legs thought he saw a familiar face.

'Glen?' he called. 'Glen? What on earth are you doing here?' But it couldn't have been Glen because the face disappeared as he staggered to his feet and by the time he was upright was nowhere at all to be seen. He forgot about Glen. He supposed he had been confused by the shock.

It made brilliant television. They didn't show the boy's face, of course, only his reaction and Jeremy turning to the camera with his hand on his cheek to ask 'Why is he frightened? What sort of a life is he living?' Then from a different part of the station he had looked hard at the camera and spoken about his concern. 'I have a daughter myself,' he said. 'At fifteen, she's grown up yet frail, knowing yet innocent, in need of protection just like the youngsters I see all round me. They've nowhere to go. They've nothing to go to. Where are the mothers?' he asked. 'Where are the fathers? Where are the homes for these children and why aren't they in them? These are questions we must ask ourselves and they are questions we must answer. They're questions Johnny doesn't want us to ask. Poor, poor Johnny!'

They had decided to call the boy with the stereo Johnny. He was just as likely to be Johnny as anything else.

'Wonderful,' sighed Neville. 'Absolutely wonderful.' Jeremy leant forward to turn the set off.

'I think it worked quite well, didn't it?' he said. 'Do you know, I thought I saw Glen at King's Cross station when we were doing that stuff with the boy. I could have sworn it was him.'

'It probably was him,' said Ruby.

'I don't think so, darling,' Penny said. 'That's out of his

way. He goes to school on the bus anyway.'

'But I've been trying to tell you for three days,' Ruby said. 'He could be anywhere. He hasn't slept in the shed since the night you sent him there. Mummy says he's been training but you don't train all day and all night for three days. He's gone away. He said he was going and he's gone.'

Penny continued to smile because it made no sense. 'Where did he say he was going? He wasn't going anywhere Ruby. He was just talking. It was just flash talk, I expect.'

'Well he's gone,' said Ruby. 'I can promise you he's gone because I have checked.' Penny bit her finger as she turned to Neville for a solution.

'He'll be at Ants' Nest's,' Neville said.

'Of course he will,' she agreed.

'He won't,' Ruby said. 'Because Ants' Nest is in a home. He has been put away. Glen told me so himself. He hasn't gone to Ants' Nest's and he isn't in the shed and he's taken the money from his football boot because I looked. He's run away. Not that it matters much to any of you. It only matters to me. He was right. You are disgusting, everyone of you, yes even you Mummy. You have a problem and I think you need treatment.' With that she ran from the room, leaving the others to take up any attitude they could lay their hands on, whether it flattered them or not.

Chapter
Twelve

Jeremy's report made the papers. The *Mail* ran three column inches on page eight. 'Newsman Hit By Runaway Boy,' it said. Penny reading only the headline thought it meant Glen. 'I don't think he should have called Glen a runaway,' she said to Neville. 'We don't know that he has run away and it makes me look terrible.' She was confused by lack of sleep. She had tossed and turned all night, worrying about dubbing and editing and Dave's refusal to let her persevere with her interview with Brenda, the curtain sewer, when surely her interviews were central to the whole enterprise. 'What does Jeremy mean, anyway? If anyone's going to be hit by it, it would be me, not him. He's only a stepuncle, after all.' Neville who had brought the paper up to her in bed stared at her fondly.

'The story isn't about Glen,' he explained. 'It's about Johnny, the boy at the station who knocked Jeremy over. You know the one. You were watching, weren't you?'

'No, actually,' said Penny. 'I've got an awful lot on my mind at the moment with the film reports.' She hadn't confided her difficulties to Neville. Neville might have reassured her that they were wrong and she was right and that she must stick to her guns but she was frightened to

116

admit even to him that things weren't going as well as she'd hoped because the confidence might have seeped down the corridor to Fern whose ridicule she simply couldn't have stood.

'You're not worried about Glen, are you?' Neville enquired. 'It would be silly to worry about Glen. He's a big lad and quite able to look after himself.'

'I know,' smiled Penny. 'But what about the money in the football boot? Do you suppose Ruby made that up? I'm sure Glen wouldn't be so silly as to leave money in his football boots. I mean he wears them all the time. They wouldn't fit, would they, if there was money in them.'

'I'll tell you what,' Neville said. 'If I get the chance I'll telephone his school sometime during the day just to make sure. You don't want him carrying money around with him. It's damn silly, even for a boy his size.' But before Neville could ring the school, the school rang Fern.

The headmaster wasn't at all pleased to find he wasn't addressing the boy's guardian and he was even less pleased to hear that the boy's mother, far from being dead, was alive and as careless to the boy's well-being as he had believed the guardian to be. Not much of this was clear to the girl from the *Sun* who had tactfully moved to the conservatory door when Fern seemed unable to keep the conversation as short as she had promised.

'I don't understand the confusion,' Fern said in tones that might have been Hungarian and were most definitely frigid. 'He has been living here with his mother and stepfather while their own house is being renovated. It is quite simple. I don't know why you thought his mother was dead even though it is a common mistake, I believe. And I certainly don't know why he hasn't been at school for the last three days. He is most definitely not with me.'

She had been speaking quietly, almost inaudibly but the girl from the *Sun* thought she detected an element of fury and was keen to discover what might infuriate a woman who seemed to have everything: a gorgeous house, a gorgeous husband, a gorgeous daughter if the photos on the kitchen wall were anything to go by and on top of that, apparently, a simply stunning career in soft-porn poetry in the offing.

'I can only repeat that I don't know where he is. I haven't seen him myself for three days and I suggest that if you want more information you contact his mother at work.' Fern snapped. She gave the headmaster Penny's number and hung up then she strode into the conservatory with a smile so dazzling that the reporter, who was doing her best to write the number on her wrist without seeming to do so, knew that something was up and wondered how long she could decently hang about to find out what it was.

She watched and she listened and she charmed Fern with small anecdotes about her own inadequacies as the photographer took pictures of Fern on the swing. 'Cross your legs, would you dear?' he said as the reporter idly chattered and he gave the swing a shove so that Fern's dress rode up above her knee and she felt extremely uncomfortable.

'Hang on,' she laughed. 'I'm a poet, not a page three girl.'

'You're alright,' said the photographer. 'Lots of our readers go for glamorous grannies.' It might have shortened Fern's temper even further than the headmaster's phone call had not the reporter smoothed things over.

'Don't worry about him,' she said. 'He can't help himself. They'll probably use a head and shoulders, anyway.' That reporter worked as hard as she had ever done to find the story she thought was behind the story and she was no laggard. When they had gone, Fern felt she had done quite well. She had spoken quite candidly about showbusiness, child-raising, literature, interior design and sex education. The reporter had been an awfully friendly girl. She had completely understood how difficult it was to be landed with bits of your husband's family at a time when your career was about to take off. Not that they had discussed it on the record, just in passing. 'You've seen Miss Penny,' Fern had said. 'What you see is what you get.'

'I thought Miss Penny died ages ago,' the reporter had said. 'Isn't that terrible?'

The headmaster finally reached Penny in Dave Caster's office to which she had retreated with Dave after a stormy viewing of How We Get Curtains. He interrupted a tearful scene. 'But I'm not even in it,' Penny was sobbing. 'The whole point was to have me in it. I'm not even there.'

'It's for you,' Dave said, handing her the phone. She shook her head and turned away but he kept on holding the phone under her nose so that she had to take it. It took her several exchanges to grasp the nature of the call.

'Oh I see,' she said. 'You've been speaking to my husband about Glen's money.'

The headmaster assured her he had not. He said he had been speaking to a woman whom he understood was not Glen's guardian but step aunt who had no idea where the boy was. 'I know nothing of any money and I know nothing of your husband,' he snapped. 'But I am very concerned that nobody seems to know where the boy is.'

'He should be at school,' said Penny, thinking fast. 'Have you looked in his classroom?'

'Mrs Brewster,' said the headmaster. 'Glen is the best athlete in the school. He knows he is expected to run, hurdle, jump, put and throw for us on Saturday and he has not put in an appearance since Monday. We are concerned. We phoned his home to be told no one at home knows he is missing. No one has seen him for three days. Glen is not the sort of boy to run out on his responsibilities. I am fearful for his safety. I think it's time the police were called in.'

'Oh dear,' said Penny. 'Oh dear. I will have to talk to my husband. We will come to the school. Could you do nothing until we get there? Thank you for calling. I will be there as soon as I can with my husband.' Then she replaced the phone and eyed Dave Caster icily. 'My son is missing,' she said. 'We are calling in the police. If you feel this is a good time to cut my career to ribbons then go ahead. I trust your judgement entirely.'

Neville had left the house shortly after Penny so missing the headmaster's call which Fern took and then Penny's when she tried to find him urgently. He had gone to Marty Cork's to see Kenny Vertigo who greeted him enthusiastically. 'Well,' he said. 'Who's a clever boy then?'

'I just wanted to thank you for your help,' Neville said shaking Kenny's grey and crumbly outstretched hand.

'Think nothing of it,' said Kenny. 'They loved you.'

'Good,' said Neville. 'Good. I loved them. You can tell them I loved them too.'

'You'll be able to tell them yourself,' said Kenny. 'But I'm pleased. I'm very pleased. I told you how much ... yes, of course I did.'

'How's it going?' Neville nodded in the direction of the house.

'Not bad,' said Kenny, 'not bad. We should be able to get some men over to your place next week. They might knock a few walls down to be getting on with. Mind you, you're alright where you are, aren't you, with Jeremy?' He flicked at the caked grime on his fist and bits of it fell to the ground where he sifted through it with his toe as if looking for a finger or two which may have come adrift.

Neville decided not to say whether he was alright or not where he was. Kenny was terrific but you had to be careful. 'He's doing his pilot today, isn't he, a mistake if you ask me, Neville,' Kenny said, 'but there you are. *Chacun à son goût.* And I'd better be getting on with my *goût* and all or I'll never get to Mandarin Street.'

Neville thanked him again and, feeling a little lost without access to the cab or to Madge and not keen to return home, decided to look in on Jeremy's pilot, a step he would never have taken had his own career not looked healthier than it had in years and his standing in the community not been stronger and surer than he could ever remember it. He could walk into any television studio in the land, he felt today, with his head held high. *Ravish* was the best thing to happen to him in years, even if it hadn't quite happened yet. For the first time ever he felt like a star.

So unusual was his step that it didn't occur to Penny he might take it and she didn't even think of looking for him at the *Tempting Fate* office. She rang Fern repeatedly and when Fern told her for the third time that Neville had not returned she said, 'Glen's headmaster is calling in the police. Glen is needed for Saturday's athletics and he hasn't been seen anywhere for three days.'

'Surely you've seen him,' Fern said unkindly. 'You are his mother.'

'That's got nothing to do with it,' said Penny. 'You put him in the shed. I haven't been able to get to the shed lately because I have been extremely busy.'

She waited and when she realized Fern wasn't going to sympathize she felt very tired. Matters seemed to be beyond her and all she could do, she gathered at her end of the phone, was look for bits and pieces to collect and somehow restore. She didn't know where Glen was. She had no sense of his death. Surely he wasn't dead. Her not having seen him for three days felt normal. Surely his absence was normal. He was such a capable boy. 'You might let Jeremy know because the papers will be on to it before long and the timing for him is terrible.' Alone and fending for herself, Penny's voice had dropped a couple of octaves and her IQ seemed to have risen thirty points or so. Fern found this disconcerting.

'Why for Jeremy in particular?' she asked.

'You don't need trouble in the family the day you pilot a rollicking family show,' Penny said flatly. 'The same as I don't need a runaway son when I am a model mother.'

'Quite,' said Fern. They allowed another brief silence to hang between them during which Fern decided that trouble in the family wasn't all that good for a newly discovered poet either, ginger or no inspired ginger, especially if it led to the shed and who put the boy in the shed in the first place. 'We could always tell the school to mind their own business,' she said. 'We could find Glen for ourselves and tell them he was sick in bed all the time.'

Penny thought about it. 'How find him?' she asked. 'Where?'

'I don't know,' said Fern vaguely. 'Wherever we think he might be. He won't be far away. We can say we know where he is because we're certain he's close at hand, can't we?'

'We could,' Penny agreed. 'But what if he is in trouble? What happens if he is in deep trouble.'

121

'Penny,' said Fern. 'You are his mother. Do you think in your heart of hearts that Glen is in deep trouble? Of course if you think he is then the police must be brought in because they have skin divers and specialists who can scour the bottoms of lakes and so on. We've thrown Jeremy's wet suit away unfortunately. But if you suspect, as I do, that's he's skived off somewhere to get away from all that running and jumping and the pressure the school has put on him, then I think we are entitled to look after it ourselves.

'Do you know Fern,' said Penny, gripped at once by the notion, 'I think you are right.' And comforted in a way she never imagined she might be by Fern she telephoned the headmaster immediately. 'Good news!' she cried so heartily that no one would have doubted her jubilation. 'There's no need for you to call the police. We have found him. He was in bed where I thought he might have been all along. He's just not in the bed I thought he should have been in. He was in someone else's.'

'Girl trouble,' spat the headmaster. 'Wouldn't you know it? Well make sure he's in tomorrow and tell him I've no patience with cowardice or adolescent lethargy. Nor do I want to hear any talk of depression. I have my own glands to worry about. There are medals to be won and he is the man to win them. Tell him that will you. I want to see him tomorrow without fail.'

'That won't be possible, I'm afraid,' Penny said. 'It's quite out of the question. We've had to call in the doctor and I'm afraid Glen is suffering from physical and nervous exhaustion. You've been pushing him far too hard, you naughty man. The doctor said if he was me he would come down on you like a ton of bricks but luckily for you I am not him. I'm not going to say another word about it. But Glen must have complete bed rest for a week, at least. Then we'll review the situation. It's lucky for all of us we found him when we did. There's no knowing what may have happened otherwise.' It was an extremely satisfying call to make and very gratifying it was for Penny to hear the headmaster chastened and the positions reversed. She was slumped in Dave Caster's office, enjoying the aftertaste when the phone rang again and a woman who may have been the headmaster's secretary asked if this was the number for Miss Penny Brewster.

'Miss Penny speaking,' said Penny pleasantly.

'Oh Miss Penny,' said the reporter. 'This is the *Sun* newspaper. I hope you don't mind us troubling you at work but we've heard that your son is missing and we wonder if there's anything we can do to help.' It was very silly to put the receiver down in such an experienced muckraker's ear but that was what Penny did because she had come to the end of her tether, her striped knitted tether which held her together while the cameras rolled but gave way like anything in humble four-ply when the tension was overwhelming.

She rushed from Dave Caster's office and into Robin Powder's without knocking which was unfortunate because she charged bang into the middle of a hoot of laugher and Dave Caster screaming 'You were right, you were right. I admit you were right. She is absolutely useless and we will stick to galloping from now on, I promise.' He had the grace to stop laughing when confronted with Penny's ashen face and horrible grimace and he leapt to his feet. 'Penny,' he cried. 'Come in. Sit down. I was just telling Robin your terrible news. Is he found? What do the police say? Do you want Publicity to handle it or will Madge field the press queries?'

'Perhaps you should have time off from the show,' said Robin who was no longer smiling but standing and taking Penny's arm. 'Would you like time off to deal with the crisis? Believe me I know how taxing this is. And I'm sure Bunty will send her deepest love.'

Penny adjusted her own features from horror, loathing and fear to joy, laughter and relief. 'False alarm,' she said. 'He's been found in bed. There was nothing to worry about after all.' It was a shame she hadn't thought to tell that to the *Sun*. That way she might not have made such a headlong entry into the conversation between Caster and Powder and she might not have been confronted so baldly with their derision. But she hadn't, so she did and now there was no denying the jam she was in. Since there was no Neville to guide and support her, she did the only thing available to her which was to take a taxi to the *Tempting Fate* office where she imagined

123

that Jeremy, despite his pilot, despite the irony of a stepson running away within days of his revealing the horror of teenage runaways, would help her.

In the taxi she penned a short note to Merilee Bawdle. *'Dear Merilee, Thank you so much for your good wishes concerning my theatre and film work. Let me reassure that* Kidding About *will not be changed at all and you have nothing to fear from any 'dangerous new format''. On the contrary, after consultation with the producers I have decided that it would be unwise for me to appear bodily in our film inserts. I feel it could unnerve the tiny viewers who might imagine I was lost or something. I do think it's important to make their security paramount, don't you?'* She felt better once that was off her chest. She even began to believe the Glen was lying in a bed somewhere and that he would turn up before long saying all he had needed was a break from the shed and from hurdling.

Fern, sensible and realistic though she generally liked to imagine herself to be, did her level best to persuade Ruby that this was indeed the case and that she and Penny had not deceived the headmaster who was an interfering old goat anyway. 'I mean what sort of man would run a school for difficult boys anyway?' she asked. In her heart of hearts she didn't have a clue where Glen was and nor did she care when he was so transparently good at looking after himself and no longer posed a threat to her daughter. 'He will turn up,' she said. 'And to be honest, Ruby, I have an awful lot to worry about nowadays without having to think about him.' She wished she hadn't told Ruby of the lie. Ruby was quite amazingly strict when it came to the truth. She had imagined quite wrongly it might give her a laugh when she seemed so short of them lately.

Ruby said nothing. She gazed at her mother with her clear, youthful gaze, undiluted by the need to dissemble and she bit into an apple. 'What?' she enquired. 'What have you to worry about?'

Fern turned to her daughter and studied her carefully. Then she said softly, 'Come here' and she guided her to the wrought-iron table upon which she laid her basket full of flowers and her secateurs. 'Sit down,' she said. In another age in just such a scene she might have prepared her daughter for marriage. 'There is something I want you to know. It's time for me to break the news anyway and you,' she crooned, smiling beautifully into her daughter's sweet face, 'are the first to hear it.' For the sake of the occasion she chose to put Ralph Fantoni clear from her mind.

She was brief, concise and quite unhampered by false modesty. 'My life is about to change,' she said and she explained about the poems, her talent and the astonishing way in which she was about to be shot to stardom. 'When all along it seemed as if Daddy was going to get all the fame and glory,' she concluded. Ruby seemed depressingly unmoved, unimpressed by the interview that was to appear in the *Sun* or her mother's inclusion in the next edition of *Listen I'm Talking!* 'What do you think?' Fern asked to prod some excitement and pride from her daughter. 'Do you think I'm clever, or not?'

'You're very clever Mummy,' Ruby said. 'I always knew you were. You can take something for change of life, you know,' then she left the table and the garden altogether and although Fern called after her she made for the garden shed and locked herself in. Fern sighed and decided that one of the penalties a mother must pay for success was a child's resentment. It had certainly been true in her own case. She had resented her mother and her mother hadn't even been a poet.

Chapter
Thirteen

Ruby ran away while Fern was rehearsing sentences for her radio debut next morning and Penny was discovering that she had missed Jeremy and Neville by a minute. With a small black rucksack over her shoulder, a few pounds in her pocket and a gloriously uplifted expression on her wonderful pale face, she strolled out the gate and down the road, knowing precisely where Glen would be and what she would say to him when she found him.

'I certainly wouldn't describe them as pornographic, definitely not pornographic at all,' Fern was whispering to the carrot she was dicing. She was preparing supper as well as her lines, 'I think spicy is a more accurate word. I suppose I am spicy by nature.' She laughed brazenly. The carrot had nothing to say to that.

'But you must know where they were going,' Penny was shouting at the young production assistant who had told her they had gone somewhere for a celebration drink. 'I am Miss Penny, Penny Brewster, Jeremy's sister-in-law. He is with my husband. They would want me to join them.' And the production assistant had nothing to say to that. She didn't know where the Brewster brothers had gone and she didn't believe this was Miss Penny. She had read ages ago that Miss Penny was dead.

'Brilliant,' Neville was saying in the limo as it cruised up Bayswater Road. 'I thought you were brilliant. You had just the right ... what ... what would I call it? Just the right touch.'

'Thanks,' said Jeremy. 'It did go well, didn't it? Bloody good production of course. I'm the first to admit that. Julian's done a first rate job. Thanks Julian.'

'You're welcome,' said Julian who was sitting sideways in the front by the driver in order to chat easily to Jeremy in the back. 'But really, full credit to you. You were absolutely marvellous. Brilliant, as Neville says. We've got a winner on our hands, no doubt about it.' He twisted his neck to look at Neville. 'And Jeremy tells me you've got something big in the pipeline as well.'

Neville cast a cautious look at Jeremy and wondered why he couldn't keep his big trap shut. It wasn't his news to broadcast and for all he knew the news mightn't have been good. It could just as easily have been that Neville had fallen short again. It wasn't, thankfully, so he could afford to be gracious. 'Hope so,' he said. 'Which reminds me. I need a lawyer, Jeremy. They asked who was representing me and I said I wasn't represented but I had a lawyer who sorted things out for me.'

'Good idea,' said Jeremy. 'I use a lawyer. I've always used a lawyer as a matter of fact. There's no point in me having an agent, not with my contacts. I can get my own work, thank you very much, and a lawyer can preside over the fine details.'

'Your details are very fine indeed,' Julian laughed. 'He's driving a hard bargain, I gather from Contracts. They haven't reached an agreement yet.'

'What's your man's name?' Neville laughed companionably. He felt at ease with his brother again, now that he was his equal. A game show host was the rough equivalent of an actor in a big budget film, even if the actor's status might be shorter lived. He felt almost elated. Mandarin Street might never have the grounds or the conservatory Jeremy had, but at least their affairs were sufficiently similar in calibre to be handled by the same lawyer.

127

'Vertigo, actually,' Jeremy said. 'He's a cousin of Kenny's. You probably know him, do you?'

'Bloody Kenny,' Neville laughed again. 'He's amazing. No, I don't know him. But I think I should. I'd like to. Could you arrange a meeting, do you think? I'm going to need him with any luck.' He trusted Kenny. If Kenny said *Ravish* was in the bag then in the bag it would be. He wasn't so elated that he didn't catch the flicker of irritation that played about Jeremy's eyes and lips, however.

'What's wrong with your own chap?' he asked looking out the window, less than engrossed suddenly in Neville's professional welfare.

'I don't have an own chap,' Neville said. 'That's the problem. I've only just stopped having Madge though she doesn't know it, poor old thing. I haven't had time to approach anyone else. The only lawyers I know do conveyancing and divorces. I want a contracts man. Vertigo is obviously a contracts man.'

'Mmm,' said Jeremy. 'Right, here we are. Let's get some bubbly into us. I think we all deserve it.' It would never have occurred to Jeremy that Ruby might run away. He didn't even know Glen was missing.

Fern was far more vigilant a mother than Penny. She discovered Ruby's absence when she called her for supper just as she discovered that Penny, Neville and Jeremy were all, also, absent. She searched the house and grounds for her. She looked under the collapsible bed in the garden shed. She hammered on the spare-room door calling Neville and Penny. She telephoned Julian Fortescue to enquire after Jeremy. No one was anywhere, not even Julian. No one phoned her to say they would be late. No one cared that the supper she had prepared for them was sitting in small matching dishes in the oven, unlonged for.

A poet is a worrier by nature because her imagination allows her to consider every possibility. Fern's imagination, within the limits of her own vested interests, ranged far and wide which wasn't that far and wide when it came down to it.

To begin she told herself that Ruby had been run over or seduced by a drug pusher. Then she put two and two together and decided that as everyone was missing, which was simply too great a coincidence to be ignored, they must all be somewhere together planning to surprise her. Any minute she told herself there would be a call from one or other of them asking her to meet them and she would be summoned to a fabulous party to celebrate the discovery of her talent and the launch of her career. Ruby would have tipped them off. Ruby was a great one for surprises.

So reasonable did this seem that she took the dishes from the oven, put the contents into plastic containers and told herself they would all freeze well. Then she went upstairs to shower, dress and tong her hair, leaving the door of her *en suite* open so that she could hear the phone when it rang. It didn't ring.

She towelled herself dry, arranged her hair into delicate curls down her back, dressed in a smart silk suit and still it didn't ring and still no one came home to have the contents of the small containers slung at them while they were still unfrozen. After a while she rang Ralph Fantoni. There was no denying she was on the verge of tears. She could hardly control herself. She prayed that Rebecca wouldn't answer the phone. She had nothing to say to her about banking, the children or anything else.

'Ralph, thank God,' she gasped into the receiver. 'Can you come over? I need to see you, badly.'

'Who is this?' said Rebecca. 'Ralph isn't home. Who is this? Fern?' Fern hung up at once. If Ralph wasn't home, she said to herself, then he must be at the party as well. There could be no other explanation. There had to be a phone call eventually. She would do some work while she waited. No sooner had she lit the candle and arranged her special paper and pen on the kitchen table than there was a knock at the door. 'They've sent a car for me,' she whispered happily. She checked herself in the mirror. The hair was curl perfect, her skin flawless.

It wasn't a chauffeur. It was Ralph. 'Hullo, Fern,' he said. 'Rebecca asked me to call by to see if you had any sugar.' He spoke as he came through the door but his eyes and ears were straining for the sounds about him. There were none. 'Are you alone?' he asked and deciding she was before she could answer, he grabbed her to him and lunged at her lips, kissing her so hard that she fought back in rage and finally shoved him away.

'My lipstick,' she cried. 'Why didn't you go and buy sugar? There are plenty of shops open.'

'Don't be silly,' he said. 'It was an excuse. I thought the rest of the family would be here. I had to see you. I haven't seen you for days. I've missed your voice, your touch, your smell. I wanted to be near you.'

'Oh,' she said. He smiled at her.

'Bud tells me you're on the road to stardom and everyone's clamouring for you. Papers! Radio! Television!' He took her in his arms again. 'Didn't I say that's how it would be? Didn't I?'

'I don't remember,' said Fern. 'No, I don't think you did.' She was thinking how short he looked and how unsophisticated compared to Bud, how soft around the edges, how out of town.

'You're going out,' he said. 'You look beautiful. Your hair is beautiful.' He tried to grab a clump or two but she dodged him.

'No,' she said. 'I was but now I'm not. You might as well come in and have a drink. I was about to have one.'

'Where's everyone else?' he asked.

'I don't know,' said Fern. 'And I don't care.' The urge to cry had abandoned her, like everything else. Wherever they were, she was certain they all were together and if they chose not to have her with them, so be it. She would go on alone. She would do the radio tomorrow and she would make it the best radio anyone had ever done. She would make sure it lead to more and to television and to more newspaper stories and she would get her poems read right across the world so that everyone would know who Fern Brewster was and every schoolchild in the world would have to memorize *The Organ Grinder*.

'That's a car,' said Ralph. 'Quick, get me a cup of sugar.'

'Fantoni,' cried Jeremy, blasting through the door on a

130

wave of euphoria and champagne. 'How decent of you to come and keep my lovely wife company. Neville was worried that she might be alone and pining for me but I said no. She is awfully self-sufficient. Didn't I, Neville?'

'Where are Ruby and Penny?' Fern asked. She was quick to see that the party had been a private one, that it hadn't been in her honour and that Ruby could well be under a bus or in the arms of a drug pusher. She didn't care where Penny was.

'I give up,' said Jeremy. 'You tell me. Where are ... no hang on. Let's offer it to the other side. Neville and Julian. Where are, listen carefully because the answer I'm sure is in the question, for a bonus of five, where are Penny and Ruby?'

No one laughed. No one dared. Julian said, 'Well now I've seen you chaps safely home, I'll be off. Must get back to the answerphone. You can lose a million in a crucial five minutes, you know.' He laughed and his bulging moustache bobbed unappealingly.

That made Neville laugh because he was nervous as well as drunk. Fern was terrifying, standing in the kitchen as she was, dressed in finest silk with her long hair curling down her back and an expression of solid metal upon her face. Ralph Fantoni was terrifying, just standing there. There was going to be trouble he could tell. There was bound to be trouble with Ralph in the kitchen at that time of night and Fern dressed to kill. 'Stay,' cried Jeremy. 'I'm sure Fern's done plenty of supper for all of us, haven't you, wee Stubble? And you haven't asked how the pilot went? That's the sort of wife she is Fantoni. You're well out of it. Here I am, embarking on the most exciting new step in my career, a step that could lead to untold wealth and riches and she doesn't even enquire if I went well.'

'No need I'm sure,' Ralph said politely. He wasn't easily bullied, despite his height. 'And of course she now has her own career to occupy her.'

'Shut up,' said Fern. She could, of course, have not said shut up. She could simply have diverted everyone with her fears for Ruby and Penny, or just Ruby. But she was keen to shatter Jeremy's complacent view of her limitations and so she did.

'What career?' he smiled. 'You're not going to open a shop or something like that, are you? Shops are the most godawful bore. I don't think it would be decent for a wife of mine to own a shop, do you, Julian?' Julian didn't want to have to consider such a question. It was far too complicated. He wanted to leave. He moved forward to kiss Fern on the cheek so that everyone would know he was leaving.

'Now you are asking,' he grinned. 'But whatever you do,' he murmured to Fern, 'is bound be a triumph.'

'It's not a shop,' Ralph said. 'You can find out what it is on the radio in the morning. She's on *Listen I'm Talking!* Tune in. You'll be astonished.'

Julian already was, a bit, they could all see. 'I will,' he said, as he hurried into the garden. 'I will. *Listen I'm Talking!* It's at nine, isn't it? I will. Bye everyone. Well done, Jeremy. And good luck, Fern.' Once again he forgot to mention Neville. It was too rude for words.

'Where is Ruby?' Fern said again. 'I'm serious, Jeremy. She isn't at home and she didn't say where she was going. She didn't even say she was going. I thought she was with you.'

'Why would she be with me?' Jeremy said. 'I've been at work all day and it went so well that Neville and I went off with Julian to drink some champagne.'

'Penny upstairs?' Neville enquired, anxious to take his leave of the awkward business as well. 'There haven't been any calls for me today, have there, Fern?'

'Your wife rang three times and Glen's headmaster once.' Fern said. 'Penny isn't upstairs. I told you. I thought she was with you.'

'Oh Lord,' said Neville, clasping his forehead in sudden concern. 'She never goes out on her own. Something must have happened. She must be in some sort of trouble. I'll ring the studio.'

'She is in some sort of trouble,' Fern said. 'With Glen's headmaster. Glen hasn't been to school for three days and the headmaster needs him for the athletics. He wants to bring in the police.'

'Oh well!' Jeremy shouted. 'That's wonderful, that is. Absolutely terrific. Masterly timing. Slap bang on top of my

132

final missing-children piece, my step-nephew dips out of his school and the police are called in. Penny is probably at the police station right now. You should be with her Neville. Someone should be with her. Maybe Robin has sent someone from Publicity. Get on to Dave Caster, Neville, and see who is with her. There's no knowing what nonsense she will be telling them.'

'She isn't at the police station,' said Fern. 'She lied. She told the headmaster Glen was at home, suffering from physical and emotional exhaustion. All that will be in the papers tomorrow in the interview I gave to the *Sun* today.'

'What interview?' asked Jeremy in alarm. 'What have you told them?' It's my career you're tampering with here, Fern. A letter is one thing, an interview is something else altogether. You've been around long enough to know that family troubles aren't for the papers.'

Ralph sniggered. Fern couldn't resist a smile herself. 'Shut up, Ralph,' she said. 'The interview has nothing to do with you,' she informed Jeremy calmly. 'It's about me, my career, actually. So is *Listen I'm Talking!* tomorrow. I'm sorry to spring this on you, Jeremy, but you may have to share the limelight with me for a little while. Herbert Harris says I am the most interesting poet of my generation.'

'Well done, Fern,' cried Neville, 'Well done. That's fantastic. And I don't blame you a bit for keeping quiet about it. You should only blow your own trumpet when you're absolutely certain the notes will be loud and clear. You could always write a decent poem. I remember that from years ago.'

'When?' asked Jeremy. 'When did you write poetry? I've never seen you write a single poem in eighteen years. You're having me on.' Ralph sniggered again. This time Jeremy wheeled on him.

'I think you should go home, Ralph. I'm sure your wife will be wondering where you are. Fern is my wife and I would like to talk to her without snickering from you for a short while. Come back tomorrow.'

'Could you excuse us, Ralph,' Fern said sweetly. 'Perhaps you wouldn't mind driving me to *Listen I'm Talking!* in the morning. Would you do that?'

133

'Ah, I'd like to Fern but it's a little early,' Ralph said. 'I have to do the younger children's school run. I'm sorry. Truly. I could come and collect you, though. How would it be if I picked you up after the recording?'

'I'll drive you in, Fern,' said Neville.

'No, I'll take a taxi. Ralph can come to pick me up.'

'I will take you there and back,' cried Jeremy. 'I am your husband. I am the one who should take you both ways. Whose doing it? Is Sam doing the interview? Sam's an old mate. I could come along and keep you company. It might be fun if we both went on.'

'It wouldn't be fun,' said Fern. 'It's my publicity and I don't want you coming on spoiling it. You don't know anything about my poetry. You have nothing to contribute on the subject of my poetry. Ralph could contribute more than you. He already has. You've been far too busy with your own affairs. I'll take a taxi there and Ralph can bring me home.'

'What affairs?' Jeremy gasped and it's possible that he might have lashed out at Ralph to punish him fair and square but he was distracted as they were all distracted, by Penny crashing in through the conservatory crying, 'Get the champagne out from the fridge downstairs, Fern. I have something to celebrate.'

'Where have you been?' Neville called to her. 'What on earth have you been doing? I've been worried sick. I was about to call Robin. I thought you must have had a terrible accident.'

'Is Ruby with you?' Fern demanded. 'Ruby is nowhere to be seen.'

Penny laughed, girlishly she thought and she raised her hand to fend off the questions. 'One at a time,' she shrieked. 'One at a time, if you don't mind, please.'

'What did you have for dinner, darling?' Neville asked anxiously. 'I hope you haven't been trying to drink on an egg again.'

'I've had no dinner. I've been having a business meeting. I don't know where Ruby is Fern because I have been at work all day. You are her mother. Surely you know where she is. Perhaps she is in bed, with Glen.' It was intended as a joke.

Penny herself had considered it witty in the scant fraction of a second the remark had hovered on the tip of her tongue. She thought she was making a family joke about the whereabouts of the missing boy and the lie she had told the headmaster. But Fern failed to see it.

'Dear God!' she said. 'She has gone to find Glen. I should have realized. We will have to call the police. Jeremy! You will have to call the police. Ruby has run away to find Glen. She is in desperate moral danger. You don't know. I didn't tell you. You don't know what we are up against. The boy is disgusting. Oh God, Ralph! Phone the police. Jeremy is too drunk to reach the telephone.'

Ralph should have gone home when asked to do so. But he couldn't. He was compelled to stay by the pageant he was witnessing in Fern's magnificent kitchen. He wondered how he could capture this mood in red and yellow dribbles. He wondered if the mood would vanish the minute he put brush to canvas as it so often did. The abstract was perfection. The reality was distortion. 'Certainly,' he said, taking the receiver from the wall. '999, that's our best bet, I think.'

'Put that phone down,' Jeremy commanded. 'And leave this house at once. This has nothing at all to do with you. I want you to leave. You can collect Fern tomorrow if you must but for the time being, disappear. Now!' He advanced on Ralph but Ralph held his ground. Neville wanted to say something but could think of nothing.

'No,' said Ralph. 'I don't think I should. We appear to have two missing children here if I'm not very much mistaken and I believe it is my duty as friend of Ruby's and as a concerned citizen to poke my nose in where it isn't wanted. The welfare of minors is at stake. Tragedies happen when people like me walk out on situations like this.' Ralph was misguided here. He had imagined he was taking Fern's part in staying.

'Situations like what?' Jeremy snarled at him. 'You don't know what you are talking about. Now get off my property or I will have the police come and throw you off.'

'Very well,' said Ralph smugly. 'Call them.'

'That's enough Ralph,' said Fern whose tonged curls were hanging down her back quite limply now from excessive emotion. 'That's enough. We've a family emergency here but we have to try to deal with it like civilized people. Jeremy, Ruby has run off with a boy whose sole interest in life is sex. He keeps filthy magazines under his bed and God alone knows what else. I dread to think what he was up to in the garden shed. It makes my stomach heave. You have to find her. Someone will have to find her.' Her voice began to tremble. 'Oh God. What will we do? Who can we turn to? Only the police know how to track down missing people.'

'No,' said Neville, relieved at last to have something to declare. 'What about The Salvation Army?'

'What are you talking about,' screeched Penny so that her voice hit the conservatory roof and threatened to shatter it into tiny pieces. 'Glen is not a sex beast. What are you all talking about? He is a normal, red-blooded, good-looking boy and I'm not at all surprised at Ruby for throwing herself at him. They are healthy children.'

'She would never throw herself at him. She wouldn't throw herself at anyone. Ruby isn't interested in sex,' Fern cried. 'How dare you say anything so repellent about my daughter! You are disgusting.'

'No Fern, you are disgusting,' said Neville, suddenly seized by the need to defend his wife and her kin despite his brother's attachment to Fern. 'You and him ... you are disgusting.' He nodded at Ralph. 'What you are up to is disgusting.'

'What are you talking about?' Jeremy said quietly. 'What are you insinuating, Neville?'

As a clever diversion Fern cried, 'We're looking at incest here, Jeremy. Ugly, underage incest. And it's our daughter we're looking at, not some cheap little tart in the *News of the World*. Do you want Ruby in the papers for committing underage incest? You have to find her. Someone has to find her or we're all for it. I don't have to spell it out.'

'Christ!' said Jeremy.

'It's not incest,' Neville pointed out sanely. 'They are only step-cousins.'

'Doesn't anyone want to hear my news,' Miss Penny cried. 'Toby Gospel has offered me the lead in his revival of *L'l Abner*. Isn't it wonderful?'

Chapter
Fourteen

If she slept well that night it was only because, as Neville had suspected, she had had rather a lot to drink. Unable to find Jeremy and Neville, she had gone to see Madge McGuire and Madge had been so pleased to see her she had broken open a bottle of gin and telephoned Toby Gospel. 'Guess who's sitting by my side at this very minute?' she had demanded of him. While he was guessing she had put her hand over the receiver. 'He's desperate to get you, absolutely desperate. He would kill for you. He said so only this morning. And you'll be over the moon. It's a musical! What do you have to say to that?'

'Not too much tonic,' was all Penny had had to say. Madge had long ago lost her capacity for lifting Miss Penny's spirits.

As she slumbered, and Neville next to her tossed and sighed and wondered if Fern would order them from the house now he had betrayed her arrangement with Ralph Fantoni and when, if ever, he was going to be offered *Ravish* formally, Fern and Jeremy talked into the night. Fern was teetering on the very edge of her side of the bed to avoid the pungent old champagne fumes that were fleeing from her husband. 'I'm hurt, Fern, I'm desperately hurt.' Jeremy said. 'Ralph

Fantoni! He's so short! Why show him your poems? What does he know about poetry? I love poetry. You know I do ... Wordsworth, Byron and the rest of them.'

In his teaching days his subject had been Geography but he had always been quite strong on relationships and how to survive them. He chose not to enquire too deeply into the precise nature of Fern's relationship with the tiny graphic designer because it didn't suit him to.

'I couldn't, that's all,' Fern told him. 'They weren't something I could show you. I'm sorry, Jeremy. Maybe it was because Ralph was so short. I don't know the psychology of it. He was interested, that's all.'

'Oh hang on!' he cried. 'You can't accuse me of lack of interest. You didn't even remember I had made the *Tempt* pilot today. You didn't ring, you didn't leave a message. You didn't even ask.' He raised himself on an elbow to frown at his wife. 'I worked my butt off today, Fern. I put my credibility as a performer on the line and you didn't even notice.'

'I can't always be noticing, Jeremy,' Fern replied, turning her head because he was speaking in gusts. 'I have to devote some time to myself. I'm a performer too, as you now know, and I was putting myself on the line today. The line is a tricky place to be when you're new to it, Jeremy. I couldn't risk falling off. I couldn't risk looking up.'

'Is this how it's always going to be now?' Jeremy asked, hearing in his wife's turn of phrase the ambition and commitment he had recognized in himself so long ago. 'Things will never be the same again.' And he fell back onto the bed in a melancholic heap.

The repercussions of Fern's career had put Ruby's disappearance in the shade. If she was with Glen, then technically, Jeremy had told himself, she hadn't disappeared, whatever Fern thought about Glen's lust. If she was with Glen she was okay, even if she should have told them where she was going and for how long. That was kids, though, wasn't it? Fern hadn't seen it that way, of course. But he had told her to come to bed. They had no choice. She should come to bed if she wanted to be fresh for *Listen I'm Talking!* in the morning. Ruby would be alright. That's what he had said because he

138

wanted to thrash out the poetry and have her tell him how her career would affect him.

Having no more to think about the career, which seemed pretty well a *fait accompli*, Jeremy remembered Ruby. 'To be frank, Fern,' he said, as Fern at the mention of Ruby threatened once again to run into the night, to summon the police and to choke the life from Penny with her stupid striped scarf, 'I don't see what we can do anyway. If she was in danger from Glen, the danger has passed to become a fact. She has a very good mind of her own. She will do what she wants to do and when she wants to do it.'

'But not that,' Fern said. 'I know Ruby. She wouldn't. She's far too sensible for sex before university. She's my daughter Jeremy. I know her.'

'I know, I know. But what I'm saying is if she wouldn't she hasn't and if she would she probably already has. That's all I'm saying.'

'But where?' Fern cried sitting bolt upright and confronting him despite the fumes. 'Where is she? We have to find her. I need to know she's safe.' Jeremy didn't know where she was. He said knowing probably wouldn't make all that much difference. 'Of course it would,' Fern squealed. 'If we knew where she was we could bring her back. We could talk to her. We could find out what's wrong.'

'We already know what's wrong,' Jeremy said. 'Come on Fern. Stop pretending. She wants Glen. She liked having him in the shed. She knows you don't want Glen in the shed and she will only come back if Glen comes back. Do you want Glen back?' Fern didn't. She loathed the boy.

'Your loathing him only makes him more attractive,' Jeremy pointed out. He had shone at relationships in teacher-training. 'If you ask me, the most sensible thing we can do is sit tight. She'll soon get sick of him, then she'll come home alone of her own accord.'

It was a neat solution. It avoided any need to fall out with Ruby, any need to alert the police and any risk of attracting unsavoury publicity at a time when none of them needed it. A small question mark hung over Ruby's soundness of limb but Jeremy was quick to counter it.

'She is a big girl,' he said. 'He is a big boy. They can look after themselves. Look, I saw all those children at King's Cross station. It's not exactly warm, but it's dry, they won't be short of company, there are plenty of social workers prowling about the place to keep an eye on them and there's no shortage of phones if they want to call home. Let's give her twenty-four hours. Let's think again if we haven't heard from her in twenty-four hours.'

Fern couldn't help but see the sense in it. If she could put her fears for Ruby aside for twenty-four hours she knew she would be able to get through her maiden broadcast and establish her career firmly in the public eye. But it was hard. She couldn't help tormenting herself. She had never dreamt that Ruby might one day think so little of her that she would run away from her without so much as a kiss on the cheek. Her heart was broken, she told herself. She would never get over it.

She went to sleep, telling herself she would never get over it and when she awoke in the morning, she was surprised and relieved to notice how fresh she looked, how clear was her mind and how keen she was to get to work. An hour or two later, she was delighted to find how well she functioned in the face of such extreme pressure. So were Ralph, Bud and Sam, though only Ralph was aware of the pressure. Sam was especially relieved that Bud hadn't handed him a lemon.

Poets, even poetesses, could be very dicey first thing in the morning. But the poems were a triumph. Even the celebrities around the table who were brought together weekly to listen to the sound of their own voices applauded *The African.* They laughed at Fern's jokes, were curious about her inspiration and seemed keen to embrace her as one of them. It was a rare thing. They so seldom liked to embrace anyone who wasn't entirely sure of success. A couple remembered her from university and those that didn't said they did. Fourteen listeners rang into to complain, three to congratulate the station for having the guts to broadcast her work and two newspapers rang to ask if they could interview her. They were referred to Arabella who was handling all her publicity.

'We'd like to see a lot more of you, Fern,' the producer said as she prepared to leave. 'How would you like to become a regular. We might try a Verse for the Week, or something. Could you write rude, topical lines to order do you think?' And on her way out the door, a secretary chased after her.

'There's a reporter from the *Sun* on the phone,' she cried. 'She says you might want to talk to her. She said to say Missing Persons to you so I will. Missing Persons.'

'Tell her I've left,' said Fern, then she climbed into Ralph's car and was driven away at slow speed because Ralph was a cautious driver, even when he had a star in his car.

Neville and Jeremy heard *Listen I'm Talking!* while they took toast and coffee in the kitchen. They had staggered out of bed specially to listen together because Fern's debut seemed to require some sort of ceremony involving more than one of them. Neither of them mentioned the night before. No words could express what either of them felt because what they felt was a mystery to them both. Neville smiled from fear every time Fern spoke and Jeremy said, 'Shush', although his brother's smile was wordless.

'She's doing well, isn't she?' Neville said in the musical interlude, 'Ikki Okka Ukka', an African Symphony for Sticks and Cans in honour of Fern's poem.

'Shush,' Jeremy hissed as Sam crooned, 'A truly delightful blend of the primitive and primitive, wouldn't you say, Fern, very similar in style to your own work.'

'Christ,' Jeremy said as the phone rang. 'Tell them I'm asleep,' he instructed. 'Tell them I can't be woken.' But it was for Neville. It was good news. *Ravish* was his if he wanted it and could he please give them details of his lawyer. It was a blissful minute. It was a moment to squeeze dry.

'Jeremy,' Neville called softly altough he wanted to scream for joy. 'Jeremy, excuse me.'

'What did I tell you,' Jeremy snarled, as he had snarled at Neville when they were boys. 'I am asleep.'

'I know,' said Neville, 'I know you are asleep. But can you let me have Kenny's cousin's number? If it's not too much trouble.' He was aware that the ice of the evening before was thin and he couldn't really risk skating across it.

'Not now,' Jeremy muttered, waving him away with his

arm. 'Tell them to call back later.' Neville hesitated.

'Uh, hi,' he said. 'His name's Vertigo but I don't have his number with me at this very second. No, not Kenny. His cousin as a matter of fact. Yes, I know. He's amazing isn't he?' Then struck by the sudden thought that they might try to contact the lawyer before he could approach him himself he added, 'Look, I'll tell you what, let me get back to you. I'm in the shower with the portable phone at the moment, absolutely soaking and starkers but as soon as I can get out and dry myself I'll be able to talk sensibly about everything. And also, are you there? I want to say how delighted, how delighted I am to be working with you. I think *Ravish* is the most important British film to be made this century. No, really!' Then though he felt he could fly, he crept back to his chair at the kitchen table. 'Get the gist of that?' he said to Jeremy.

'I thought you said *Ravish* was in the bag yesterday,' Jeremy said. He was as impressed by Neville as Fern was by him.

His temper hadn't improved greatly by the evening. His day was exceptionally trying. Several people congratulated him on Fern's performance, all of them claiming never to have suspected her of being so intelligent, talented or witty. Even Julian Fortescue said, 'She's a good-looking woman, too.'

'Why would I marry anyone who wasn't intelligent, talented or witty?' he said to them all. He was worried about Ruby as well. What would become of Ruby now she had a working mother? He wasn't happy about working mothers, whatever he had written about Juanita Hobbs and Peesa Pizza. The principle was different with her. His own mother had worked with his father, it was true, but he had never liked it. He had hated not having her undivided attention when he needed it and he was sure that was how Ruby would feel too.

He came home early to check that Fern was where she should be. He handed her a drink as she lay on the floral *chaise* in the conservatory before supper. They were quite alone because Neville had steered Penny carefully up to the

142

spare room half an hour earlier, by-passing Fern in the sitting-room, saying, 'We're retiring early. I might come down and boil an egg or two for us later.' It wasn't an especially natural thing to do when both their children were missing and if tragedy didn't throw them together, then the joy of success should have. But this was a sign that they were mad. They behaved in a mad way. In joy and in grief they kept as clear of each other as they could manage although they were related and under the one roof. 'What are we to do now?' Jeremy asked, sipping his drink and studying his wife carefully.

He continued to stand. He had the advantage standing. 'The twenty-four hours are up and there's still no sign of her. I might as well admit, Fern, I'm uneasy. We're going to have to do something about it.'

'What did you have in mind?' Fern asked. 'And for God's sake sit down. You make me nervous, hovering there.'

He didn't sit. He began to prowl. 'You'll have to find her, won't you,' he said, revealing in his voice all the edginess of the day. 'You're the mother. The house and family are your responsibility. I have a new show to see to and you know how delicate that is. It's down to us. We're going to have to tramp the streets to find her. The more I think about it, the more I think it's our duty to tramp the streets. You'll have to tramp the streets.'

'Which streets in particular?' Fern asked languidly. Acclaim had strengthened her. She wasn't even a tiny bit edgy. The twenty-four hours had equipped her well to cope with her missing daughter. In twenty-four hours Ruby had become in Fern's mind a rebellious teenager who was determined to find out about life the hard way.

'Don't be flippant. I don't know how you can be flippant when it's Ruby we're talking about,' Jeremy said. 'You know very well what streets. The streets she is most likely to walk along.'

'Oh those streets,' said Fern. 'I will take the *A to Z* and walk along every street in London then because she might walk along any of them and I will call, will I? I will wander up and down them calling "Ruby! Ruby!" You think that's the best way to find her, do you?'

'You amaze me, Fern,' Jeremy said. 'Ruby is your daughter. How can you treat it so lightly? God knows what trouble she might be in.'

'Jeremy,' said Fern, poking at the ice in her glass with a dainty index finger, 'what you said to me last night made perfect sense. She will turn up on her own when she is ready to. I think we should sit tight and wait.'

'And how long will you wait? We could be waiting till the cows come home. I won't tolerate indefinite waiting. It will get out any day now and I won't be discovered waiting.' He sat, finally, in a pale yellow and lime banana chair and he sized up her resistance and the likely outcome of his haranguing her further. 'I will wait twenty-four hours more and that's all. Then you will have to do something.'

Fern didn't say, 'Or what?' because she knew that it would only embarrass and enrage him and she still cared for her husband though his status was now less important to her. 'We will give her another twenty-four hours,' she agreed.

In the spare room, no one spared a thought for Glen. His disappearance seemed somehow less urgent. It was more natural. Penny's thoughts were devoted to being less than whole-hearted in her delight for Neville's news. 'Oh,' she said. 'What is it, a talking extra or what? How wonderful for you though. Lots of people are going to be in *Ravish*. Toby says he would like to be able to offer you something in *Abner* but he doesn't think it's for you and I have to say, darling, I agreed with him because accents aren't your strength are they?'

'Oh, darling!' said Neville whose day, unlike Jeremy's, had been an exceptionally fine one. 'Do you think it's really wise, I mean in light of what he has just done to me, do you think you should commit yourself to Toby? His track record is awful, let's face it, and now you've got your filmed inserts you don't really need theatre work, do you?' He was happy to flatter her because Terence Vertigo had agreed to handle his contract and Splendid Productions had informed him that a public announcement concerning casting was imminent.

'What do you mean?' Penny said crossly. 'I'm not just a children's presenter stroke journalist, you know. I am an actress. And actresses act. I need to get to a live audience. I

144

must have a live audience sometimes or I will shrivel and die. You know that. You've said almost as much to me. And anyway, Madge wants you to phone her. She was asking about *Ravish* and I said I didn't know what was going on and she said she'd been trying to get hold of you for a week and that Splendid were being evasive.'

'I'm not with Madge anymore,' Neville said. 'I haven't told her in as many words but I've let her know. I haven't been in for days and as we've both always said, body language says everything, doesn't it? I wanted to avoid a scene that would have been painful to both of us. Surely she's cottoned on by now.'

'What do you mean?' said Penny. 'Not with Madge. Of course you're with Madge. We've both always been with Madge.'

'I know,' Neville agreed, 'though you've only ever been a bit with her. You know you have. You've arranged most of your own stuff for years.'

'Who are you with then?' said Penny. 'I must say, Neville, it's a very funny thing for you to do without telling me.' She stopped looking at herself in the tiny mirror in her hand and she gazed into his handsome face which she saw was younger, firmer and more distant than she remembered it from the morning. 'What's going on between us?' she whispered. She took his hand. You never usually do anything without telling me.' She began to cry. 'It's ever since we moved into this disgusting house, isn't it? Your family are evil. I felt their evil influence the minute I met them. They have driven Glen from me and now they are taking you from me. I'm so frightened.' She shuddered. She could act, a little. She sobbed. 'Oh no,' she said. 'We've been cursed. We should have stayed at Bucket Road. We could have built a jacuzzi in a log cabin in the garden.'

Like Jeremy, Penny was unnerved by the strange shift of power in her normally smooth-running life. Neville told her she was being silly. He said she must dry her eyes, eat up her toasted sandwich and have a good night's sleep. Everything would be fine in the morning, he told her, and she believed him because in the past it had always been so.

145

But by morning, matters hadn't improved a single iota for her though they did look up for Jeremy. He was in several papers ('Newsman to Tempt Fate') and he also took up a large part of the piece on Fern whose enormous photograph appeared under the heading 'Rhyming Granny Swings For Joy'. Neville's film was announced ('Iceman Up For Major Role') but no one had anything to say about her, not even that she was up for the fifteenth time for a Fertile Fruit. As the others poured over the papers, she dallied in the bathroom, preparing for work and she examined her cleavage for consolation. It offered some but not much.

She wanted Neville. She wanted him to come upstairs, put his arms around her and say she was his dear little Penny and the best little number on the small screen and that it would be her turn next week when Toby announced *L'l Abner*. But he didn't and she knew he wouldn't anyway because morning though it now was, it was as clear to her as it had been the night before that he didn't believe *L'l Abner* would see the light of day. He didn't believe for a minute Toby would make her a West End hit. His faith now was invested entirely in himself.

She might have cried again had she not known it would ruin her for the morning and she had a programme to do. They were showing How We Get Curtains today, without her in it. Dave was ramming her failure in her face. His failure, she told herself. She had coped perfectly well with the filming. He was the one who had collapsed under the strain. He was the one who hadn't come up to scratch. She would go and see Robin about him and have him taken off the show. He was every bit as useless as she had thought he was in the first place. She took a deep breath. There wasn't a lot to look forward to, she told herself, but she had to go on for Merilee and for all those other mothers who loved and admired her. She wouldn't give in. She would ride the storm and float out the other side on a rainbow.

This was easier said than done, she found when she turned up for work. She smelt the atmosphere immediately, the air of rejection, the winds of change. Almost no one would speak to her except Angelica in Make-up and all Angelica had to say was, 'Never mind.'

146

'Oh no,' she whispered to herself in the lavatory. 'They're going to drop me. I can tell.' She might have gone under to it, she might have given up and allowed herself to be submerged by the tide of opinion against her had not the reporter from the *Sun* tackled her as she left the *Kidding About* set and said, 'Miss Penny, you're every bit as good as you were when I was a girl fifteen years ago.' She didn't utter a word about Penny hanging up on her.

She was such a nice, friendly, sympathetic girl, far too young and inexperienced to be horrible about anyone, Penny told herself as she invited her to come and have a cup of coffee with her in the canteen. 'My office is such a tip we might as well join the horrible masses,' she said, confidently. She thought she had a nose for nasty reporters. This one sipped orange juice and said how much she liked television. She wrote about television people because she loved them. She told Penny how she had interviewed Fern only the other day and she had found Fern, well, cold to be honest, and a little hard, though she knew she shouldn't say anything so indiscreet to a relative.

'Oh we're not related,' Penny said, anxious to put at ease anyone so young and innocent. 'She is married to my husband's brother. All we have in common at the moment,' she added carelessly, though her heart was pounding with the enormity of what she was about to do, 'are missing children.' And so the reporter dragged the story from her painful truth by painful truth, though there was less truth than pain when it came down to it and there wasn't a great deal of pain.

'I could tell something was wrong,' the reporter gasped when Penny finished her story. 'I knew it. I could sense it.'

Both children disappeared under mysterious circum-stances, first Glen, then Ruby. Neither had left a note. Both had seemed carefree and happy. They had been there one minute and gone the next. The parents were all beside themselves, but they were soldiering on, they had to. There was nothing else to be done.

'But why haven't you told anyone before?' the girl asked. 'Surely the publicity would have helped to find them.'

Penny, who had taken out a handkerchief to twist

147

anxiously between her fingers, stared into it and said so softly that she could hardly be heard, 'We've been told to say nothing. For obvious reasons.'

'I see,' said the reporter. And saw what she wanted: an astonishing tale of glamour, wealth and heartbreak. 'Showbiz Kids Kidnapped. The Shows Must Go On.' She would deliver it to the nation within twenty-four hours.

Chapter
Fifteen

Whatever everyone said, Fertile Fruits were coveted. There weren't many people in television who didn't long for a fertile apple, banana or in some cases mango to go on their mantelpieces or into their specially commissioned mahogany award cabinets. The annual presentation ceremony may have been tackier than a sideshow but it had prestige and those involved in it had clout. Robin Powder had clout.

He had worked on the very first awards and over the years had developed a special relationship with Fertile Fruits so that, although his rise through programming had taken him away from production, he remained at the helm of the yearly bunfight. He decided who would host the show, who would present the awards, how the awards would be presented, which high-stepping girls would dance in what feathers and what heart-rending special awards should be made to whom, and everyone knew he did. This gave him a standing in the television community which otherwise he wouldn't have had at all.

For six or seven years in the early days of her nominations, Miss Penny had tried to persuade him to further her claim to a grape at least. 'You know the real judges are the people,' he had told her. 'And you know the people don't know me from a bar of soap. I would give you all the awards if it was up to me,' he would say to cheer her up. And she had come to accept that he was right but with every passing year she grew more frantic.

To be pipped at the post on so many occasions was almost worse than never to be nominated at all. After eight years a newspaper had joked, 'Eight times a bridesmaid, never a bride' and after thirteen years another had quipped 'Thirteen times a bridesmaid, never a bride.' She had almost become a joke.

It seemed to her, after she had shown the reporter from the *Sun* to Reception, that if she couldn't win an award this year she never would. She penned a quick note to Merilee Bawdle, then she marched on Robin Powder's office. This year she deserved an award. This year she would get one. She wouldn't be dropped. She would fight on. She would put How We Get Curtains behind her.

She strode along the corridors with assurance, her shoulders back, her chest high, even if it was camouflaged by a more than usually generous scarf. She paused only to slip the letter to Merilee into the *Kidding About* out-tray. '*Dear Merilee,*' it said, '*By now you will have heard my ghastly news and you will be wondering how I am and how it all will affect the show and the awards. Well, Merilee, I am fine. I was devastated to begin with and I could hardly raise my eyes to look at myself in a mirror, but I am over that now. I believe I am in God's hands and that God would want me to soldier on. So I will. I have a brand new musical coming up called L'l Abner, more of which later. I think I told you that I have decided to remove myself from the film reports and though they are the less for it in some ways I am sure it is actually for the best. Your own trooper, Penny (Miss).*'

'You can't go in. He has someone with him,' said Yvonne, the secretary who had never before blocked her access to the Powder room.

'Who is it?' Penny smiled. 'There can't be anyone he's seeing now I can't see too. It isn't his time for seeing people. It's almost lunch time.'

'There is someone with him, though,' Yvonne said. 'If you would like to leave your name and number he will try to get back to you.'

'Ha, ha,' said Miss Penny, then, deciding she really didn't want to treat the matter lightly, gave Yvonne a shove and pushed past her.

'Come back' Yvonne yelped. 'How dare you! I'm sorry, Robin. She pushed her way in. I couldn't stop her.' Robin was sitting in his large chair peering out the window, on his lap a clipboard to which was attached a sheet of paper given over entirely to doodles of cats. He was quite alone.

'Penny,' he cried as if Penny was the very person he had been longing to see all morning. 'Come in, sit down. That's quite all right Yvonne, thank you.' Yvonne went out slamming the door behind her. 'I watched the show this morning and I want to tell you that I thought it was absolutely smashing. You were quite right of course. The Curtains insert gave it just the right lift and I must say it blended in perfectly with that porky boy getting caught up in the puppet theatre, didn't it? He'll have to go that boy. He never watches where he is going. I gather you've had a marvellous offer from Toby Gospel.'

Penny smiled as he pulled the chair out for her and she sat down as if all that was on her mind was smiling and sitting down. But she was listening, watching, taking note, sizing up. She was no slouch when it came to tactics and she reckoned she could spot a Powder tactic almost before he had thought of it himself. She waited until he had finished speaking before turning to look him full in the face then she buried her head in her hands and began to sob, quietly, with her shoulders heaving gently under the weight of the enormous scarf. If there was a single criticism that could be levelled against her own tactics it was that she didn't have many of them up her sleeve.

'Glen has run away with Ruby and we don't know where they are,' she gurgled as incoherently as she dared. 'Oh God, Robin, what am I going to do? He's been missing three days and they are being so horrible about him. They are calling him depraved and ... and ....'

151

'Which ruby?' Robin asked. 'I thought Glen was found in bed. You'll have to stop crying because I can't understand what you're saying.' He fished a packet of tissues out of his desk drawer and handed her one but she didn't stop sobbing. She couldn't.

'Jeremy and Fern's Ruby,' Penny wailed. 'They say it's all his fault and I don't know where he is. Oh Robin, I'm so frightened. He was in bed but now he isn't. He wasn't when I said he was. I only said he was because I was so frightened. Where is he? Where's Ruby? Who's holding them against their will? What am I going to do?'

'Did he need the money?' Robin asked. 'It can't be as bad as all that. It won't have been very valuable, you'll see. Look you'll have to stop crying because mascara is running all down your face.'

Eventually it was made clear to him that Ruby was Jeremy's daughter, that she had vanished with Glen, that there was an unpleasant suggestion of incest, made in the family in a moment of anguish, and that there were grounds, definitely solid grounds, for fearing for the safety of both children. 'This is terrible,' he murmured. 'Absolutely terrible. What are the police doing? Surely it would help if Jeremy made some sort of public appeal,' he said, and in so saying had dawn on him a series of possibilities which prompted him to buzz Yvonne to summon Magda from Publicity. 'We will deal with it,' he said to Penny. 'Poor, poor Penny. Leave it to us. We will deal with it.'

Magda from Publicity grasped the situation almost immediately and, thrilled to find herself in the centre of so glorious a circumstance when all she had been doing all day was telling television journalists that she didn't know who was getting this year's Golden Fertile Melon, she decided that the *Sun* should have the story exclusively for one day only. She sent for the reporter to be more fully briefed. Miss Penny, Magda explained to the reporter, would like to launch a nationwide appeal for the missing children through her newspaper.

There was no denying the heartbreak. Miss Penny, for years the most popular figure in children's television and shortly to be rewarded with a special award for unequalled services to the industry, was bereft. Robin Powder, chief executive producer of the Fertile Fruits Television Awards, wasn't prepared to confirm or deny the award because he couldn't, naturally, given the objective position he had to take up in relation to the Fertile Fruits but he was certainly prepared to say it was a definite maybe. It was the least he could do in this whole horrible business.

The appeal brought tears to Magda's eyes as she composed it. 'I am in torment. I beg you to free the children. They are innocent. They have done nothing to deserve this nightmare. At least give yourself the satisfaction of knowing that you have liberated young lives on the threshold of ...' Magda paused here, and unable to find a powerful enough word to convey the future stuck in 'life'. 'PLEASE, PLEASE listen to the words of a suffering mother.' Penny wanted to add 'No Kidding About' but Magda advised her against it.

After she had been photographed with the baby picture of Glen she kept in her make-up purse and with pictures of an entirely unrelated baby which wasn't smudged with lip gloss and after they had taken a few for luck of her galloping across the *Kidding About* set with her dress up around her thighs, Magda advised her to go home and take the phone off the hook. Penny said, 'You are right. I'm exhausted.'

She saw no need to alert the rest of the family to what she had done. They would only try to steal her thunder she told herself and she needed as much thunder as she could get at the moment. They were all alright for thunder.

'Is there a police spokesman I can liaise with?' Magda asked.

'No,' said Penny and Magda was prepared to leave it at that. The *Sun* reporter was also prepared not to pursue the police perspective because she sensed it was not in the best interests of the story. But she did pursue Fern, Jeremy and Neville because theirs was an overview she was certain could only enliven the debate. She began pursuing them the minute she got back to her office and she was still at it hours later with time running out.

She tried Fern at home, at the *Listen I'm Talking!* office and at her publishers but she couldn't find her. Fern was

153

experiencing her first professional deflation, tramping a street or two, testing public reaction to the Rhyming Granny. She told herself she was looking for Ruby but she didn't seriously expect to find Ruby in Harrods or window shopping in Bond Street. Public reaction was disappointingly poor. Either people didn't read the *Sun*, she told herself, or they did and forgot what was in it or they didn't forget but they didn't care either. No one recognised her.

She inflated again after a while. As she hailed a taxi and caught sight of her reflection looking cool and clever in the taxi window she told herself it was a good thing. It was loathsome to be called a Rhyming Granny. It was embarassing, undignified and horrible. Bud had been wrong to think it was a good idea to give an interview to the *Sun* when the *Sun* didn't give a fig for her poetry. She decided to go and see him and tell him. She would tell him that in future publicity really should not be so indiscriminate and he might take her to lunch. She imagined Bud's neat brown hand on hers across a pure white linen table cloth.

Jeremy was also on the move and so beyond the reach of the *Sun* reporter. She tried him at home but found the number so engaged she guessed the phone was off the hook, at the *Tempting Fate* office, the newsroom and then the newspaper office where he might have been writing his column. But he was in none of those places. He was lunching Juanita Hobbs again because she had been in the pilot audience and had accosted him after the show. He had been touched, he told Neville who asked why she was there. 'She's a sweet kid. I really should buy her lunch sometime.' They were at Langans. So was Neville. Neville was with Marty Cork and Terence Vertigo.

'Marty, hello! What motley company you keep these days,' Jeremy was crying just as Fern was climbing out of the taxi and the *Sun* reporter was being told to find the lot of them, they had to be somewhere and that she could come off the story if it was too much for her. 'Juanita, this is Mr Cork and Mr Vertigo and I think you met my brother at the studios, didn't you? At the *Tempting Fate* pilot. Which I've just done. And just as a matter of interest Terence, though I don't want to

154

intrude, I gather there's still no signature on the contract.'

Terence frowned. 'It's in hand,' he said.

'That's good enough for me,' Jeremy cried, laughing unnecessarily. 'Well, we won't keep you from your business. I'll catch up with you later.' And though he didn't blush or in any way reveal embarrassment or irritation, to himself he cursed, not for appearing to be out with a floozie or even because he couldn't behave as naturally with the floozie as he would have liked, again, but because his brother was lunching two men he would have liked to be lunching and none of them had shown the slightest inclination to have him to join them.

'Had old Talcum on the phone this morning,' Marty said, just as Fern was being told that Bud Fenchurch was in a meeting but would call her at home later that afternoon if that was alright with her. 'He wants to know if our boy here will present one of the Fruit awards this year.'

'Put him on to me,' Terence said. 'I'll talk to him. I don't think it would be a bad idea though. What do you think?'

'Suits me,' said Neville, wondering if it would cause any problems with Penny or what would happen if he was called upon to give Penny or Jeremy an award but Terence hadn't been talking to him.

'I'm just wondering whether it is,' Marty said. 'He's a rogue that Talcum. He can sometimes throw it back in your face, know what I mean?' And Terence said he did but Neville didn't and wished he did. They agreed that perhaps they should give Talcum the benefit of the doubt just as Fern climbed into another taxi to go home. Neville relaxed. What was it to him? His contract was signed, sealed and delivered.

Across the restaurant Jeremy said to Juanita that he thought she would make a very good model but it wasn't something he knew a lot about. She needed to find herself an agent and suddenly he didn't care whether she found an agent or not because, gorgeous though she was to look at, she was boring him to death and he would much rather have been talking to his brother or even his wife. 'No thanks,' he said in response to her invitation to go back to her house. 'I think I'd better go back to mine. I'm absolutely knackered.' And when she appeared to think she might be going with him added, 'My wife's expecting me actually.' At roughly the same time the *Sun* reporter finally found a photographer and headed out for the Brewster address to doorstep whoever turned up because surely one or other of them would sooner or later.

Penny was in the spare bath when Fern let herself in and found the phone off the hook. She didn't hear Fern calling through the house and as Fern didn't expect to find Penny at home she failed to look in the spare room. She replaced the phone and took herself to her own bath to devote herself to the calm and beautiful thoughts a new poet needs when she has a child missing and a publisher less overwhelmed by her promise than he appeared to be even the day earlier. Neither of them was inclined to stagger down the stairs in a state of undress to answer the door when the *Sun* knocked loudly and the *Sun*, seeing no one through the windows, guessed they were all still out.

They were both in their bedrooms, dressing and contemplating their futures, when they were disturbed by the sound of merry chatter as Jeremy welcomed the reporter and the photographer into his home crying, 'What, a follow-up is it, to the story of the Rhyming Granny? You want me to be the Rhyming Grandad, do you? You're in trouble there though, aren't they Neville? No grandchildren at all, I'm afraid. I'm not even sure Fern has any, has she? Where is she? She'll make us all some tea ... Stubble!'

'Congratulations on your *Ravish* role,' the girl said to Neville. 'They say it's going to be a wonderful film.'

'Thanks,' beamed Neville. 'It looks pretty wonderful to me.'

'Oh,' said Jeremy, 'So it's my older brother you're after. Well watch out Big Brother, a pretty young thing like this can run rings round an old ham like you. Where's Fern, I wonder? She didn't say she was going out. Did she tell you she was going out, Nev?'

Fern appeared on the stairs, followed by Penny. Both of them were quick to recognize the reporter and assume she was there on their account. They hurried to greet her, 'I hope you haven't been waiting long,' said Fern.

'I thought we had finished the interview at the studio,' Penny said. 'Did Magda suggest you come out here?'

It was almost beyond the girl, who might not have been as young as she looked but was a baby compared to the Brewsters. 'To be truthful,' she said, 'I want to talk to all of you.'

'Why?' Penny jumped in. 'I think I've told you all that can be said at the moment. We agreed you had all you needed for the time being.'

'What about?' Neville asked. 'What's up, Pen? What about?' No one paid him the slightest bit of attention.

'Unfortunately my editor didn't see it that way,' the reporter said, smiling ruefully.

'Oh dear,' said Jeremy. 'Editor trouble. You'll have to give way, Penny, I know what editors can be like. You must give the poor girl a break. What was the interview for, anyway? Are you doing something on her little film stories?'

'Nothing like that,' said the reporter. 'We're running a large piece tomorrow on your missing children.'

The silence was less stunned than stunning, the reporter was to remark later to the photographer. For one astonishing minute, she thought that Miss Penny was about to be torn to pieces by her in-laws. Not that anyone moved towards her or even threatened to. You could simply see the hostility. But it was only for a minute.

'Oh Penny,' said Neville. Fern and Jeremy, faster than he was to perceive an opportunity, realized at once that anything they said would be taken down and used to whatever ends the reporter chose and they adapted their positions accordingly. Fern opened her mouth to speak but saw words forming in Jeremy's and trusted him to take the lead.

'I see,' he said. 'I see. You had better come into the drawing-room.' When they were all seated he spoke as an extremely good teacher of geography. 'I'm sorry the story has broken when it has,' he said. 'For the children's sake we've been trying to keep it as quiet as possible. I'm not sure how much you know but I'm sure you appreciate that they are in danger.' Breath was heard quite plainly gushing from Miss Penny's diaphragm as the reporter nodded, as relieved as

157

Penny that he wasn't issuing a denial which would have ruined everything.

'Have you had any message from the kidnappers?' she asked.

Neville crossed to stand by Penny and he put his arm around her shoulders to protect her from the enormity of her lie. Fern, fearful though she was for Ruby's safety and steeped in hatred though she was for Glen, felt a pressing need to laugh irritate the insides of her cheeks. Jeremy, controlled as only a television news reporter can be, said, 'There has been no message. We are waiting and praying.'

'It isn't a simple case of two teenagers running away together?' the girl enquired carefully.

'Certainly not,' said Fern. 'Glen disappeared five days ago and Ruby two days later. They scarcely knew each other.' She moved towards the pretty art-deco sofa and sank slowly into it. She sighed gently and the others said nothing, appreciating her performance because they realized now that whatever she said, whatever any of them said, their lives depended on it, if not their physical lives, their professional lives. 'There are some crazy people about,' she said. 'Unfortunately we have all been in the public eye this week, though Penny not so much, and it's just possible it's triggered something. God knows what! They've simply disappeared. We don't know why. We don't know where to and we don't know with whom. All we know is they are gone and we are distraught.' Taking their cue from her, Jeremy, Neville and Penny all composed their features to look distraught.

'Her composure was amazing,' the reporter said to the photographer when they were on their way back to the office. 'Quiet dignity, I call it. What would you call it?'

'Bollocks,' he said. 'It was only instinct.'

Chapter
Sixteen

'There's nothing to be achieved by taking it out on Penny,' Neville said when they were all alone together. She had fled to their room the minute the newspaper people had left, leaving Neville to defend her from their wrath. But there was no wrath. There was merely a tempting circumstance, the very same circumstance that had appealed to her in the first place when the girl from the *Sun* had confronted her at work. It had grown more attractive to Jeremy and Fern with every passing sensitive question.

'We will have to call in the police, now,' Jeremy said with a good humour Neville was not prepared for.

'We'll say we didn't report it at once because we thought they would turn up and we didn't want to waste police time.' Fern agreed.

'That's it,' said Jeremy. 'I will tell them that I'd had some experience of runaways at King's Cross and I decided that under the circumstances there was no real cause for alarm. Are we agreed then?' So the police were called and by the time the story broke next morning, steps were already being taken to find the missing children.

'Newspapers are amazing,' said Inspector Mallard,

carefully balancing a cup of Fern's coffee on his lap in the conservatory, unwilling to take another sip in case it killed him. 'Where did they get this kidnap stuff from?'

'They read what they like into anything,' Jeremy agreed.

'I suppose you ought to know, Jeremy,' the Inspector said, chuckling. 'Now then, let's go over these details again. Your brother and his wife moved in with you a couple of weeks ago while their new house was being decorated. Renovated. Which was it, decorated or renovated? It's not especially important. I just wondered if you had the name of a good builder. Vertigo, is it? Thanks very much. Their former address was Bucket Road; their address to be is Mandarin Street. I think I'm right in that, aren't I? The boy disappeared, ah,' the inspector referred to his notes 'six days ago now, taking with him his kit bag and possibly some money from a football boot though this seems unlikely since his mother says he never kept money in his football boot and the boots are where he left them.'

He discreetly reached across to the enchanting wicker table glazed in the softest of pinks and relieved himself of the coffee. 'It's unfortunate that your wife decided to redecorate the shed shortly after he left. It would have been a great help to us if she had left things exactly as he did. Did she decide to redecorate for any particular reason? No, I see. Well, she hasn't got very far with it anyway, has she, just the egg-shell base before she begins the stippling.' He took his job very seriously. There wasn't a detail he didn't cover. He noted the *Men Onlys*, Ruby's visits, which were regular or infrequent depending which mother you spoke to, the boy's physical prowess, Penny's interest in jacuzzis and even the egg Penny ate for dinner the night everyone fell out.

It was the same old story of forbidden teenage love, he thought, gleaning the bits and pieces as he did from each of them separately. What one didn't tell him, another did because, he was interested to note, there was little love lost. He had to laugh when he read the paper. He really did. They couldn't have got it much more wrong.

It had covered the front page, a wonderful human-interest story that touched the hearts of anyone who had ever watched television. Two beautiful, gifted children plucked from the security and privilege of their home for God knows what reason to God knows what Fate, leaving behind four desperate parents, beside themselves with worry and grief, clinging to the hope that their babies would be spared, determined to carry on despite the tragedy and to bring pleasure to the millions who had come to rely on them.

What heart wouldn't ache for Jeremy Brewster famed for his compassionate news coverage, recently transferred by popular demand to Light Entertainment? The early morning news showed a clip of his Runaway Children report and remarked sadly on the cruel irony. The afternoon papers, having sought press releases from Arabella, were able to speak with some authority about the blow to Fern, newly acclaimed poet of her generation.

Photographs of Neville with Marty Cork were rushed from the offices of Splendid Productions though they were discarded in favour of a head shot of Neville, capturing the vulnerability that had won him the *Ravish* role in the first place. *Kidding About* had never had such an audience as it had that day. Hundreds and thousands of viewers who remembered seeing Miss Penny as a child were delighted to find she hadn't died and were agog to see how she would perform when there was so much sadness and worry in her life. They looked in to see if she would gallop. Would a woman, beset by grief, gallop? She did. She knew she had to. The nation wept. It was a wonderful day.

The Brewsters, distressed though they were, revelled in the attention they received, counting themselves lucky that not much else was happening in the world and that public sympathy drew from those who could have been most critical, praise which was deserved enough but which otherwise might not have been so forthcoming. They each gave interviews to reporters who stopped them outside their home, their offices or the restaurants to which they went to comfort each other.

They spoke of tragedy, grief, stress, parenthood, their horrible anxiety and of course, *Ravish*, *Tempting Fate*, *Kidding About* and a forthcoming book of poems. They couldn't say enough how grateful they were to the wonderful British police force and out of the public eye, they laughed with Inspector Mallard at the way the media machine stormed on, careless of precise details, determined to make the most of what seemed to be happening to four personalities of whom any news was something on a slow day.

Fern was asked to write a verse for Ruby for the next *Listen I'm Talking!* She consulted Arabella who was now in constant touch. 'What do you think? Maybe I should maintain a dignified silence. It isn't very seemly to pen a few rude lines about a missing daughter.'

Arabella said, 'Yes.' She didn't know. It's hard for girls handling a poet's publicity to speak with authority because they get so little experience. 'I see what you mean,' she mused. 'But then again, you don't want to lose the contract. They did say a poem a week so it would be a shame to miss out on your first one. There's always someone waiting to step into your shoes, you know.'

'I know,' said Fern thoughtfully. It was slightly peculiar she admitted to herself but she had always known it would be. Fame is a peculiar burden to bear. But it's a choice you have to make and she had made it. She had opted for it and now she had to accept it for what it was. She took out her special roller ball pen and her special lined paper. The phone rang. It had been ringing all morning. She had wanted to take it off the hook but Neville had said, 'Better not. We don't know who it's going to be.' And she had taken his point.

'The children might try to contact you,' Inspector Mallard said who was on his way out the door at the time. After thirty-six hours on the case he let himself in and out.

'Oh quite,' Fern had said.

'Yes quite,' Neville had agreed. This time it was her mother.

'What's going on, Fern?' she demanded. 'I'm stuck down here and everyone tells me you've been on the wireless and now Ruby is kidnapped. What on earth are you up to?' Fern's heart sank. Another mother would have been pleased to have a daughter acclaimed as a poet.

'I'm not up to anything, Mother,' she said. 'Ruby isn't kidnapped. She's just taken off for a few days and we don't know where she is. You know what teenage girls are like. And I've written a book of poems which is going to be published soon so I had to go on the radio to talk about them. That's all. Sorry I haven't been in touch. I've been very busy. How's Mrs Plantaganet?'

'She's standing here, right by my side, waving a newspaper in front of me. Ruby and the boy have gone, it says. Well you only have yourself to blame, Fern. You let the child go her own merry way and now look. If you weren't prepared to look after her yourself you should have sent her away to school. That's what I did with you because I had the business to run when your father died. It was hard but it was for the best. What sort of poems?'

'Just the usual,' said Fern. 'Listen Mother, I have to go. There are a load of people here. Are you eating your dinner? Good. I must fly. I will ring you later.' Then she collapsed at the table and took up her pen again. She wished there were loads of people there requiring her attention. She felt like talking. She wanted to know what the world was making of her in the newspaper. She wanted to ask someone, anyone other than her mother, and she hadn't a clue what to write. What sort of lines were they expecting, anyway. Rude thoughts on a missing daughter?

She put her pen to the paper:
'I once owned a jewel,
As precious as life.
She was only on loan ...' She couldn't think of anything subtle. All that rhymed with life was knife.

'Fern, Fern are you in?' called Bud Fenchurch who had found his way through the back door. She rushed from the kitchen to meet him, pulling a tendril from the scarf on her head because she thought, on consideration, that no hair on her face at all was too severe. 'Oh you are, thank God. I can't tell you how sorry I am, how very, very sorry. And you came to see me but I was in a meeting. Those bloody awful meetings. I wanted to get back to you yesterday and the day before but I couldn't. You know how it is and as soon as Arabella put the papers in front of me this morning and told me what the situation was with *Listen I'm Talking!* I said to my secretary, "Cancel everything for the rest of the day. No I don't care if it's Enid Blyton, nothing is more important than this" and I jumped in a taxi to get here as fast as I could.'

He kissed her lightly on both cheeks. She took his hands and led him into the kitchen. She thought how delightful it was to treat him like a lover when he wasn't a lover but claimed a position in her life as intimate as anything a lover was entitled to. 'Coffee?' she purred. She took her work from the table and put it gently on the dresser. 'I've been working,' she said. 'To take my mind off things for a bit.'

'Oh Fern,' he said. 'That's brave. That really is. Do you want to talk about it?' He was tall, broad and tanned. He had been on the sunbed that very morning. He liked to surprise people with his tan when what was expected of anyone to do with poetry was skin the colour of skimmed milk.

'It's a poem to Ruby,' she said. 'For *Listen!* I haven't finished it yet.'

'Do you want to talk about Ruby?' he enquired gently.

'I'm not sure,' she said. 'I'm finding it hard to give it an erotic reference. It doesn't feel right. But I suppose if I work on it I'll manage something.' Even Bud was startled. Here was a woman who only days before had had scruples about allowing anyone to read her work let alone use her tragic daughter to promote it.

'I don't know that it would have to be erotic,' he said. 'I think they will understand if it's not.'

'Probably,' said Fern. 'But I can't help thinking that it would be wrong to move out of my genre. I've made a bit of a name for myself with cleverly concealed erotic references and I don't want to lose ground by being even for a split second the same as any other sentimental poet. It's a question of strategy, don't you think?' Bud thought then nodded.

'Look, as you've brought it up,' he said, 'it was something I was going to mention while I was here. It wouldn't be a bad thing at all, while you are so much in the public eye, for us to bring the publication date forward. It may seem unfeeling but believe me, Fern, opportunities like this don't present themselves every day and I'm sure that when Ruby turns up again, and I know she will any minute, she will see the wisdom of it. We can get it on the streets in two weeks if we all go like the clappers.' Fern grabbed her pencil and wrote the word 'clappers' on the edge of a newspaper lying on the table, with her picture on its front page. She thought it had possibilities. Then she smiled broadly at Bud.

'Wonderful,' she said. 'What do I need to do?' He took from his briefcase her folder with those poems marked which he wanted amending and he asked if she could possibly finish the work by the next day at four. She said she thought she could. Then he handed her a sheet which he stressed was only a draft from Arabella, containing a programme for Publicity which would involve a nationwide tour if she felt she was up to it, the week after next and in the meantime he encouraged her to keep going with *Listen I'm Talking!* which he assured her was a major breakthrough for her as a poet and a real chance not given to many. No one mentioned Ruby again. Bud could see now that Fern was not a time-waster. She was a professional.

Robin Powder was using precisely the same term in reference to Penny at a small press conference given to announce details of the Fertile Fruit Awards. 'We're going to tell you everything you want to know except the winners names,' he had laughed as he had laughed every year since the awards had started and he had made the reporters all sick with the joke. This year, however, they had laughed along politely because they had a real story to concern them. Was Miss Penny at last going to be rewarded with a special fruit for services to children's television and did it have anything to do with her missing son?

'That, if I may say so,' Robin said, 'is a pretty callous question and not one I want to dignify with an answer. But I would like to say this, Miss Penny, Penny Brewster, has brought joy to millions of children for seventeen years and for the last fifteen of those seventeen years she has been nominated for one of these awards. It would come as no surprise to any of us, I'm sure, to find that this year, her professionalism, her staying power, has been rewarded. Miss

Penny is a true professional and I salute her.'

'Here, here,' the corps agreed. It was better than an embarrassed silence.

'Is there any news of Miss Brewster's son?' someone asked.

'I'm afraid not,' Robin said. 'The police are searching for him and for his step-cousin at this very moment and Miss Penny is persevering as best she can. I'm sure many of you will have seen this morning's show and have been as moved by it as I was.'

'Any chance of a few words with Miss Penny,' they asked.

Robin shook his head. 'Sorry,' he said. 'But I believe there will be a photocall in the car-park in half an hour. Now I think that's all for the minute.' But he was addressing their backs. They had all fled from the boardroom in order to get the best possible view of Miss Penny in the car-park. Only one or two bothered to look down their sheets and see that two other Brewsters were featured in this year's awards. Jeremy, father of the missing schoolgirl, was nominated for his Widow's Plight story and Neville was to present the Fertile cherry to the weathergirl of the year.

Miss Penny appeared in muted tones and even the stripes on her scarf, small and discreet under the circumstances, were sombre. She posed silently for the cameras and tried to take Magda's advice which was to say nothing. Magda had said that it would be silly to make further appeals when the one had been so powerful, even if it had been diluted by the three other appeals. But the questions thrown from the reporters behind the photographers were so tempting Penny couldn't resist them. She shot a quick look at Magda in the wings and said, 'I don't want to answer questions because I find them too painful. But I could make a short statement.' The body of snappers moved in on her, vying for angles up her nose and beneath her scarf.

'I want to thank you all for your concern and I would like to thank everyone who has telephoned with support for me and my family in this terrible time. We are trying to carry on as normal and we are waiting and praying that our children will be returned safely to us. The police are doing their best and we have great faith in them. I especially want to thank

Toby Gospel who is sticking by me and who insists that I will play Daisy Mae in *L'l Abner* come what may and that we will be opening in Guildford in the Autumn. That's D-a-i-s-y-M-a-e. Thank you.'

She went directly home after the photocall, driven by Magda who said she would man the phone for the next few hours or so. 'I really think you must watch what you say and to whom,' she advised as she swung into the drive and pulled up alongside Fern's dainty cream convertible. 'It's so easy to have your words twisted and misinterpreted.'

Inspector Mallard was back in the conservatory. He had returned not long after Bud had left and though Fern had indicated she was desperate and having the greatest of difficulty finishing her poem to Ruby, he had said he needed a few words because there did appear to be some sorting out to do.

'Ah,' Fern cried on seeing Penny. 'Here's the very woman you need to see. Penny, Glen's headmaster apparently says that you told him Glen wasn't missing but in bed. He says you told him you found him in bed and you had the doctor to him and he said the boy was suffering from mental and physical exhaustion. That can't be right, can it? I know Glen hasn't been in bed in this house at all and we certainly haven't had a doctor to him.' Fern played with the loose tendril that dropped from her scarf as she spoke. No one would have taken her for a bare-faced liar, not even the Inspector. He thought Penny was a bare-faced liar but he liked the look of her better.

'Hullo Inspector,' Penny said putting out her hand. 'This is Magda from Publicity. She's come home with me to man the phone. We've been plagued at work and we hardly like to take it off the hook.'

'The children might try to phone,' he agreed.

'Exactly,' Penny said. 'Would you like a drink or something Magda?'

'I'll get you both some coffee,' Fern said moving quickly to the kitchen spurred by the fire from Penny's eyes.

'Now tell me again, Inspector, what is the problem?' Penny sighed.

He repeated the headmaster's story giving Penny plenty of

167

time to think and terrifying Magda who could see all sorts of difficulties with a special award if her charge continued the way she was. She felt she should save the day for Penny who was most clearly in a spot but she didn't know how to. When the phone rang she hurried off to answer it.

Penny leant forward on the *chaise longue*, towards the banana chair on which the Inspector had slumped. 'To be utterly honest,' she said, 'I told the school a most terrible lie. I was so anxious not to get Glen into trouble,' she said. 'I know I shouldn't have and I wouldn't have made your job harder for the world. To be frank I completely forgot I had told it. Unluckily, my son is his school's champion athlete and that ghastly man had been hounding him. There was a meeting coming up in which he was expected to win everything for them and I thought well if that's why he has disappeared I'm not going to make matters worse. So I told the headmaster he was sick in bed to shut him up.' Tears formed in her eyes. She really was very lucky when it came to her tear supply. It was her greatest theatrical asset, wasted on Daisy Mae if Toby Gospel had but given it a second thought.

'I quite see,' said the Inspector getting up. 'It makes complete sense to me. Thank you very much.' Magda hearing him leave walked purposefully back into the conservatory.

'That was Kenny Vertigo,' she said.

'Oh, for me,' said the policeman.

'No,' said Magda. 'Sorry. For Neville actually. He said to tell him he is starting on Mandarin Street today and the first walls will be down by tomorrow.'

'I don't know where Neville is,' said Penny.

'Oh dear,' said the Inspector. 'It's like a disease, isn't it.'

Chapter Seventeen

Neville was with Terence Vertigo, as it happened, agonizing over the details of his contract with Splendid. 'As far as they're concerned you're an unknown, that's what it amounts to,' Terence was saying. 'We might have pushed for a fee plus a percentage but I think it's better this way. There's enough here for all the jacuzzis in China.' This made him laugh.

There was a family resemblance between Terence and Kenny, same name, but where Kenny was known by almost everyone in the business, Terence was not. Terence was known only to those who knew those who knew those who could guarantee that the chunk of their income he took was sizeable. His speciality was contracts but he was experienced too in what Fern called strategy.

'They've been trying to get you all morning,' he said to Neville of Splendid Productions. 'About your son. What's the story there?'

'The story is, he's gone,' Neville said. 'My sister-in-law didn't like the shine her daughter took to him and she didn't like the magazines he kept under his bed. They fell out so he took off.'

'Fern,' said Terence. 'She's a good-looking woman. She's a good cook too.'

'I like her,' Neville said. 'But she's an acquired taste.' Neville spoke assuredly, unhindered by the need to defer to anyone now the contract was signed. The contract gave him confidence and brought to his well-shaped features a glow that others only get from love. He was no longer fearful of Fern whose number he was certain he now had. She hadn't said a word to him about Ralph Fantoni, not a single word, not even a hurried 'How dare you?'

'She was on the radio the other morning, reading poetry,' Terence said. 'I never thought she was a poet. I always thought she was an interior decorator. Funny that! So what happened to her daughter?'

'She ran off to find my stepson,' Neville said.

'Which way did she go?'

'Search me,' Neville shrugged, a request which struck Terence as being enormously funny.

'No thanks,' he said. 'We'd better call them back, then.' He phoned Splendid Productions who wanted to know if they should issue a press release and what they should do about the twelve separate requests for television interviews they had had. They thought Neville should do a couple, at least. They would have done a couple for the pre-production publicity, missing children or no missing children. They wanted to know if Neville would make himself available.

'I'll dictate a release,' Terence said. 'And we'll do two of the interviews.' Then he hung up. 'By the way,' he said, shoving across the desk three scripts and an invitation to Neville to open a fête in Kent, 'these came in for you during the day. You're in demand.'

'How on earth did they find their way to you? No one knows I'm with you,' Neville said.

Terence winked. 'Search me,' he laughed. 'Search me and you'll find my cousin.'

'Kenny Vertigo rang for you,' Magda told Neville when he arrived home in a limousine with darkened windows, having passed the police guard which was now on the gate to keep the press at bay. 'To say he was starting on your house today. And Madge McGuire who wants you to call her urgently. All the requests for interviews I've passed on to Splendid. And

Jeremy rang. He wants you to ring him at work.'

Jeremy was slumped in the large easy chair in Julian Fortescue's office with Julian and Nancy Dipswitch from Publicity. 'One doesn't want to sound too callous about it, of course,' he was saying.

Julian held up his hand. 'Doesn't sound even a tiny bit callous. The point is, Jeremy, you are in the public eye and so you have an obligation the others don't have. I don't want to exaggerate but your tragedy is the whole country's tragedy. The whole country wants to know what is happening.'

'I know, I know,' said Jeremy. 'I'm only too well aware of it.' He closed his eyes to indicate the force of his awareness. 'Of course we would all like a bit of privacy but we're not entitled to it. What we have to decide is what to do for the best.'

Julian, sitting on the edge of his desk, looked at the list in front of him. 'Well this is the choice,' he said. 'The God spot want a guest appearance. That's just thoughts for children and parents in trouble ...'

'I'm not sure about that one,' Jeremy said. 'It's very down, isn't it, when I'm now Light Entertainment. Light Entertainment is up. And I don't want to be linked with failure at this stage of the game, really, Julian. It's not my style: one failed parent to a nation of failed parents ... what else?'

'News want a follow-up: the personal perspective. You mentioned Ruby in the King's Cross feature and they want an appreciation of Ruby. On the question of up-ness, I think you'll have to accept that the mysterious disappearance of your child isn't up, is it? It's not an up thing to have happen. I wouldn't worry too much about keeping it up. I don't think from *Fate's* point of view that the country seeing your human, sensitive side is a bad thing. I can see your problems with the God spot which really is very low key. I'm not sure God would help *Fate* as much as News can, publicity-wise. Think about News. Five minutes of you back at King's Cross, wondering aloud would be no bad thing.' He waited for Jeremy to commit himself but Jeremy wouldn't. 'And then there's Marty Cork which is the important one, of course.'

'Yes,' Jeremy agreed. 'But I want to talk to Neville. It

171

would look absurd, all of us trooping onto the set or even if we were all introduced in a line of sitting ducks on the sofa. We can't have four distraught parents. Well, we can, but I don't want to be one of them. At least two of us wouldn't get a word in edgeways. I'll ask Neville if he and Penny wouldn't mind doing something else. Maybe we should offer Neville the God spot.'

'Marty wants Neville. There's the *Ravish* connection to consider, I'm afraid,' Julian pointed out, then in response to a muffled shout from his secretary next door yelled, 'Who? Oh right, put him through. It's Neville now,' he said. He smiled at Nancy Dipswitch who smiled back but said nothing. She hardly ever did. She made notes but she hardly ever spoke.

Jeremy picked up the phone. 'Brother,' he cried. 'What news upon the Rialto? It's heavy going, isn't it?' Neville told Jeremy about the scripts. Jeremy told Neville about the God spot. 'It's not something I feel I can do at this point in time. I thought you might like to do it.'

'No thanks,' Neville said. 'Terence is handling my stuff for me. The God spot won't get a look in. He's being firm about it, I'm afraid.'

'Is he?' said Jeremy. 'He's handling your publicity is he? I didn't think publicity was his bag. What's he want you to do about *Cork's Popping*?' Jeremy smiled at Julian to impress upon him that he wasn't even remotely peeved that Terence was looking after his brother's interests while he was having to look after his own.

'Cork's what?' Neville laughed.

'I know,' said Jeremy. 'It's not *Who Can We Talk To Now* anymore. It's *Cork's Popping*. New image. Crass isn't it? What are you going to do about it?'

'Haven't the faintest idea,' said Neville. 'But I suppose that will be one I'll have to do. I know there are two newspaper profiles, one in the middle of the market and one up.'

'Interviews,' Jeremy said.

'No profiles, you know profiles. They are interviews, of course, in their way but they're more analysis, aren't they?'

Jeremy didn't care to comment. 'The difficulty with Marty Cork,' he said, 'is that if we all go on we're going to look very silly. They've asked us all but I think it would be mad. On the other hand it would be mad if one of us didn't do it. One or two of us. For the children's sake. We probably should have one from each family.'

Back at the house, Neville smirked. The upper hand was a very pleasant hand to hold. 'It's difficult,' he said. 'Penny from our family should do it, obviously, because she's Glen's mother. But I suppose Marty will be keen to have me because of the *Ravish* connection and I don't suppose two from one family and one from the other would look right, would it? It would look as if one parent didn't care.'

'That's true,' Jeremy agreed. 'I suppose it should be all of us.'

'What did you want to talk to me about?' Neville enquired.

'What? Oh the children. Any news of the children?'

'Not yet,' Neville said. 'But Inspector Mallard is working like a beaver.'

'Good,' said Jeremy. 'Good,' though he felt it was less than so and he was right, to a point. Inspector Mallard had been tracking down Glen's friends. He had found Ants' Nest in his home for delinquents and because Ants' Nest found it difficult to relate to anyone called Inspector, the circumstance which might have been brought to a speedy conclusion, took a protracted turn. 'He said he was doing a runner. He said he was going to Israel,' the boy said. 'Or Manchester.' So more hours passed than should have without the missing children being found and the hours became days and the children didn't seem to be anywhere in Manchester, or kidnapped or even remotely inclined to make their presence known.

Robin Powder told Dave Caster that, given the success of How We Get Curtains, he wanted to put even more 'zip' into *Kidding About* and he thought it might be fun for Miss Penny to take the show to Sunderland where she had such a huge following.

'Sunderland!' Dave bellowed.

'You should see the votes that have poured in from Sunderland,' Robin said. 'She has a fan there who's headmistress of a primary school. I think we should do the show out of the school. All we need are lights and a piano.

'And permission from the education authority, and permission from the parents and a huge insurance and an OB unit. I thought this was a low budget show.'

'Even low budgets can stretch to make a point,' Robin said. 'Get your skates on, Dave. Publicity is ready to announce it. I want to go with it while the show is hot.' Never, in twenty years of *Kidding About*, had the show ever before been described as hot. The move thrilled Penny to bits. She sent Magda out to buy three new scarves.

It was over supper, forty-eight hours after the police had been called in and thirty-six hours after the story had broken in the *Sun* that the first suggestion of a clue appeared. Kenny Vertigo brought it when he called around on his way home from Mandarin Street. 'Marty says you're all going on the show tomorrow,' he said.

Jeremy, Penny, Fern and Neville were hunched over at the kitchen table barely able to speak to each other so concerned were they with their own business. They had tried to talk to each other but it hadn't been satisfactory, talking when no one was listening. Penny squealed, 'Who? I can't. Not tomorrow. I'm going to Sunderland tomorrow. We're doing two *Kiddings* out of Sunderland in appreciation for all the support they have given me over the last two days. No one mentioned doing *Cork's Popping* to me.'

'Nor me,' said Fern. 'Is someone supposed to have organized it with Arabella? That girl is so slow. Bud will have to do something about her. Honestly! Did you know about it?' she snapped at Jeremy.

Neither Jeremy nor Neville had mentioned Marty Cork to their wives because they had persuaded themselves there had been nothing to mention. 'No point in building their hopes up, is there?' Jeremy had said to Neville on their way back from an evening stroll to the gates to see how the poor reporters were faring. 'Julian said it was on the cards but not definite. He certainly didn't mention tomorrow,' he said to Fern as Kenny smiled at them all affectionately. 'I thought they had the Russian jugglers and the expelled diplomat on tomorrow.'

'You may be right, Jeremy,' Kenny said. 'It's a funny old game.'

174

'I'm going to telephone Arabella now to see what's going on,' Fern said. 'How can I possibly get these poems done, go on *Listen!* and do *Cork's Popping* all by tomorrow? They must be crazy.'

'Finish your dinner,' Jeremy urged. But Fern couldn't. It wouldn't wait. Penny couldn't eat either, for trying to decide what should come first, Sunderland and glory or Marty Cork and glory. Should she go for quality or glory or bear in mind the ratings.

'How's the bomb site?' Neville asked smoothly, less ruffled Kenny was pleased to see than any of the others by the strain of the limelight.

'A mess,' he said, standing up to go. 'But I thought you ought to know that even though we've tried to make it secure you've got visitors. Tramps are sleeping there at night by the looks of things. There's not much we can do if we don't catch them but I thought you might like to know anyway.' Then he was gone and if it crossed Jeremy's, Neville's or Penny's mind that this was a clue, then it crossed very quietly and received no attention. If it occurred to Kenny that the visitors were significant, he said nothing. Why would he when there was loyalty at stake, work at stake and a sizeable chunk of a growing income to be considered.

For days, Madge McGuire had been considering the same sizeable chunk and it seemed to her that she was being very badly served by a boy whom she had been saving from penury for the last twenty years with judicious loanings of her taxi. She told herself and everyone who came into her office that she didn't expect thanks, she had been too long in this business to expect thanks, but she didn't expect to be cast aside like a worn out jumper either just because something new in cashmere had turned up.

There wasn't much anyone could say to that when it was obvious to them that if something in cashmere turned up they too would sling aside a worn out jumper. Who wouldn't? But they listened to her anyway because she was a good old stick and it did seem hard, not that Neville Brewster should have moved away from her but that he had moved away without so much as a 'Nice knowing you.'

She had given up trying to contact him she told herself, though every quarter of an hour she dialled a number in the hope of finding him at the end of it. She had her pride. She had also given up trying to reach him through Penny who had returned to being her distant self now her son had run away and she was back in Robin Powder's good books again. Sitting at her desk, playing with the Instantaxi telephone panel and gazing at the map on the wall in front of her, Madge devoted hours and hours to deciding just what to do about Neville Brewster and what would be in it for her when she did it.

'Satisfaction,' she decided at last. She would have satisfaction and she knew just how to reach him where he would be most aware of feeling reached. She dialled the little girl reporter on the *Sun* intent on giving the story to her exclusively because she was such a nice little girl. She would show Neville what happened to actors with ideas above the expectations of their agents. She chuckled to herself and on being told the same little girl was off for the day but would be in later in the week she decided to bide her time. She might as well savour the idea, she thought. It was such a good one.

All the papers ran some sort of Brewster story next morning, most at length. There is something uniquely compelling about private tragedy in the face of public triumph. Most of them cleverly combined news of the children which was scant with news of the parents which was plentiful. It was hard to escape the poignant fact that disaster had struck just as all four parents, talented, beautiful, prosperous and blessed as they were, were embarking on exciting new projects.

Curiously, Neville seemed to fascinate them most. Fern said it was because *Ravish* was the most newsworthy of the projects, Penny believed it was the Marty Cork connection and Jeremy remarked to Julian that Terence Vertigo was a wily manipulator. Neville himself put it down to the quality of the head shots Splendid had provided and the certainty that he was on the verge of the greatest success.

But all of them had a very fair run and not a single reporter had asked them or even looked as if they might be on the brink of asking for the story behind the story. The story they printed was the one the Brewsters were sticking to: that the children had gone and were being sought and that everyone was desperately concerned. There was no question of anything sinister on the home front. Both schools had reported that the Brewster children were clever, well adjusted and carefree, without a reason in the world to scarper, in Ruby's case because it seemed to be true and in Glen's case because the headmaster was too terrified of being responsible for the boy's misery to suggest anything otherwise.

It was plain that these two happy children had gone and that they hadn't returned because something or someone was preventing them. Just what this something or someone was, was the story behind the story and the press waited for it to be revealed at police briefings. None of the Brewsters had uttered the word kidnapped in as many letters because there had been no letters or any communication of any sort from anyone. But kidnapped was what the children were believed to be.

Inspector Mallard who had maintained a sensibly low profile in the early hours, hadn't ruled it out. He had simply said, 'All that can possibly be done to find these children is being done' and when asked why they had disappeared and whether there was serious cause to fear for their safety would say only, 'Why they have vanished is so far not known and of course there are fears for their safety as there always must be in cases of this sort.'

It was enough to keep the tragedy alive. But if Inspector Mallard believed it was a tragedy, it was less of a tragedy and not the same sort of tragedy as the rest of the world would have it. As Miss Penny was boarding the train for Sunderland, Neville was opening the fête in Kent, Fern was explaining the significance of her Ruby poem to a reporter from a woman's magazine and Jeremy was recording 'Fate fate fate fate fate fate fate I'm tempting, tempting fate' for rush release, a reporter from the Early Evening News put the question to the Inspector bluntly.

'There's absolutely no suggestion of them having been kidnapped,' he said impatiently. 'We are appealing to the children to come forward as they must be aware of the

177

trouble they are causing.' He didn't say how he had ruled out a kidnap or even that he had never suspected there might have been one which naturally he hadn't. And he spoke without warning or consultation, catching Arabella, Magda, Terence, Julian and Nancy Dipswitch all completely by surprise. He hadn't indicated to a single Brewster that he was about to make a surprise statement or even suggested to them that their troubles were over because he knew they never really believed they had any. This is where they were all wrong. Their troubles were only beginning.

Kenny Vertigo caught the tail end of the interview as he came in from work. 'Hang on,' he said to his wife who was shouting at him for getting in early when she had been expecting him late. 'You're in luck,' he said to her when the item was over. 'I have to go out again anyway.' And he drove as quickly as he could back across London to Mandarin Street which was in an even bigger mess than he had described to Neville. He made his way across the rubble and up into the loft. 'Are you up here?' he hissed. 'Kids?' He knew they were.

'Kenny?' called Glen cautiously emerging from behind an old wardrobe which had been in the loft for generations. 'I thought you'd gone home. What's up?'

'Listen,' said Kenny, brushing the dust from the grime on his trousers. 'The police are appealing for you to come forward. They know it's a domestic. It's just a matter of time before they come to get you. You're not going to be able to hang on here for much longer or anywhere else if it comes to that.' Ruby appeared from behind the wardrobe as well.

'Tea?' she asked. 'I'm just making us a cup. Want some beans?'

'No thanks,' said Kenny. 'I was just saying to Glen here. You're going to have to think about coming out. Apart from the police, it won't be safe here after tomorrow because I want to knock that wall down over there and, even though I've never had an accident in my life, I won't be able to answer for a high wind.' He laughed. He wanted to sound persuasive. He could see himself in trouble if he was caught concealing missing children. He might even find himself on a kidnap charge which was something he was fairly certain his cousin could relieve him of but even so. His wife was not an easy woman.

'We've decided never to go back home,' Ruby said. 'You've seen them. They are disgusting.'

'They're alright,' Kenny said. 'They're only working. Anyway I've got to get back. Think about it. I'll fix it for you if you like. But you'll have to come out soon otherwise we'll all be in trouble. O.K.?' Publicity was all very well in Kenny's book. Everyone could do with a bit of publicity now and again. But there came a time when you could get too much of it, and too much of it was nearly always the wrong sort.

Chapter
Eighteen

In Sunderland, Angelica from Make-Up said to Penny, 'It's good news about your boy. The police are wonderful, aren't they?' Angelica had watched the early evening news while Penny had been in the bath. They were due at Box Road Primary within the hour for a run through.

'I think a bit of cleavage tonight,' Penny said. 'For a change. I adore the police, Angelica. They are saints.' She peered into the mirror at which she was now seated, wearing her gold satin robe and absolutely nothing on her face. 'God, not a blackhead,' she groaned, then she squealed.

'I've missed it,' she wailed. 'Oh Angelica, You should have called me. Was I on it?'

'There was a bit of you, the side of your face. You couldn't really tell it was you. I could, of course, because I know your face. They mentioned that you were coming up here though and there was a lot of your husband. He's terrific looking, isn't he? Much better looking than his brother. He was talking about *Ravish* and that play he did about Iceland and then he said how much he loved Glen and what a good relationship they had always had. He said he taught Glen how to sprint. It

180

must be wonderful for you, having a husband like that, when it's not his child.'

'He didn't. Glen taught himself to sprint. Glen's father is very athletic.' For a minute Miss Penny looked dreamy, remembering the muscles Glen had inherited but she pulled herself together as Angelica began to work on her face, applying congealing cream to the lines and block out cream to the blackhead.

'Then they had that policeman who was on before, saying that the children hadn't been kidnapped and they must come forward because they were causing you and the others such distress. I must say, Penny, I think you have been terriby brave, I don't think I would have been as brave as you if it had been my child. I think I would be in a wet heap by the phone.'

'That wouldn't achieve much, would it?' Penny said. 'We all have work to do and the police have their work to do. Their work is to find the children. Thank God they are getting on with it.' She looked brave and she sounded brave but a horrible little bubble had formed in her stomach when Angelica had mentioned Inspector Mallard and it began to swell. It was similar to the bubble Neville had described to Fern on their first night under the one roof. It had nothing to do with the show coming out of a primary school in Sunderland.

If Inspector Mallard was saying it wasn't a kidnap and he knew they knew it wasn't a kidnap, what was he going to say it was. Sooner or later someone was going to have to account for the children's disappearance and the accounting made Penny nervous. She told herself to stop it. She told herself that nerves would spoil one of the most important events in her career if she wasn't very careful. To do the show before a live audience of her greatest fans was an achievement almost but not quite beyond her wildest dreams.

Jeremy, Fern and Neville all suffered similar discomfort as a result of the Inspector's interview. They all wondered what he meant by it and what he would say next because his going along with the kidnap theory when the kidnap theory had provided such excellent mileage had always seemed too good to be true.

181

As soon as the *Fate* theme had been done to everyone's satisfaction, Jeremy had his driver take him to the police station where he ran up the steps two at a time for the benefit of the sturdy bunch of photographers, cameramen and reporters who had been assigned to follow him. Inspector Mallard had gone home for the night, he was told. There was no further news of his daughter but the officers all had high hopes of finding her soon. They were following up several leads from the reconstruction of her last sighting at the bus stop. The public had been marvellous in their response. This made Jeremy nervous too. What public? he asked himself unreasonably. He was used to thinking of the public as an audience, not as a body of vultures determined to swoop in on his private life and undermine his public image.

His irritation surprised him as he left the police station. He was tired, he told himself. He was exhausted. He had nothing to fear. What could he possibly have to fear? 'No, nothing to report,' he told the waiting press.

'Any idea why she ran away?' someone yelled. He smiled.

'If she wasn't unhappy at school, might she have been in some other trouble?'

'Is she in love with her cousin?'

'Has she had lots of boyfriends?'

'Would you describe yourself as a strict parent?' He kept on smiling as he trotted rapidly down the steps and he jumped into the car crying, 'I'm tired. I want to be at home with my family. We are all desperately worried as you can imagine.'

It is a curious thing, the way in which the public eye can see a villain where only a minute before it saw a hero. But if you court fame, you court scandal and the merest whiff is enough to draw to the limelight a whole swarm of vile moths keen to take part in the transformation. They hurl themselves on the hero, nibbling at him and splattering him with muck until he can no longer be recognized for what he once seemed to be. In the case of the Brewsters, the moths began to beat their wings within minutes of the Inspector withdrawing his support for the flimsy substance of the story that had been woven about them.

If the children were not being held against their will, then they were staying away of their own free will. If they were staying away of their own free will, there had to be a reason. The sickly-sweet odour of something not being quite as it should have been in the house of heroes drifted from the conservatory and across the beautiful landscaped gardens, past the half-stippled shed and out the gates to where those who had spun the yarn in the first place waited. Their trained noses caught the scent and they took off after it, careless of the dark corners into which they were lured in order to release the moths.

Someone found Ants' Nest well before Madge McGuire was able to give an exclusive to her little girl on the *Sun*. Freshly restored to the bosom of his mother, he was spilling the beans as he chose to call it, just as Merilee Bawdle was throwing herself into Miss Penny's arms, regardless of the open mouths of her pupils.

'This is the happiest day of my life,' she cried as Miss Penny tried to protect her hair and make-up with a quick and deftly administered slap with a scarf. 'I've planned two magnificent days. It's absolutely perfect. Except,' and her eyes filled with tears, perhaps from genuine emotion or perhaps from the scarf 'for poor little Glen. Oh Penny! When I think of Buck. Poor, poor, little Glen. And no father either. Like Buck.'

'Merilee,' Penny agreed. 'Thank you but I don't think we should ...' She patted the proffered hands. 'How wonderful. How wonderful to be in your wonderful school.' Then she turned to survey the voters in the hall who were crammed into chairs almost one on top of the other to allow for maximum galloping space and she said, 'How lovely to see you here, this evening. I'm so looking forward to *Kidding About* here and to having great fun with all these marvellous children.'

'Samantha,' Merilee called crisply. 'Samantha, step forward. This is Samantha Mogul, Miss Penny, whose mother is our parent governor. I wrote to you, I think, about her. Samantha is eight but I feel she is quite short and she is very keen to lead the galloping because she has done so well in tap and modern and she leads our junior marching squad.'

Samantha stepped forward, a small child in some respects it was true, but in others she was quite unusually large. Her head, for instance, was large, as were her teeth. She had exceptionally large teeth for an eight-year-old. 'Mrs Mogul has been the Miss Penny Vote Co-odinator for Sunderland East,' Merilee pointed out significantly. 'We are lunching with her and one hundred other fans at a small buffet in your honour tomorrow.' The bubble in Penny's stomach inflated a little more.

'Well done, Samantha,' she said. 'You go and stand by the piano.' As the rehearsal proceeded and Samantha's entrée into showbusiness seemed assured, Ants' Nest concluded his interview.

'Yeah,' he said. 'Glen's always been neglected at home. He thought he would be better off in care with me. He wanted to pay money to get in. But I had to tell him it wasn't on. I said he would have to get out and commit a crime or foul deed first. Or else he could denounce his mother. But he wouldn't. He pretended his mother was dead. It was easy because he never saw her.' He gave a great interview, Ants' Nest did and he wasn't unreasonable. He didn't price himself out of the market as Juanita Hobbs so very nearly did.

Juanita dropped a note to Roy, Jeremy's editor, asking how much he would give her to keep her mouth shut. Jeremy Brewster, she could reveal, so-called distraught father, man of compassion, defender of the weak, laugh a minute, couldn't keep his hands off her when she agreed to have lunch with him after he had written about her.

'He promised me a career in modelling,' she wrote. 'He said I was wasted in pizzas. He tried to get me into bed but I told him I had my reputation to think of. If you don't believe me,' she added, 'plenty of people saw us at Langans. Even his brother. None of this need ever be mentioned again if you contribute to my son's school fees fund. At the moment it is short by ten thousand pounds.'

Juanita's note was in the post, being sorted, as Penny slept in Sunderland, unaware of Ants' Nest's interview, unaware that the bubble in her stomach was expanding even as she slept because she had gone to bed horrified at the prospect of

184

Samantha, sickened by the school hall and sure that Dave Caster was right. 'We shouldn't have come,' he had said all night. 'This is ridiculous.'

When Neville telephone her in the morning she was in severe pain. 'It must have been something I ate,' she said. 'And I was trying to be so careful.'

'You must lie face down on the floor and bounce,' Neville advised her. 'And if that doesn't work, massage your stomach downwards the way I do. Alright?'

'It's horrible up here,' Penny said. 'We should never have come. I should never have left London. Merilee is going to drive me mad.'

'Never mind,' Neville said. 'It's only for a day or two. And all you're missing is the *Cork's Popping* interview. You don't have to worry about that, I'll make sure you get a good mention.' He was in high spirits. Ants' Nest's interview had yet to appear and Madge McGuire was only at that moment getting through to the *Sun* to say it didn't matter if the girl wasn't there, she would talk to anyone.

'What?' Penny roared so that Neville had to take the phone from his ear. 'What do you mean? No one asked me about the Cork interview. I wanted to do it. I should do it. Glen's my son after all. And even if you have got *Ravish*, I've got a Fertile Fruit nomination and *L'l Abner*.'

'I know,' said Neville. 'Everyone knows. But it was a last minute thing. Penny? Pen? Are you there?' She wasn't. She was off the phone and down the hall to Dave Caster's room and she was hammering on his door.

'Dave,' she was crying, 'Dave. Open up. We have to get back to London. It's an emergency.' He came to the door in his dressing gown, eating toast.

'They've found your boy!' he cried. 'That's wonderful. Congratulations! Didn't I say he would turn up in the end?'

Penny stifled her faint embarrassment with impatience. 'It's not that. We are still hoping and praying. I have to get back to do the *Cork's Popping* interview tonight. We had better cancel this morning.' She marched into Dave's room and picked up a piece of toast from his breakfast tray. 'When did you order breakfast?' she enquired. 'I thought we were all eating together in the dining-room.'

'Have mine,' he said as she did. 'We can't go back. Robin would never agree to it for a Cork interview. We've spent a bomb on setting this lot up.'

'I can just do this morning, then,' Penny said. 'I won't do this afternoon's recording. I can just about get out of here and back to London in time. One show out of Sunderland is plenty. You said so yourself. You said no shows out of Sunderland was plenty.'

'They've gone to so much trouble,' Dave argued. 'We will ask Robin.' And they tried to ask him all morning off and on but Robin was out and about on Award business so Penny acted on her own judgement and she charged through the live show, galloping better than she had galloped in years with Samantha bringing up the rear. Then she dashed back to London forgetting the recorded show in which Samanatha had been promised a leading part, abandoning the buffet, with Angelica in tow so that her hair could be Carmenned on the train. She didn't even look back which was unfortunate. Had she, she might have witnessed scenes of puzzlement, of desolation, and of rage.

Nothing Merilee could say about the pressures and whims of showbusiness or the desperation of a mother worried sick about her only son could calm the fury or make up for the waste of time, food and nervous energy. Mrs Mogul, Astrid Mogul, parent governor, mother to Samantha, vote co-ordinator, and former showgirl herself, put in calls to the Entertainment Editors of three national newspapers and she tipped them off in no uncertain manner. They were besieged with calls about the Brewsters that day. Where a day earlier they had been asking themselves how long the bandwagon could roll, today they were taken aback by the venom that inspired so many to want to sever its back axle.

The Ant's Nest interview appeared in the final edition of an afternoon paper which hit the streets while Penny was galloping away from Sunderland. It provoked a rush of blood to the feet in the throng of reporters outside the Brewster's house and a couple dodged around the back, and out of sight of the policeman guarding the drive, clambered over a back

186

wall to surprise Fern and Ralph Fantoni in the garden.

'You know I love you,' they heard Fern murmur to Ralph. 'You know I do but you must be patient.' Fern told Ralph she loved him not because she did, she didn't really, but because she believed she loved Bud who was too dangerous to love and she felt she owed it to Ralph anyway not to be too dismissive too quickly in the face of her astonishing success.

'What are you doing here?' Ralph demanded of them as they fell in a heap onto the lawn. 'You are trespassing. Fern go and get the policeman, I will stand guard over them.'

'We just thought you might like to see this,' one of them said, waving an early edition at Fern. 'Is it true that you forced the boy to live in the shed while everyone else lived in the house? Is that the shed?'

'I'll get the policeman,' Fern said. She felt entirely calm. So did Jeremy when he was informed by Roy that Juanita Hobbs was attempting to blackmail them. 'She says you tried to get her into bed.'

'She's making it up, of course,' said Jeremy. He sighed. 'Poor little brat. I suppose she thought she could cash in on my publicity. What have you said to her?'

'I told her to get lost.' Roy said. 'She wants ten thousand pounds. She'll probably go somewhere else.'

'No one will touch it, will they?' said Jeremy. 'It's plain scurrilous.'

'I wouldn't count on it,' Roy advised. 'Have you seen the afternoon papers?' Roy felt just the slightest bit apprehensive. His paper had reported the missing children with quiet dignity and a certain sense of bereaved involvement since one of the children was the daughter of their star columnist. But he had been uneasy about the fuss.

He hadn't liked the spirit with which the Brewsters had thrown themselves into the publicity. It did nothing for Jeremy's credibility, he thought and Jeremy's credibility reflected on the credibility of his paper. He certainly didn't like the tone of the Ants' Nest interview. Not that any of it was directed against Jeremy but he might be considered cruel by default in not intervening when his wife put the boy in the shed. Still, it was too soon to tell what was going to happen.

187

He had heard on the grapevine that Jeremy was certain for a Fertile Fruit this year. He wouldn't want to be seen to be unfair to an award winner, not when his daughter was missing, not on the strength of allegations made by a former pizza parlour worker and a delinquent. 'I'd keep your head down for a bit,' he suggested. 'Any news of Ruby?'

'We're hoping and praying,' Jeremy replied.

Late editions of the afternoon papers carried with the Ants' Nest interview paragraphs about Penny walking out on her show in Sunderland. Dave Caster was quoted as saying valiantly the strain was getting to her but it was noted that she was listed in the TV guide to appear on that night's *Cork's Popping*. This wasn't fair. The TV guide hadn't known that she was a last minute starter because no one had told it. It had only been guessing. The implication was that she had intended to walk out on Sunderland all along. Inspector Mallard was saying that the police were looking forward to bringing the whole sad story to a speedy conclusion. It put Marty Cork in a very difficult position indeed.

'My difficulty,' Marty explained to Terence Vertigo, 'is that I'm going to have to ask them about these stories so the whole tone of the interview has to be a bit challenging. It just can't be all tea and sympathy as we thought. Do you follow me? I mean I can't skate round it, can I, or I'll look a prat. So where does that leave young Neville? We can't have the star of *Ravish* sitting on the sofa looking like a child abuser, can we? I know it's not his son and the paper didn't accuse him of neglect or imprisonment but it won't look good, will it?'

'Quite,' said Terence. 'But it will look even worse if they pull out now. Leave it to me. Challenge away but challenge sensibly Marty. You don't have to wage war for a known delinquent or even for Sunderland.'

Luckily for Neville, Madge's story of the callousness of the boy she had plucked from obscurity, which might have enhanced the view of him as a child abuser, didn't appear until the following morning so he was able to lean forward on the sofa when Marty Cork challenged him and persuade the nation that he was a worthy star for the most exciting British film in years.

'Glen was not stuck in the garden shed. It's almost laughable. Jeremy and Fern' — he smiled gently at both of them along the sofa — 'gave him his own apartment in the grounds which my sister-in-law stippled for him especially, though she didn't finish it in time.'

'I've had rather a lot on,' Fern admitted with a small wry but captivating laugh.

'He was not a neglected child,' Neville continued. 'Poor old Ants' Nest Murray is a sad kid who would say anything for money. Penny has been a wonderful mother, bringing him up alone in the early years even though she was working flat out on *Kidding About*.'

'I did my best,' Penny said in a tiny voice, squeezing Neville's hand. 'And if you are watching Glen, please, please come home. If there is something stopping you from coming home, please, please get a message to us. We will do anything.' A tear rolled down her face. She was exhausted from so much travelling. And with the careful use of family pictures and a dear little video of Ruby kicking a ball by the garden shed and with considerable self-restraint which enabled the Brewsters to refrain from speaking of themselves even once, they restored themselves in the public eye and Marty Cork felt perfectly able to have a drink with all of them after the show without compromising himself at all.

Chapter
Nineteen

The reprieve was temporary. By morning the moths had done their work. Madge had slung a great bucket of mud at Neville. Ralph Fantoni had denied in letters inches high that he was Fern's lover, Ants' Nest's mother had claimed everything her son had said about poor little Glen was true, Astrid Mogul had accused Merilee Bawdle of vote rigging and Juanita Hobbs had denounced Jeremy as a philanderer when he had been pretending to be a grief-stricken father. It looked bad, really bad.

Robin Powder was beside himself, prowling about his office far earlier than he was used to prowling anywhere. Yvonne and Magda were also beside themselves as well as beside Robin because he had roused them from their beds to help him deal with the crisis, even though rain poured down as it had never poured down and the wind had ripped at their clothing as they'd struggled through the early morning and they were soaked to the skin. They made the sacrifice because Fertile Fruits, their bread and butter when you came to think of it, were looking rotten to the core. With only days to go they had to face the fact that the yearly publicity binge for the fruits, the industry and the stars themselves smelt like fermenting carrots.

'Look at that weather,' Robin sighed. He tried to think. He watched the rain and he asked himself what he could do. What was he to do with the orange he had lined up for Jeremy, the adulterer, and the raspberry already inscribed to Penny, the bad mother and cheat? How could he uninvite Neville, the ruthless, when he had leant on both Marty Cork and Terence Vertigo to get him to present one of the night's top awards though he'd only offered the weather-girl in the first instance? It was simply too terrible to be true. A Fertile Fruit was nothing if it wasn't a reward for decency, clean-living and public acclaim. The public had withdrawn its acclaim, yet he couldn't withhold the fruits, or could he?

'Of course you can,' Yvonne said. 'Just tell them there's been a recount.'

'It's not as easy as that,' Robin said miserably. He was thinking of Marty Cork and Terence Vertigo. 'You're too young to understand, Yvonne. We need a salvage job,' he said to Magda.

She wasn't hopeful. 'The trouble is there are so many of them. You might save one, but not the other.' This was all too true.

'Get Terence Vertigo for me,' he said to Yvonne. 'And if he's not in his office find him. It can't wait.' Early though it was, everyone was looking for Terence that morning: Jeremy, Neville, Marty, Splendid, the newspapers keen to hear what he thought about Madge McGuire. But Terence was nowhere to be found. He was on a building site with his cousin.

He had been in constant communication with his cousin from the word go, from the very minute that Kenny realized where the children were hiding. He wasn't a hard man. Even a hard man wouldn't have kept news of missing childrn from desperate parents. But he had seen no desperate parents, only grafters, desperate for a bit of media coverage.

'He's not taking my calls,' Jeremy said. He turned from the phone on the wall and confronted his family who were collapsed in various poses of despair and dejection about the

191

kitchen and the conservatory. He didn't know what damage Juanita Hobbs had done. He didn't want to know. He intended to sit tight and consult Terence since Terence was his lawyer and had been long before he was ever Neville's.

'You'll have to go to work, Penny,' Neville said. 'You're already an hour late. 'It's nearly ten, now.'

'I can't,' said Penny. 'I can't face anyone. They will all be whispering behind my back and calling me a cheat. I hate that Merilee. Why hasn't anyone contacted me to support me? Robin should have rung, or Dave, or Magda. I can't take the silence. I can't go in. They will have to do it without me.'

'Don't be silly,' Fern said. 'Who else can do it? Besides, they might have been trying to reach you while Jeremy was on the phone. I think you should go in, Penny. It looks bad for all of us if you don't. I'm going to get on with my book. We can't afford to let the papers touch us.'

'It's alright for you,' Penny mumbled. And it was in a way because the only scandal to touch Fern that morning had concerned Ralph whose denial had been everything she might have wished it to be, given the nature of the work she intended to be known for. The nastiness concerning the shed had been dealt with by Neville the night before, as far as she was concerned, and if the madwoman Nest was going to insist upon it, then it was for the public to decide who was telling the truth. She could afford to be quietly confident. Who would believe the mother of a delinquent against the word of a poet?

'The post,' Jeremy said as mail arrived through the door.

Only Fern had the energy to pick it up and put it on the table. She sifted through it, removing letters addressed to her and she tore open a pale green envelope she knew was from Bud. 'At least he's communicating with me,' she said.

It was a short note, penned before she had given her side of the story on *Cork's Popping* or Ralph had issued his exciting denial. '*My dear Fern,*' it said, '*What a pig I have been. I can see now I was being cruel to expect you to produce a book when I know all your energy must be diverted to the recovery of your daughter. Please don't worry. There is positively no urgency. You must take your time. Take as long as you like. Take a year or two. Write what you can when you can and keep in touch. Your devoted, Bud.'*

'What's it say?' Jeremy asked, intrigued by his wife's pallor and the hint of suicide about her mouth.

'It says, "Get lost",' she said.

Neville finally telephoned Dave Caster to say that Penny had dysentry from Sunderland and would not make the studios that morning. 'She couldn't risk violent movement, if you take my meaning,' he said. 'It's the first she's missed in seventeen years.'

'Give her our love,' Dave replied.

'Didn't he want to speak to me?' Penny asked.

'No,' Neville admitted. While he was on his feet he dialled Terence Vertigo's number again. 'Still out,' he reported.

The Vertigos hadn't so much connived in the disappearance of the children as been aware they were safe. It had been plain to them that everyone's best interests were served by their staying in the loft for as long as possible, and since the time was now right, due to circumstances beyond their control, they tipped off the police who had been to Mandarin Street earlier, oddly enough, but found nothing.

While Terence and Kenny negotiated with the children, the Brewsters continued to sit in the kitchen and the conservatory, needing to be near each other, needing to watch each other in case one of them gained an advantage at the expense of the others or even at no cost to anyone except the peace of mind of those who remained without one. They read and reread the papers, gasping at the untruths, the wild exaggerations and the slanders, threatening law suits and wondering where on earth Terence was since he was the only one who could seriously advise them. They watched the repeat of *Kidding About* which Robin Powder ran in Penny's absence.

'He is deliberately humiliating me,' Penny moaned. 'He is pretending I am dead' for it wasn't even *Kidding About*. It was a *Kid's Corner*, featuring the galloping of the first Miss Penny, made at a time when the current Miss Penny was still Maureen Cartilage.

'She died of syphilis,' Fern remarked. Other than that, no one spoke. They had gone into shock. Fern didn't ask about

193

Juanita Hobbs, Jeremy didn't ask about Ralph, Neville didn't deny Madge McGuire's accusations and it didn't occur to anyone to enquire about Samantha Mogul. They all sat, fixated by the music and movement, lost in their own sense of betrayal, waiting.

While the rain pelted across the gardens and the wind dragged at the trees, they waited. The curtains remained drawn, the blinds down, the door locked. Despite the weather, reporters hovered at the gate, also waiting. They roared into action as Terence Vertigo arrived with Inspector Mallard just as the gallopers flopped into Kid's Corner and faded to black.

'Thank God you're here,' Jeremy cried, letting them in. 'We couldn't decide what we should do for the best.'

'Quite,' said the Inspector.

'They've been found,' Neville noticed cleverly. 'Where are they?'

'We could remove them bodily but we decided not to for the time being,' the Inspector said. 'Mr Vertigo has been very helpful. Both Mr Vertigos as a matter of fact.' He placed himself at the bottom of the table as the lawyer took a seat at its head.

'My cousin found them over at Mandarin Street,' Terence announced. 'It seems the boy has been there all the time. Israel was a red herring. So was Manchester. So was King's Cross Station. You thinking you saw him at King's Cross Station was some sort of telepathy.' Everyone stared at Jeremy but no one spoke. 'They aren't anxious to come home but we seem to have arrived at a basis for agreement.'

'Ruby's always been very sensible,' Fern said.

'I don't know what we're going to do about all that stuff in the papers,' Jeremy ventured.

'One thing at a time,' Terence remarked. The deal was this. 'They want you all to come over to Mandarin Street to agree to it before two witnesses. There must be no publicity attached to the meeting and no parent should attempt to exploit it before, during or after. The boy must be allowed to come back to the house and given a bed in the study and they want to enjoy their friendship without any interference from any parent. Mrs P. Brewster must stop galloping and

194

Mrs F. Brewster must receive treatment for kleptomania. I think it's clear enough and not too extravagant under the circumstances.'

'What kleptomania?' Fern asked.

'We've always galloped,' Penny said.

'Seems reasonable to me,' Jeremy said. 'What do you think, Terence?'

'I think the sooner they are home the better for all of us,' he said. So it was arranged.

Inspector Mallard agreed to keep the press away in the interests of security and because of the delicacy of the situation and half an hour later, when Penny had changed into a long, fresh scarf and some pale make-up and Fern had arranged her copper tendrils, Terence drove the Brewsters in a limousine with darkened windows to Mandarin Street past the road-blocks and up to the house with which Neville and Penny had fallen in love and had planned to turn into a palace.

'Bloody hell,' Jeremy said. 'How long have they been in here?'

'All the time,' Terence said. 'So I gather. They've made themselves quite cosy if you like dirt. Ah, Kenneth. Are they ready?' Kenny, in a suit to honour the occasion and in his capacity as chief negotiator, had come forward to meet them. There wasn't a camera or notebook in sight. There was no one in sight. Even the neighbours had been asked to make themselves scarce.

'I think so,' he said. 'Step this way. Sorry about the mess. It's much worse in this rain. They want Terence and me to witness the terms then they want to talk to you in private for a minute or two before coming out. I said that was alright. I hope you don't mind. You're looking very nice today Miss Penny.'

'Thank you,' said Penny. She put herself in mind of Jackie Kennedy at the President's funeral.

'Great,' said Neville. 'The work's coming along well. Look Penny, that's where the jacuzzi is going to be.'

'No,' said Kenny. 'That is the kitchen.'

They climbed the filthy stairs without benefit of bannisters

195

and through rooms with nothing significant in them in the way of floorboards until they came to a hole in the ceiling, above which was the loft. A rope-ladder hung from it, like a condemned man's noose. 'Hullo children,' Penny cried. 'We're here, darlings.' Her friendly pitch was ignored.

Glen and Ruby talked to their parents via the Vertigos as the wind swept the dust about the ramshackle rooms. They stayed in the loft, behind the wardrobe and they insisted their parents stay below as if eyeball to eyeball would dilute the seriousness of their intent. They were very businesslike. Ruby refused to comment on the final clause concerning the kleptomania and Glen wouldn't say whether there had been money in his football boot or not. They simply stated the terms one by one, more or less as Terence had described them. From beneath the hole at the foot of the ladder, their parents could see very little choice. Their lives were in ruins. If normality was to be restored to them they needed their children back. The agreement was made. Glen and Ruby declared themselves satisfied and the Vertigos withdrew. As they gingerly made their way back through the far-from-waterproof wreck, Jeremy began to climb the ladder.

'I'm coming up,' he said. 'I'm not talking to you down here.' There was a slam as the Vertigos left through the front door. 'Ruby, stand by to take a passenger on board.' There was a small cry of protest and then a horrible rumbling and shaking as the ladder began to rock and Jeremy began to flap in mid-air.

'What's that?' shrieked Penny. The floor beneath her began to tilt and the wall on her left to shift bewilderingly.

'Run for your lives,' someone called from below and those that could, did. But the children couldn't and neither could Jeremy. He could go neither up nor down until the ladder finally gave way, hurling him to the ground. As he clambered to his feet, the wind gave a final shove to the wall which Kenny had said he couldn't guarantee and the loft in the palace-to-be in Mandarin Street collapsed, trapping the Brewsters and all their hopes for the future. It no longer mattered that they were lean and desirable, that their faces glowed and their hair shone. Had it occurred to them, they might then have traded places willingly with anyone suffering from obesity or wrinkling.

Neville, Fern and Penny survived, clinging to each other in the kitchen as everything around them swayed in the dust and rain and wind. They stared at each other in horror and disbelief, their eyes bulging white in their muddied faces. 'Oh God,' Neville said, 'Oh no.'

'Jeremy,' Fern called. 'Ruby?'

'Glen!' shrieked Penny, all the months and years of neglect rushing before her eyes as she cried for the return of her baby boy and a life she could live over again, better. Then it was still and all they could hear was the wind, the occasional splat of debris, the rain and the distant voices of the Vertigos calling to anyone who might be able to hear.

'Shush,' said Neville. 'Listen.' They listened. The cries of the Vertigos outside calling for them and summoning help grew more insistent. 'Oh God, let them be quiet,' he said. 'Be quiet,' he screamed. 'Be quiet!' He put his hands to his eyes and concentrated in the silence, straining for a sound. He strained for an image. He strained for something from his past, for the gift his parents might have given him. He prayed for a vision, God knows why when all his life he had only ever wanted to act.

'Neville,' said Penny. 'Oh Neville.' But he brushed her off and moved forward suddenly.

'It's alright,' he said. 'I can see him. I know where he is. Stay here. There is a way up to him. I'm going to get him.'

'I will come too.' said Fern.

'Stay here,' Neville said. 'You are safe here.'

'I don't want to be safe here,' Fern argued. 'I'm coming too. I want to find them. I'm going to come with you.' So they all edged forward together, in pursuit of Neville's vision, crawling through the gap in the kitchen wall and out into a mass of rubble. 'Jeremy,' Neville called. 'Jeremy.' But no one replied. 'Shush,' he said again. 'It's alright,' he said, 'he is alive. I can hear him.'

'I heard nothing,' said Fern.

'You can only hear the Vertigos,' Penny agreed.

'He is alive.' Neville insisted. 'The ladder has saved him.'

And he pushed on as fast as he dared, knowing where he was going, bringing the others with him, risking all their lives by the shift of his weight on surfaces that couldn't be trusted. And they found him, as Neville had said they would, lying under the ladder, alive if not precisely well.

'Hullo,' Jeremy said, bemused, 'Who brought the house down?'

'Daddy?' Ruby called, peering through a tiny crack above their heads.

'Thank God,' said Fern. 'Are you alright, darling?'

'Glen,' Penny sobbed. 'Oh Glen, Glen.'

'I'm here, Mum,' Glen called. 'We're alright but there's not much room.'

'He's trapped by the wardrobe,' Ruby said. 'And I can't get it off him. Can one of you come up here and help me?'

'There's help coming,' Fern said. 'I can hear them outside. They will be here soon.'

'But he can't breathe,' Ruby said. 'Mummy, he can't breathe. You'll have to come and help me. He'll die.'

'I'm coming,' Neville said. But he couldn't. He was far too big to squeeze himself through what was left of the hole.

'Keep breathing, Glen,' Penny cried. 'Keep breathing. I'm coming.' And she tried but her chest was not much smaller than her husband's and her legs were too long. 'Don't worry, darling,' she cried. 'I will sing to you.' And she gave him a burst of 'Five Little Ducks'. 'It's the right weather for it,' she laughed. 'Hang on, darling.'

'Mummy! Quick,' screamed Ruby. And Fern being slim and short was able to get through the hole and she managed it as fast as any mother who is urged on by panic in her child's voice and fear. Together she and Ruby tugged at the wardrobe.

'We need rope,' she yelled. 'Can you see any rope?'

'My scarf,' said Penny and she had it off, exposing the treacherous neck without a single thought for how it would look. They used it as a sling and Glen was released just as firemen appeared below them urging them to stay put and not to move because to move would endanger all their lives.

They were found huddled in two small groups, Neville and

198

Penny cradling Jeremy in their arms and Fern and Ruby cradling Glen. Their survival was a mystery to those who had tunneled through to them. They gave no credit to the gifts which come into their own in an emergency. Fern had the gift of shortness and Penny the gift of scarves. Neville later denied he had any gift at all.

Inspector Mallard kept the press back until the Brewsters had been brought out. Glen and Jeremy were carried out on stretchers and the others came in rugs into the rain which continued to pour down. Then he allowed them to come forward as the family were helped into the ambulances which they boarded in the blaze of light created by the flashes of the photographers.

Questions were fired at them but nothing too difficult and all Neville would say was, 'We have had a lucky escape.' There were photographs the next day but no interviews, not even with Kenny Vertigo whom it was guessed might be sued for failing to ensure that the building was safe before allowing anyone into it.

'I don't know where this leaves us,' Robin said to Magda next morning when the rain had stopped and the sun was shining.

'Back where we started, I think,' she said and he was inclined to agree with her.

Chapter
Twenty

No one ever gets back to where they started because what has happened between starting and going back changes everything. Starting points may look the same but they are not the same. At the Brewsters', for instance, Jeremy may have gone back to News when Light Entertainment didn't like *Tempting Fate* after all, but Glen was on a camp bed in his study. Fern may have gone back to writing her poems in secret but Ralph Fantoni had disappeared from her life. The filmed inserts may have been dropped from *Kidding About* but so had the galloping.

Days had passed since the roof at Mandarin Street had fallen in on them, crushing the circumstances which, in gathering momentum, had threatened to destroy them. Confused days had passed, during which they had been torn between counting their blessings and counting the cost. They weren't so mad that they couldn't see their blessings. They were still alive, weren't they? Like any other family, they were grateful for that and in the privacy of their own four walls they had striven to be like any other family.

Jeremy and Glen had spent a day or two in hospital, recovering, during which Ruby was reconciled with her mother, her mother was reconciled with Glen and Glen was reconciled with his mother. The brothers had always been reconciled to everyone and everything so they were able simply to look on, smiling, unable to believe that they had read each other's minds in the ruins of Mandarin Street and unwilling to say they might have because they had always poured scorn on their parents' act.

No one mentioned fame or the need for it, but beyond the four walls steps were being taken to bring about a reconciliation with the public. If Terence Vertigo had given the wall a shove himself, he couldn't have orchestrated a salvage job better. Sympathy is a wonderful incentive for forgiveness. There is no surer way for a hero to regain his former glory than by becoming a victim and as Jeremy and Glen had languished in hospital, victims, together, Juanita Hobbs had been branded an ungrateful fibber, Samantha Mogula was recognized for being an unspeakable little show-off, other former taxi drivers spoke out in defence of Neville's defection from Madge and the garden shed was played down as well as a garden shed can be.

Naturally, sacrifices had to be made. *Tempting Fate*, for one, was sacrificed because Light Entertainment cannot abide a scandal and the contract had never been signed. *Listen I'm Talking!* backed away from Fern, claiming the interest had only ever been casual and dependent on the imminent appearance of a book. And of course the galloping went.

By the night of the Fertile Fruits Award Ceremony, the Brewsters were feeling considerably less moth-eaten than they had been before the roof had caved in yet by no means as on-top-of-the-world as they had felt before that. They were just as famous, in fact more famous than they had ever been, but they no longer knew why they needed to be. The need hadn't vanished. Needs don't overnight. They simply no longer took it for granted. Only Neville assumed he knew where he stood.

Only Neville made no claims to being back where he started because he most definitely was not. Where in the beginning he had been an actor with an uncertain future in musicals and a taxi, he was now about to star in the most important film of the year and the taxi was out, as indeed was Madge, the taxi owner who in the beginning had featured so prominently. Neville knew that he needed to be famous because film stars were famous because film stars were famous.

'Don't be silly,' he said to Penny as they dressed in the spare room. 'How will you look a fool? You're still Miss Penny. Jeremy is worse off. He's lost *Tempting Fate*. And what about poor old Fern? What hasn't she lost?' He was thoughtful in his own certainty. He tried not to let it upset anyone less certain.

'I lost an award,' Penny said, her eyes brimming at the mere thought as she arranged the slender straps of her evening dress. 'Robin practically promised. It was in the papers. Now everyone will think I'm not getting one because I'm a cheat.'

'You wouldn't have been asked tonight if they thought you were a cheat.' Neville lied. 'Anyway, what's an award? I've never had one.'

'But you're giving one,' she said. Yet she knew in her heart of hearts she could have lost her show and that to lose an award for which votes had been touted in the first place was to get off lightly.

'Look,' he said, taking her by the shoulders. 'You have to be very, very brave. Tonight is going to be difficult but if we all behave sensibly only good can come of it. Tonight we're going to squash the rumours and reclaim our dignity. The children will be with us, Jeremy's getting Reporter of The Year and you will still be among the nominees for Children's Personality. No one is pretending you weren't nominated. All you have to do is look dignified in defeat.' He kissed her quickly on the cheek. 'Now let's go down,' he said. 'I don't want to keep them waiting. Does my hair look funny?'

Even he was slightly nervous. This was the first public appearance for any of them since the accident and he knew the eyes of the nation would be on them. He wished his hair would behave itself. 'Penny,' Fern cried when she saw her. 'How brave! How brave of you to wear that dress. I lost the

202

nerve to expose my breasts years ago.'

'Really?' said Penny.

'Penny has wonderful muscle tone,' Neville said. 'Look the cars are here. Are the others ready? Oh Ruby, you look gorgeous, doesn't she, Pen? Red looks beautiful on you. Where's Glen?

'Still in the study,' Ruby giggled. 'He can't get his tie right.' Ruby wasn't nervous. She thought it was a lark. She wasn't back to where she started either because now she had Glen exactly where she wanted him and he had her.

'I'll go and get him,' Neville said.

'Tell Jeremy to get a move on too,' Fern called after him.

'I'll wait in the car then,' Penny murmured. She hated being in a room with Fern when Neville wasn't there to protect her.

'You look lovely, Mummy,' Ruby said.

'Do I?' Fern said. She didn't feel lovely. There was no one left to make her feel lovely, not Bud, not Sam on *Listen I'm Talking!*, not even Ralph. She had lost so much, she told herself that she was worse off than she had been in the beginning. At least in the beginning she had had Ralph and her secret. Now Ralph was gone, reclaimed by his wife, and the poems were public knowledge. It was hard not to be bitter.

'It's alright,' Ruby said gently. 'I believe you. I know you aren't a kleptomaniac. You were just being secretive, that's all. You shouldn't have been ashamed of your poems. I would have understood.'

'Thank you,' said Fern.

'And they're still going to do a book, aren't they?'

'I don't know,' said Fern. 'I'm not sure.' It seemed to her she might be better off without a book. What could a book achieve? A small amount of attention or even a lot of attention wasn't necessarily better than a good secret and she could remake her secret. She smiled at Ruby. 'What's a book,' she said, 'compared to a Ruby?' What's a sex-mad boy in the study compared to a Ruby? She chewed at her cheek. Glen still looked sex-mad to her, even if he was being beautifully behaved and a trifle wan.

'Right,' said Jeremy, running down the stairs followed by the others, immaculate in their dinner suits with their handsome faces spruced and keen. 'Let's go.' He wore his arm fetchingly in a sling and Glen sported a pleasing scar across his left cheekbone. Otherwise all there was to suggest that the Brewsters had been in a house fall was a cautious tolerance, though Fern found it harder to be cautious than the others.

'I'm so nervous,' Penny whispered to Neville in the car. 'I'm terrified.' She was not the Penny who had swanned into Sunderland and she certainly wasn't the Penny who had demanded filmed inserts. This was a Penny with no faith in her public now that Merilee Bawdle had written to say how disappointed she had been by the turn of events. She would never believe what the delinquent had said, she had written, but certain parents had felt very let down by the lunch and she had come to believe that it could do the school no good to be publicly associated with the suggestion of crooked dealing. She wished Penny well however.

It wasn't enough to be wished well. Without Merilee in the background Penny felt bereft. Merilee had been everyone to her. And with Neville assured of stardom, she teetered on the brink of feeling utterly abandoned. She was terrified of the background she was being edged into.

'What's there to be nervous of?' Neville said squeezing her hand. 'You have me.' Neville spoke as a husband persuaded of his worth. He was a substantial thing to have. 'Here we are,' he said and he smiled from the car. 'All right, Jeremy?'

The photographers waiting outside the theatre saw them coming. 'They're here,' someone cried. 'Quick it's the Brewsters.' Fern, Ruby and Glen climbed out of one long, low car and Jeremy, Penny and Neville from the other. 'This way, Ruby,' several voices called. 'Hey Glen!' It was the children they were interested in and it wasn't hard to see why. Holding each other's hands in the cool night air, they were almost the most beautiful things you could wish to see. They were tall and straight and lean and true and their faces were clear and alive and full of joyful expectation. Elderly ladies waiting in the gutter were lost for words.

But they didn't hang about. They all moved inside quickly

with Glen unselfishly taking Fern's arm as well as Ruby's, as a mark of their closeness whatever anyone still thought about the shed, and Penny snuggling between Jeremy and Neville, whom she believed could protect her from anything unpleasant that was being muttered on the sidelines.

'Fifteenth time lucky, Miss Penny?' someone shouted. 'What do you reckon?'

They were met by a Fertile Fruit hostess and led to their table. 'Table twenty-two,' she informed them. In view of the size of their party, they were seated on their own and Robin Powder, in his wisdom, had put them behind a pillar.

'They must come,' he had said to Magda. 'We can't ignore them. But there's no need to flaunt them. They'll get their two minutes after the last break which is about as generous as I think we need to be.'

'We're behind a pillar,' Penny said.

'I'm happier behind a pillar,' Ruby murmured. Glen said he was too. Neville, Jeremy, Fern and Penny tried to look as if they were but they weren't. They tried to look like a family entitled to the limelight and bathed in it but they felt like any other family given bad tickets for an opening night. Despite everything they had hoped and had imagined Terence Vertigo had achieved, the snub was obvious. All those who might have surrounded them in their hour of triumph were scattered about the room as far from them as it was possible to be. Neville felt it most keenly. He had most to lose.

'There's Marty,' he said. 'I must say a quick hello.' But there wasn't time. Halfway through his dash to the *Cork's Popping* table he was ordered back to his seat by a floor manager and though he tried to catch Marty's eye, Suzie Cork placed herself in his line of vision and spared her husband the embarrassment of having to recognize him in public. They sat in their less than splendid isolation through the first half, sipping at the wine that had been placed on the table for them, unaware of the fruits that were being distributed, lost in their own unhappy reveries. They didn't sip for long becaue there were only a single bottle and being nervous, they drank it in one gulp.

In the break, Neville and Jeremy were summoned

backstage with the other presenters and award winners and as they passed between the tables, heads turned away and conversations were suddenly so engrossing that the most they elicited from anyone was half a smile or a quick nod. The only exception was Kenny Vertigo who leapt from his chair and shook them both by the hand, knowing they wouldn't dream of suing him and keen to make it plain to anyone who happened to be looking. 'I've brought all the men over to Mandarin Street from the Gothic,' he said. 'You'll be in your own house in no time.'

'What do you think it means?' Neville said to Jeremy as they waited and fidgeted.

'I suppose it means he's working like stink,' Jeremy said. What it meant was that in a room full of people needing to be famous, it is the size and quality of the fame that counts. The very famous are pleased to associate with those as famous as themselves or those famous temporarily for anything fine, but they are unhappy to consort with the less famous or the notorious. They won't, not for any length of time, not intimately. It's a rule. Jeremy and Neville knew it and understood it. As Neville's name was called to present the award to the Reporter of the Year he thanked god that his contract had been signed when the size and quality of his fame had been at their peak.

As he ran lightly down the ramp to the stage, clutching the envelope containing the name of the winner, he was relieved to hear the applause, muted though it was. 'Thank you,' he said. 'I've been asked to present this award,' he said, in a voice that was as easy on the ear as anything the audience had heard all night, 'because the character I'm to play in *Ravish* is a reporter who must choose between his career and his principles. It's entirely coincidental that my brother is among the nominees but he, like all those nominated, cannot be faulted on ethics. They all work hard in an industry which thrives on half-truths, innuendo and scandal, to pursue the truth. They are ...' he paused as the film clips were shown one by one and the audience, relaxed by the taste of wine, moved by the pitch of his voice and able to be generous in a body where they could not be one at a time, murmured

206

appreciatively at Jeremy's clip. And when Neville announced him as the winner and appeared to be moved to tears himself, they broke into the wildest applause of the night, cheering and clapping and stamping in a manner that shocked them all.

At Jeremy's entry onto the stage they doubled their efforts. He smiled and nodded and when he could be heard said, 'Steady. I won't be held reponsible for bringing another house down.' And when this reduced them to laughter out of all proportion to the joke he added, 'but I do thank you from the bottom of my heart. I will cherish this melon for the whole of my life. There are, of course people I would like to thank. My producers, Terence, Roy at the paper, the whole news team but most of all I want to thank my family who are with me tonight. You may know that we have been through a troubled time lately and that we have had to survive not only private difficulties but some extremely unwelcome and hurtful public difficulties. However, we have survived and, wonderful though this melon is, nothing can match the closeness we have and we thank God for it.' Suzie Cork burst into tears. She was an odd woman.

When the brothers were returned to the privacy of their seats, Neville removed a small bulky package from inside his pocket. 'A present,' he said to Jeremy. It was the mask of comedy. 'You don't need Light Entertainment,' he said. 'Head for Arts and Drama.' And Jeremy nodded.

'I will,' he said, grasping his brother's hand. 'I will.'

The rest of the awards were nothing in comparison, except for the award to the Children's Presenter which raised an audible moan when Penny failed to win it. Robin Powder raised his eyes at Magda. 'Oh well,' he said.

You might have thought, in view of all that had gone before, that the Brewsters would have wanted to make the most of the huge wave of love and support that waited to envelope them when the lights came up, the show was over and the celebrities were herded to the bar for an elegant supper, especially when *Ravish* was still in the offing and Jeremy needed contacts in Arts and Drama. But no. The brothers rose as one, grinned at each other and taking an arm

each of a wife and child they guided their family briskly to the waiting cars and home.

Later, they sat in the cool night air at the small wrought-iron table and sipped champagne thoughtfully. 'I think it went well,' Neville said, eventually.

'They were pleased for me, weren't they?' Jeremy agreed.

'I had to laugh,' Penny chuckled. 'They were so cross when I didn't get the mango. It was almost better than getting it.' Fern sighed and smiled to herself. She had just thought of something which she would never tell anyone, ever.

In the garden shed, Glen and Ruby kissed each other. Glen counted to twenty-seven before Ruby withdrew her lips to smile up at him. 'We'll go and tell them,' she said. 'Let's tell them now.' Hand in hand they strolled across the garden to where their parents were feeling pleased with themselves.

'No thank you,' Ruby said when offered champagne. 'There's something I want to say.' She smiled at Glen and he smiled back. Fern clung grimly to the promise of her secret. 'When Glen moves to Mandarin Street,' Ruby said. 'I will be moving into the garden shed. I would like it to be my room.'

'No,' cried Fern. But Glen said, 'I know I complained but you've made it very comfortable.' He put an arm around Ruby and led her back across the garden. 'Honestly,' Ruby called over her shoulder. 'It's for the best,' Glen agreed. 'Under the circumstances.'

'What circumstances?' Fern cried. But there were none that anyone could think of.